CASABLANCA
BLUES

TAHIR SHAH

CASABLANCA
BLUES

TAHIR SHAH

MMXXII

Secretum Mundi Publishing Ltd
Kemp House
City Road
London
EC1V 2NX
United Kingdom

www.secretum-mundi.com
info@secretum-mundi.com

Secretum Mundi Publishing Ltd, 2022
VERSION 04012022

CASABLANCA BLUES

© TAHIR SHAH

Visit the author's website at:
Tahirshah.com

ISBN 978-1-912383-97-9

*This book is dedicated to the
Kingdom of Morocco —*

*A realm touched by magic,
whose landscape and whose
people never cease to amaze.*

One

THE WINDOWLESS WALLS at Acme Telesales were painted slate grey.

A sea of uniform desks filled the central hall, each one the same drab shade. The chairs were grey as well, and the telephonic headsets, and the complexions of the sales staff who wore them, and even the plastic plants.

The only splash of colour in the entire place was the baseball cap pulled down tight over Blaine Williams's blond mop of hair.

It was fire-engine red and had the word 'CASABLANCA' written in large letters across the front.

'Good morning to you, ma'am,' said Blaine into the headset microphone. 'No, no, I didn't call last week. No, not even the week before. Why am I calling? Well, ma'am, I've got an offer... an offer for the silver generation...'

Click.

Blaine dialled again.

'Hello, ma'am. Let me be blunt: Do you have trouble with your drains?'

Click.

'Good morning to you, sir! Could I interest you in a case of Drain-O-Sure?'

Click.

A miniature buzzer mounted on the left of Blaine's desk, number 52, emitted a muffled warning sound. Beside it was a black-and-white studio shot of Humphrey Bogart — with signature cigarette, fedora, and sullen stare. And next to it was an empty mug, Bogart and Bergman's cheeks pressed together on the side.

In a well-practised movement, Blaine slipped off his headset, leaned back in his chair and closed his eyes.

'For Christ's sake! Beam me up to the mothership!' he bellowed.

Two

ON THE DOT of seven a.m., an automatic sprinkler system turned itself on and began watering the manicured lawn in front of the Omary mansion. There was not a blade of grass over an inch and a half tall, nor a weed in sight.

A pair of imposing wrought-iron gates threw long, arabesque shadows over the lawn. They rose thirty feet into the pale blue sky, armoured CCTV cameras mounted above each one.

Behind the grass and the gates, the mansion rose up like a magnificent frosted wedding cake. Gleaming ivory white, it was adorned with Doric columns and Classical mouldings, and reeked of immense affluence: the kind of wealth that only a business empire, corruption, or both, can provide.

Inside, a handsome, well-groomed man of fifty-six was taking breakfast, squinting with half his attention at a pie chart on a laptop screen. His left hand was stirring a porcelain cup of English breakfast tea clockwise when his daughter, Ghita, hurried in.

'Baba, oh, Baba... What catastrophe! What misery!'

Hicham Omary glanced up and smiled absently, surprised his only daughter was awake at such a reasonable hour. He didn't say a word, because he knew an explanation would be forthcoming — one that would begin in condemnation and end in a solicitation for funds.

'How can a girl expect to get married with such imbeciles on the payroll?' Ghita moaned, as a cluster of servants fussed around her. 'I have had no choice but to fire the lot of them, every last one. We'll have to start again from scratch. It will cost a little more, but I know you'll agree to that, won't you, dearest Baba?'

Her lips stretched wide in a taut smile, Ghita blew a kiss across the table in her father's direction.

Mr. Omary's gaze moved back to the graph and, in one continuous movement, out to the landscaped garden that extended far behind the house. The sprinklers were throwing rainbows over the lawns. He was about to ask for a figure when his daughter held up a finger and exclaimed:

'I blame the working class! Damn them! And damn them again!'

'Excuse me?' said Ghita's father in disbelief.

'Well, it's they who are driving up prices! Do you have any idea how much it costs to put on a wedding?'

'I daren't ask,' Omary replied coldly. 'But after all, Ghita, it's only an engagement. How over the top does it need to be?'

Three

BLAINE WRESTLED WITH the key to the front door of his building and, after an eternity, managed to get inside. The stairwell was gloomy and damp. It smelled of rotten eggs and led up many flights through a dark, dingy twilight zone of urban squalor.

The sordidness and the stench increased with altitude.

By the fifth floor, where Blaine's poky apartment was found, the filth was especially vile, as if painted on thick like a theatrical backdrop.

Dressed in a grubby macintosh, the belt tied in a knot at the waist, Blaine began the ascent in a slow trudge. In one hand he held an old fedora and in the other, a TV dinner furled up in a crumpled paper bag.

As he approached the narrow landing of the third floor, the door to 3A jerked open. The mousy, hunched figure of a woman could almost be seen in the shadows and the grime.

'What you got up there Williams, a herd of frigging rhinos?!'

'Hello Mrs. Cohen.'

'All that banging and crashing. Every day it's worse. Any more of it and I'll get the super up there!'

'I've been at work all day, Mrs. Cohen.'

'Sure you have. And I'm frigging Mata Hari!'

'Goodnight to you, Mrs. Cohen,' said Blaine, as he lumbered upwards.

On the fourth-floor landing he came across a young, clean-cut couple standing outside a particularly battered door. They seemed uneasy, as if instinct were telling them to flee. Both turning at once, they smiled anxiously at Blaine.

Such was their fear they might have screamed.

'Are you here to rent 4D?'

The couple nodded in unison.

'Oh,' Blaine replied. 'I see.'

'Whhhhhat's wrong with it?'

'Nothing, nothing much at all… except…'

'Except?'

'Except for the rats, and the roaches… and…'

'*And?*'

'Well, surely Mr. Rogers told you…'

'Told us what?'

'About what happened to Mr. Wilson… you know… the business with the shotgun.' Blaine paused, leaned back on his heels. 'Made a helluva mess and…'

Before he could finish, there was the sound of city shoes and cheap pumps taking the stairs two at a time. After much scurrying, it was followed by the distant echo of the front door slamming shut.

A minute later, Blaine was sitting on the expansive furry couch that dominated his living room — Coors Light in one hand, a remote in the other, the Hungry Hombre platter balanced between his knees.

A few feet away stood a widescreen TV, the centrepiece of an apartment that was a shrine to *Casablanca*.

Every inch was filled with memorabilia.

There were cabinets packed with *Casablanca* knick-knacks — mugs, albums, and snow-globes, miniature figurines of the leading cast, medallions and cheap plastic

TAHIR SHAH

giveaways. There was Humphrey Bogart soap — still boxed — a stack of *Casablanca* playing cards, and a large-scale model of Rick's Café.

The walls were covered in framed posters, each one emblazoned with the movie's title and its cast. And, on the far side of the room to the left of the couch, was an enormous neon sign in vivid scarlet. Every few seconds the cursive script came alive, bathing the dim room in a warm, comforting glow.

Without thinking, Blaine clicked a fingertip to the remote, took a swig of his beer, and sat back as he did each night to munch his way through the Hungry Hombre meal for one.

The neon sign flickered on and then off as the movie's title sequence rolled in black and white.

With Blaine moving on to the Hungry Hombre dessert, there came the title of that inimitable destination — *CASABLANCA*.

Four

AN ARMY OF liveried caddies was lined up and ready at the Royal Casablanca Golf Club, each one more neatly turned out than the last.

There was a sense of utopia, as if the pristine buildings, the caddies, and the course were somehow set apart from the urban sprawl that lay just beyond the club's boundary wall. It was a mystery how the management achieved it, but the

6

noise and pollution from the churning, seething Casablanca gridlock never managed to disturb the serenity of it all.

Three men were standing in conversation at the tee.

The first, Hicham Omary, was a media mogul and the father of Ghita, society's most demanding debutante. The second was Walter Schwartzkopf, American ambassador to the Kingdom of Morocco. And the third, Driss Senbel, was a leading lawyer, and the kind of man who had made a career from ensuring that A-list oligarchs remained firmly above the law.

Stepping forwards, Senbel glanced at his Patek Philippe.

'Let's get going. Shall we toss?'

'Better wait five more minutes, until it's eight o'clock,' said Omary. 'You know how the club is with its rules.'

Senbel waved a hand easily through the air.

'It's all taken care of,' he said. 'I tipped the greenskeeper. We can tee off whenever we like.'

Omary frowned for the second time that morning.

'But surely bribery *is* against club rules,' he said curtly.

'Nonsense. It's just oiling the wheels of the economy.'

'You mean you were helping to rot the foundations of society.'

Slipping on his glove, the ambassador swivelled to face Senbel.

'I'm with Hicham on this one,' he said. 'Every payoff you give cripples this country a little more, turning good people into bad. You're scorching the roots of honest society.'

Driss Senbel tossed a shiny new ten-dirham coin and waited for it to fall onto the perfectly clipped grass.

Squinting at the king's head, he smiled smugly and stepped up to the tee.

His caddie passed him a driver.

'Are you crazy?' he said as an afterthought. 'If people like us stop oiling the wheels, the country would grind to a halt. I'd give it a week, possibly two. Then…'

'Then what?'

'Then there'd be anarchy.'

When the lawyer had swung, Hicham Omary stepped forwards. His mind wasn't on golf. It had been on curbing the extravagances of his wayward daughter, but now it had shifted to the subject of corruption. Despite his strong feelings against it, he knew full well there was nothing even he could do to alter the age-old order of things.

'I have to admit it, but I reluctantly agree with Driss on this,' he said apologetically. 'It's the system, and the system's not going to change whatever we say or do.'

The ambassador nodded to his caddie, who passed him a wood.

'What if you were both to refuse to pay any more bribes?' he asked. 'No more *baksheesh* for the cops, or for the government officials, or any of the other social detritus who demand it?'

Senbel took in the crystal dial of his wristwatch again. He sighed.

'I'm telling you,' he said, 'there'd be a revolution within a matter of days!'

Five

HUMPHREY BOGART WAS carousing with his clientele, the smoke-filled Rick's Café Américain in full swing, when Bergman strolled in. His head nestled into the beige fur of the couch, Blaine mumbled each line just before it was delivered.

He knew every one.

All of a sudden, his mobile phone bleeped. Taking in the display, he moved it in an arc to his ear.

'Hey sweetie, how was your day? Got some painting done? Oh, that's great. *Mine?* No thrills. Just a thousand calls to geriatric serial killers, psychopaths, and the suicidal. Long live Drain-O-Sure!' Blaine paused, grinned, his attention fading. 'OK. Great,' he murmured, 'see you in a bit.'

Fifteen minutes later there was a faint knock at the door.

A pretty redhead kissed Blaine on the lips as she moved through the doorway and into the sitting room. She was panting lightly, not from lust but from the climb. Behind her back was a square object the size of a bathmat. It was covered in a paint-spattered cloth.

'I've got something special for you, sweetheart,' Laurie said. 'A surprise!'

'A surprise? You know how I have trouble with surprises.'

'Go on… guess what it is.'

'I give up.'

Blaine grinned his trademark grin, his cheeks pink and full. As he did so, Laurie whipped away the cloth, smudging the monstrous purple canvas beneath. Blaine didn't react. Not for a long time.

'D'you like it, hon?'

'Um.'

'You hate it, don't you?'

'Er.'

'Tell me… tell me the truth…'

Blaine took the artwork and laid it against the far wall. He glanced at his hands, which were purple.

'I thought you could move Bogey and put it up there — you know, in pride of place,' Laurie suggested.

Blaine froze.

'*Move Bogey?*' he mouthed incredulously.

'Yeah.'

'Sweetie…'

'Yeah?'

'Bogey's not going anywhere.'

Straightening her short, slender body to seem taller than she was, Laurie glowered.

'It's damn well time you got over this whole *Casablanca* baloney!' she spat. 'It was just a B-grade Hollywood flick for God's sake!'

Blaine felt his bloodstream fortify with adrenalin. His cheeks flushing, he paused the movie, as if not wanting to subject the cast to a domestic squabble. Then, holding his purple hands into the light, he scowled towards the far wall.

'And that… that *thing*… that swirly purple gunk… You mean to tell me that you're passing it off as *art?!*'

In a flood of tears, Laurie snatched her creation to her chest. Unsure of whether to attack or retreat, she chose the first option.

'At least it's alive and it's... it's... it's spontaneous!' she snarled. 'Two things you could never be accused of being! I wouldn't let you keep it if you were the last man on earth! You don't know how to appreciate art... you don't know how to appreciate a woman!'

Six

HICHAM OMARY FED the beige calfskin steering wheel of his limited-edition Jaguar through his fingers in a turn.

His concentration was not on the road, but on the conversation that had dominated the morning's game — the subject of endemic corruption.

Halfway between the golf club and his home, a distance of a mile, he was flagged down by a uniformed police officer. Rolling his eyes, Omary eased the car to a halt and lowered the window.

'Good morning sir, you made an infraction back there,' said the officer, his accent from the Mediterranean shores of the north.

Hicham Omary groped in his pocket for a hundred-dirham note. Expertly, he used his left hand to fold it once and then again. In a much-practised movement, he leaned sideways so as to insert the square of paper into the policeman's cuff — thereby avoiding his hand.

But just before the bribe was delivered, he froze. The officer winced. He hadn't yet received the money.

'Look at me,' said Omary out loud. 'I'm as guilty as all the rest.'

'You made an infraction, sir,' the officer repeated.

'So give me a ticket.'

'But...'

'But, what?'

'But, sir, there's another way to sort out the situation.'

'And how would that be?'

The official frowned, fumbling for his pen. No one ever agreed to pay the fine. After all, the standard bribe was a quarter of the price and executed in a fraction of the time. The last thing any policeman wanted to do was paperwork. In the time it took to fill out a single form for an infraction he could bring in ten times as much in bribes — cold, hard cash he got to keep.

Omary held out his wrists.

'Let's go to the police station,' he said. 'I'm all yours!'

Seven

ANOTHER BRIGHT BROOKLYN morning, the blue sky masked by the slate-grey walls of Acme Telesales. Seated at desk 52, Blaine slipped on his headset and got down to coaxing random New Yorkers into bulk-buying Drain-O-Sure.

'Good morning, sir. I'm calling about your drains.'

Click.

'Hello, ma'am… do you have a smell in the kitchen that won't go away?'

Click.

'This is your lucky day, Miss — a Drain-O-Sure day!'

Click.

Just as Blaine was about to make the next call, the supervisor strode up, clipboard in hand.

'I want to see you in my office right away, Williams!'

'I've got five more calls to make before my break. That OK?'

'No, not OK!'

'Huh?'

'You've been suspended!'

'*Suspended?* What for?'

'You know what for… for that email to the shareholders… for damn well claiming that Drain-O-Sure's a con!'

Tugging off his headset, Blaine wiped a hand down hard over his face.

'But Mr. Seldon, we're preying on the elderly and the vulnerable. We're touting a product that's nothing but watered-down bleach… It's shameful and it's probably illegal as well.'

The superintendent whispered into a miniature microphone on his lapel.

'What's going on?'

'You're being terminated. Right now. That's what's going on.'

'What?!'

'Clear out your stuff, Williams. Security's on their way up. I want you out of the building in ten minutes!'

Eight

A PAIR OF size six Jimmy Choo black crocodile stilettos crossed the lawn, the heels sinking into the grass as they went. Strapped tightly into them, Ghita Omary struggled to stay upright as she reeled towards a group of caterers who were huddling at the far end of the garden.

'No, no, no! You imbeciles!' she cried, her arms flailing for balance. 'What are you doing with those lights? They're not supposed to be there! And change those tablecloths at once! Where did you get them — from a prison?! I don't want cotton. I want the finest silk!'

The caterers jerked to attention. They were surrounded by toppled stacks of chairs, piles of trestle tables yet to be assembled, and by miles of crumpled fabrics. One of the men, the bravest and also the most senseless, wagged a finger towards Ghita.

'We're just following orders, miss,' he said.

The next thing he knew, he was lying on the grass, his thigh having been pierced with a size six Jimmy Choo in black crocodile.

In one slick movement, Ghita withdrew her bloodied weapon, slipped it back on her foot, and turned to greet her father, whose Jaguar was purring into the drive.

'Baba! Sorry, but you can't park there,' she called loudly. 'The champagne delivery is about to arrive.'

Hicham Omary might have protested, but he was used to being dealt orders by his daughter.

14

Parking beside the kitchen door, he closed his eyes and found himself in a simple, bare-walled apartment in an old art deco walk-up somewhere far downtown. For a moment there was silence... and simplicity.

Ghita opened the car door, and her father's memory vanished.

'I'm working with idiots, Baba!' she exclaimed, dabbing a lace handkerchief melodramatically to her eye. 'I don't know what to do. One tiny mistake and tongues will wag. You know how they are — like vipers.'

'Dearest Ghita, it's only an engagement,' Omary said as he climbed out of the car, touched with a sense of déjà vu.

'*Only an engagement?* And we are *just* ordinary people, are we?'

Before her father could reply, Ghita clapped her hands, the soft skin of her palms anointed twice daily with a moisturizer from the Savoy Alps.

'I shall need some cheques, Baba,' she said, a tone of sternness in her voice.

'*Some?*'

Ghita calculated. Maths was never her strong point. She quickly lost count, then frowned.

'Just sign me the entire book, and leave them blank... I have lots of people to pay.'

Standing on tiptoes in her Jimmy Choos, she pecked her father on the cheek, her lips leaving a smudge of Chanel Rouge Allure.

'Baba, what would I ever do without you?' she said.

Nine

A SHORT, STOUT man with a waxy face and a week's growth of beard was standing in the shadows outside apartment 5B. The kind of figure you would never pick out in a police line-up, there was nothing at all memorable about him.

Blaine knew his landlord was waiting there in the darkness before he reached the landing. He could smell him, even against the stench of rotting eggs — he reeked of Turkish cigarettes.

'Good evening to you, Mr. Rogers,' he said, taking the last pair of steps in one. 'And to what do I owe the pleasure of your visit?'

'I've had enough!' the landlord growled. He limped backwards a pace and rested a shoulder on the wall.

'Enough of what?'

'Of your chasing away my potential tenants! You make this place sound like it's out of *The Silence of the Lambs*!'

Blaine untied the belt of his raincoat and got out his key. Without thinking, his thumb ran down the notches and he turned it the right way up for the lock.

'Was it wrong of me to point out the highlights?' he asked.

'What highlights?'

'Let me think,' Blaine said, stepping forward until his face was half a foot from the landlord's. 'The abundance of free vermin, the rising damp, and the curious case of Mr. Wilson in 4D.'

The fingers of Mr. Rogers's right hand formed into a fist. He might have thrown a punch, but he was too close and far too feeble. So he yelled instead:

'I want you out of here tomorrow, Williams!'

'But...'

'No buts! Just get the hell out!'

Ten

A LINE OF black limousines stretched down the street, high society streaming out of them and in through the wrought-iron gates of the Omary mansion.

The ladies were coutured in woven silk jelabas, jewels glittering in their ears and around their necks. Their husbands were impeccable in tuxedos, solid gold watches on their wrists.

On either side of the entrance, a pair of giant flambeaux were burning, their flames licking the night air. The ground beneath them was sprinkled with scarlet rose petals, picked at dawn that morning in the foothills of the Atlas.

Inside the gates, a band of musicians from Jajouka were playing, brought in by bus from the Riff. Armed with tambours, fiddles, and with simple wooden pipes, they had been the only choice that Hicham Omary had successfully made. Their music reminded him of his own Berber ancestry, and of carefree summers in the hills in Morocco's north.

The platinum spotlight of a television crew blinded the guests as they entered and ran the gauntlet of welcome.

Inside, against the scent of roasting lamb and pungent white lilies, Hicham Omary and his daughter mingled. There was much grinning, many superlatives, congratulations and kisses.

As father and daughter gave welcome, an army of waiters glided between the guests with trays laden with food and crystal flutes of vintage Cristal.

Eleven

THE REVOLVING DOOR to the street slowed as it turned the last few inches.

Blaine stumbled out, the last cardboard box filled with his possessions clutched in his hands. Balanced on the box, like an imperial crown, was his precious fedora. Tucked into the band was his most prized trophy of all — the stub of a cinema ticket from *Casablanca*'s premiere night.

With care, he placed the box beside all the others just outside on the pavement, put the hat on the back of his head, and did a count.

There were fifteen boxes in all, packed tight with a lifetime's collection of *Casablanca* memorabilia. Beside them was a single vinyl suitcase a little the worse for wear and, next to that, half a dozen framed posters, each one an original, of the same legendary film.

Blaine scanned the street for the truck that the doorman had ordered for him. With no sign of it, he picked up his oversized satchel and a plastic bin liner with a few stray clothes and went back inside to check.

'Hey, Al, he's still not out there.'

'OK. I'll give 'em a call.'

The doorman's bloated finger hit redial and his ear was assaulted by a shrill musical recording.

'I hate The Beach Boys,' he said.

Blaine tapped his watch.

'He should have been here half an hour ago.'

There was a loud grumbling sound outside, as if it were about to rain. The doorman peered out at the sky just as the dispatcher came back on the line.

'Yeah this is Al at Atlantic Avenue. We ordered a van to go to…'

'To storage in Jackson Heights,' Blaine whispered.

'To Queens. Yeah. That's right.' Al hung up the phone. 'Any minute now,' he said.

Blaine gave a thumbs up and went out to the kerb.

He did a double take.

All the boxes were gone.

The only thing left was a poster of Humphrey Bogart, with the word *Casablanca* ornamented in red along the bottom edge. The glass had been shattered, and there was a diagonal boot-print across Bogart's face.

In the distance, slaloming away down Atlantic Avenue, was a garbage truck.

Blaine's hands gripped his cheeks. He couldn't make a sound. Then, slowly, the vacuum in his lungs filled with air.

'Screw you, you bastards!' he screamed. 'And screw you, Mr. Rogers! And you, Mr. Wilson, and you too, Laurie! Screw the whole damned lot of you!'

Twelve

POISED ON THE marble steps that led down to the terrace, Ghita surveyed the guests with her best friend, Aicha.

They were both dressed in couture gowns, every inch of visible skin laden with cut jewels and gold. Ghita's neck was hidden beneath a fabulous sapphire and diamond necklace, a matching tiara weighing down her chestnut hair.

'You've got the whole zoo here tonight,' said Aicha, sipping her champagne.

'And to think that this is just the engagement,' Ghita added.

'Sweet of your father to roll out the red carpet.'

Ghita turned to face her friend, a glint of annoyance in her eye.

'And what's wrong with that? As I've told him so often, he mustn't be shy about blowing a little small change if he wants to be respected by society.'

A waiter swanned up, a silver tray of canapés in hand. Aicha took one. Foie gras on a bed of Beluga from the Persian side of the Caspian.

'This is divine. Where d'you get them?'

Ghita's glance moved dreamily through the guests below.

'I sent the jet to Paris this morning,' she said. 'We emptied half of Fauchon. But if you're serving Cristal, how can you have anything but the best caviar?' Ghita shrugged. 'Anyway, it's just money,' she said, 'and Baba can always make some more of that.'

Thirteen

HUDDLED UP AT a corner table at Rick's Diner in Brooklyn Heights, Blaine opened his satchel and spilled its contents over the table.

There was a *Casablanca* mug, a bound copy of the original screenplay, a passport, a wallet, and the studio shot of Bogart that had adorned desk number 52. Propped up in the chair across from him was the glassless picture frame, the smudged boot-print across the screen hero's face.

A waiter glided over, notepad in hand.

'What'll it be?'

'What's the special?'

'Couscous with prunes.'

'I'll take it… with fries, and a Bud Lite.'

The waiter scribbled, grinned robotically, and was gone.

Blaine sat quite still, his eyes locked on Humphrey's as he contemplated his tremendous loss. At first he felt terrible remorse, as he remembered each individual object that had been swallowed and pulverized by the mechanical monster. He half wondered whether there was any hope of making an insurance claim. But even if he had grounds, how could he put a price on a collection that had taken his entire life to amass?

The couscous arrived, fries at the side. The waiter raised the clay pot's conical lid and clenched his face in another automatic smile. All he was thinking about was the tip.

Blaine dug a fork into the couscous, moved it to his mouth, swallowed, then grimaced. Across from him, it seemed as though Bogart was grimacing too.

'Excuse me!'

The waiter rushed over, his expression taut and submissive.

'Yes, sir, what can I do for you?'

'I'm not gonna bore you with details, but I'm not having the greatest of weeks. So I came in here because couscous is the one thing I expect the universe to deliver without any surprises — especially here at Rick's.'

The waiter narrowed his eyes.

'*And?*'

'And this couscous tastes like gravel... salty gravel. It's barely even cooked.'

'We haven't had any other complaints, sir.'

Blaine sniffed aggressively.

'Yeah, well maybe your other clients are cement mixers, but I'm not!'

The waiter's cheerful facade evaporated. He loomed down over Blaine and Bogart, his fingers gnarled like talons.

'Listen to me, you schmuck!' he roared. 'I've had enough of you! If our couscous isn't to your liking, you can go screw yourself! Or get your royal ass up to some chichi Moroccan joint on the West Side! Or better still, take a hike — to Casablanca!'

Blaine was about to explode. But something stopped him, something deep inside. All of a sudden he was the personification of calm.

'That's it…' he said in a whisper.

'Huh?'

'You're a genius. What's your name?'

The waiter looked down sideways, as if expecting a veiled attack.

'Carl,' said. 'The name's Carl.'

'Well, thank you, Carl! I don't know how to ever thank you enough!'

'Thank you for what?'

'For saving my life.'

Fourteen

Arm in arm, Ghita and Aicha glided down the curved marble staircase and into the crowd.

For Ghita it was a moment to savour. All eyes were on her, the most eligible young woman in all Casablanca. And there was nothing she relished more than being the centre of attention.

A waiter hastened up, a tray of glasses arranged over the burnished surface of his tray. Ghita took a flute of Cristal. She sipped, then almost spat.

'This champagne is warm!' she scowled.

'I shall have it chilled at once, Mademoiselle.'

'Have the bottle poured away!'

'At once, Mademoiselle.'

'These people are so incompetent!' Ghita hissed at her friend.

'They don't understand about hot and cold,' Aicha replied.

'I know they don't, and that's why they're poor.'

At that moment, the sound of a massive engine revving broke above the strains of the musicians from Jajouka.

Ghita's eyes lit up.

'Mustapha's Ferrari…'

A moment later, the two women were standing at the great iron gates of the Omary mansion. Smoothing her gown after the gallop, Ghita regained her composure and straightened her tiara.

Just before the car door opened, a little girl stepped in from the street. Standing between Ghita and the scarlet Ferrari, she was barefoot and dressed in rags.

'Shoo! Get away at once, you nasty little thing!'

The child didn't move. Ghita motioned to one of the security guards, who stepped forwards and snatched the child out the way.

'What an embarrassment,' Ghita exclaimed under her breath.

The Ferrari's door opened, and a slim man with designer stubble and slicked-back hair stepped out. He was moist with expensive aftershave, as though he had just been hosed down in it.

'Your knight in shining armour,' Aicha laughed.

24

Mustapha stepped forwards and pressed his lips to Ghita's knuckles.

'I've been waiting half an hour for you,' she said crossly.

Mustapha smoothed a hand down over his lacquered hair.

'And I have been waiting for you my entire life,' he replied.

Fifteen

BLAINE STEPPED OUT of Rick's Diner into the rain.

In one hand was the poster and in the other, the black bin liner, and the satchel around his neck.

He flagged down a cab, the brake lights reflected in the damp street.

'Where to, bud?'

'JFK. And step on it!'

The door slammed, the tyres screeched, and Blaine found himself energized in a way he hadn't been in years. He checked the flight details on his phone. Royal Air Maroc Flight 201, the red-eye to Casablanca. Leaning back into the tattered seat, he stared out at the droplets tumbling down the window.

He closed his eyes and heard the sound of his grandfather calling him inside. The afternoon was filled with syrupy yellow light, the kind that only really exists in a childhood memory. His grandfather moved into the doorframe, raised a hand, and waved.

'Got something to show you,' he said. 'A little surprise.'

'What is it, Grandpa?'

'A surprise.'

Blaine took the porch steps in one, wrenched back the screen door with both hands, and charged into the house. There was the scent of banoffee pie from the parlour and the sound of vinyl crackling Billie Holiday's 'Summertime'.

'What is it, Grandpa?' Blaine squirmed. 'What's the surprise?'

The old man turned round. He was holding a glass beaker half filled with water. In the glass was his smile.

'Hold on a minute, son,' he said, draining the glass and slipping in his teeth.

Then, reaching down to the bureau, he picked up a grubby fragment of grey paper, no bigger than a postage stamp.

'When I was a young man I took a girl on a date,' he said. 'The girl was your grandma, and the date was the most important night of my life. It was on that night that I asked her to be my bride.'

Blaine sat on his grandpa's knee. He could feel the bones.

'Where did you go — on the date?'

Grandpa didn't reply at first. His tired old eyes glazed over. Then, slowly, he said:

'To see the most magical movie of all on opening night.'

'Which movie, Grandpa?'

'*Casablanca* — the finest picture ever made.' Again he paused, pushed his teeth back into place, and said: 'I want to give you two things, Blaine. The first is this little bit of paper. I'm hoping you'll look after it and cherish it.' Opening his palm, he revealed the grubby scrap of paper.

'But what is it?'

'My ticket stub from that night, from the premiere of *Casablanca*.'

Blaine took it. As he held it up close to his eyes, his grandpa drifted off to sleep.

'What's the other thing, Grandpa?' he said in a loud voice.

Blaine's grandfather stirred from his doze, confused.

'Huh? What? Oh… yes, the other thing…'

The old man put on his glasses and strained to look at the TV listings. 'The other thing is that we're gonna watch it together.'

'Watch what?'

'*Casablanca* of course! It's just about to start!'

Sixteen

THERE HAD BEEN toasts, and more toasts, laughter and even tears.

Hicham Omary had thanked his friends for honouring him at his daughter's engagement. He had lavished praise on the impending union, and regret that his wife was not alive to witness it all. As the Jajouka musicians struck up and the guests began to dance, Ghita and her fiancé slipped away into the rose garden.

'I was thinking of Australia for the honeymoon,' Mustapha said. 'The Great Barrier Reef?'

Ghita smiled.

'You read my mind!'

Mustapha was about to reply when his mobile rang. Without thinking, he took the call, his brow beading with sweat, a hand cupped over his mouth.

'Hi sweetie... How are you? Yes, yes. Can't talk now. OK. Until tomorrow. Me too. Yes, OK... I promise.'

'Who was that?'

'It was, er, my... my... cousin... Karim, I mean *Karima*.'

'And we didn't invite her? Why didn't you tell me?'

'Oh, she's not a close cousin.'

'But you're meeting her tomorrow?'

'Just for a coffee. She needs some help with something.'

Ghita moved closer, until her lips were less than an inch from her fiancé's ear. In a voice as cold as crushed ice, she said:

'If you ever lie to me about another woman, my darling, I shall hunt you down and tear out your heart.'

Seventeen

At ten minutes to ten, Hicham Omary went up to his private study and took a call from his senior editor, as he did every night of the week.

He might have taken it on his mobile, but he wanted a little space and solitude. Besides, he was tiring of the great and the good of Casablanca society.

The editor had gone over the news agenda for the main bulletin of the night. It was a formality, one that even

Omary — as owner of the channel — was not expected to change in any way.

Putting down the receiver, he paced over to the window and watched as Ghita strolled through the crowd. She was showing off a colossal diamond set on a band of Russian gold.

Beside her was her beloved Mustapha, whose good looks were matched only by his confidence, and by the size of his father's bank balance.

There was a knock at the oak door and Hamza Harass, father of the groom-to-be, swept in. In his hand was a Cohiba cigar, a luxury he clung to despite a chronic heart condition.

'Thought I'd find you in here,' he said.

Omary mumbled something indistinct. Stepping across to a bookcase lined with leather-bound volumes, he pushed a secret button made of brass. It was mounted to the underside of one of the shelves and transformed the unit into a well-stocked bar. Omary poured two tumblers of Glendullan. He handed one to Harass, his closest friend, a man with a seat on his company's board.

They clinked glasses.

'To a union between our families,' said Omary, peering towards the window again.

'You certainly know how to throw a party,' Harass replied.

'I didn't do anything. Just found the band.' He paused, then smiled. 'And I wrote a few cheques as well.'

'They make a wonderful couple. So in love.'

Omary cupped the single malt in his hand, warming it.

'I worry about her — I worry about Ghita,' he said.

'Look at her, you've given her everything. She's elegant, beautiful, intelligent.'

'But she's not streetwise,' Omary sighed, taking a gulp of his Scotch. 'She's never been touched by the real world. Never taken a taxi let alone a bus, never had to rough it — never even gone shopping for food, or anything, except for luxuries and designer brands.' Omary fell silent and sighed again. 'She has never starved,' he said.

'And is there shame in that?' Harass asked.

'Perhaps not. But it weakens her... and leaves her open to attack.'

Eighteen

DAWN BROKE OVER Africa, its light brighter than anything Blaine had ever witnessed. Squinting through the half-shaded window, he peered down at his first glimpse of the Dark Continent. Beside him, Bogart was strapped into the empty seat, the tread of the boot-print a little less obvious than before.

What an adventure! Blaine thought to himself. First time to Africa and on an adventure in search of his true love. He looked down at the parched landscape below. His grandfather's picket-fence smile was overlaid on the canvas of desert. The old man would be pleased — pleased that a little ticket stub had led to an obsession — and that the obsession had in turn led to adventure.

Flight 201 descended fast through a clear blue sky, banked sharply over water, and flew in low over a vast metropolis — all gleaming and white like a distant paradise. There were straight boulevards edged with pin-prick palms, dazzling villas and apartment blocks laid out in radiating lines. And there was a sense of order, as though the city below the metal wings was inspired by something divine.

'Casablanca,' whispered Blaine to himself. 'At last…'

His eyes welling with tears, he touched a hand out to Humphrey, and gave thanks to the universe.

The tyres touched down with a thud and a trace of smoke.

All the passengers leapt up. In a maelstrom of movement, they fought each other for their cases and their abundant packages of duty-free.

Taking his lead from the others, Blaine grabbed Bogart and elbowed his way down the aisle. Before he knew it, he had clambered down the staircase and was treading with uncertain footsteps over African soil, or rather, cement.

In the terminal building, an immigration official drew deeply on his filterless cigarette, exhaled, and asked:

'*Combien de temps restez-vous en Maroc?*'

Blaine jabbed a finger at his passport.

'American,' he said. 'You speak English?'

The official stubbed out the cigarette and blew out a last lungful of smoke.

'What is your age?'

'Twenty-nine… my date of birth is in the passport.'

'How long you stay in Casablanca?' he asked, in a voice deepened by a fondness for Gauloises.

'Um, er,' Blaine faltered. 'Not quite sure. I got a one-way ticket. You see, it's a last-minute trip.'

'What the name of your hotel?'

'I don't have one. Not yet.'

The official lit another cigarette despondently. He flicked through the empty pages, clicked down the stamp, and slid the passport back across the counter.

'Welcome to Casablanca,' he said.

Nineteen

AT THE BACK of the Omary mansion, the empty bottles were piled up, the catering staff gorging themselves on leftover canapés. The last of the guests were stumbling out to their cars, a little the worse for wear after all the chilled Cristal.

Ghita stood at the gate, kissing cheeks and giving thanks. She was irritated that Mustapha had left early amid a whirlwind of excuses. The owner of the catering firm moved cautiously from the shadows and received the full force of Ghita's wrath. It was late and there was no one else to savage. But, having been in the business for many decades, he knew how to sidestep the insecurities of the city's *nouveau riche*.

Stooping to the point of grovelling, he kissed her hand, and declared:

'Miss Omary, allow me to say that you were a radiant princess tonight.'

Her vanity never quite satiated, Ghita's wrath melted. She blushed, the colour lost to the darkness.

'Do you really think so?' she giggled.

There was a crash of bottles in the distance and the caterer slunk off to bark orders at his team. All alone for the first time that night, Ghita strode into the mansion, slipped off her stilettos, and searched for her father.

She found him in his study nursing a second glass of Glendullan, his bow tie undone. He seemed a little depressed, but it never occurred to Ghita to ask why.

'They have all gone, Baba,' she said. 'I think it went well.'

Hicham Omary's eyes creased in a smile. He wasn't listening.

'For the wedding we will definitely use another caterer,' said Ghita. 'Mr. Hamood and his band of merry men were incompetence personified.'

'What's that?' asked Omary distantly, staring into mid-air.

'The caterers… they're imbeciles. And they're liars and they're thieves. I shall insist that they are all fired. It'll teach them a good lesson.'

Hicham Omary took a sip of his whisky. His eyes slowly focusing, he took in his daughter, who had slumped down in a leather armchair across from him.

'Do you ever think of the families they support?' he said softly.

Ghita frowned.

'Their lying, thieving relatives? Why should I spare a thought for them?' she said, rubbing a hand over her heel. 'Damn those shoes. You'd think that Louboutin could design shoes that didn't pinch.'

Again, Omary sipped. He patted the place on the sofa beside him.

'Come and sit with me,' he said.

'Oh, but I'm tired, Baba. I think I shall go to bed.'

Omary patted a second time, repeating his request a little more forcefully.

'There's something I want to ask you.'

Ghita crossed the room and sat down on the sofa.

'What is it, Baba?'

'Tell me something…'

'What?'

'What is the greatest suffering you have ever known?'

Ghita pressed her hands together, touching a fingertip to her lips.

'Is this a joke?' she asked, a little confused.

'No, just a question.'

'Well, if you are asking, I'll tell you. It's enduring that terrible car you gave me. It's made me a laughing stock. It almost broke down again last week. And that chauffeur you gave me is a scoundrel.'

'Which car?'

'The white one… the one with those little silver rings on the front, like the Olympics.'

'An Audi.'

'That's it. It's German, and quite unreliable.'

'Ghita, can I tell you something?' said Omary, resting the empty glass on the table to his left.

'Yes, Baba. Oh, is it a surprise? You're giving me a new car? Well, would you give me a new driver at the same time? Tawfik's such a wretch.'

Ghita's eyes lit up.

'Oh! Thank you! Thank you!' she exclaimed, kissing her father's cheek, and leaving another smudge of Rouge Allure.

'Listen to me,' her father said coldly. 'When I was your age I had holes in my shoes. I had never taken a taxi. My feet were covered in blood from walking. I was thin as a pole.'

'Poor Baba.' She leaned forwards and kissed him again.

'I don't want sympathy,' he said. 'I just want you to understand.'

'To understand what?'

'The value of money.'

Ghita sat up straight.

'Oh, I do,' she said. 'I know the cost of all sorts of things and think it's bordering on the criminal what they charge. I was just looking at a jacket at Gucci. They're asking a king's ransom.'

'And the cost of milk? How much is milk?'

Ghita shrugged.

'Well, I suppose it depends on how much you buy.'

'A litre. For a litre of milk.'

Another shrug.

'A few dirhams, I suppose.'

'How much exactly?'

'Dearest Baba,' Ghita giggled. 'I've never bought milk.'

'Why not?'

'Because there are people to do that.' She yawned. 'Now, I'm tired, so terribly tired. I shall go to bed.'

Omary stood up and walked to the window. He peered down into the darkness, where the strands of coloured lights were being taken down and the trestle tables folded away.

'How would you survive without all of this?' he asked.

'Without what, Baba?'

'Without the luxuries you take for granted every moment of the day?'

Again, Ghita giggled, a giggle tinged with apprehension. She wondered what her father was getting at.

'I am quite sure I would survive very well, Baba.'

Hicham Omary turned slowly to face his daughter. He looked at her hard, taking in the tiara and the jewels, the couture gown and the perfect manicure.

'Without me bankrolling your lifestyle and your whims, I'd give you five minutes out there in the real world,' he said.

Ghita emitted a faint squeak — the seed of a giggle. Then she fell silent, realizing her father was for once deadly serious.

'I don't need money to survive,' she said faintly. 'But it just makes life, well… nicer.'

'So you are telling me that you would survive quite happily out there without the funds I provide — funds you plough through without a second thought.'

'Of course I could survive, dearest Baba.'

'But for how long?'

Ghita touched an index finger to her lower lip, the nail polished in rosebud red.

'For ages, I suppose.'

'For a day… a week… a month?'

'Yes, yes… at least that long.'

Omary took a step closer to the sofa.

'For a month?'

Ghita widened her eyes and nodded very gently.

'Yes, I'm sure I could survive for a month. After all, how hard could it be?'

'I don't believe it!' shouted Hicham Omary, slamming his palm down on the sofa's wooden arm. 'I don't believe you could survive without my money or your fancy friends.'

A tear rolled down Ghita's cheek as her face flushed with emotion. She had never seen her father angry before, let alone annoyed at her — and on this most special of nights.

'Then I'll prove it!' she exclaimed.

'How?'

'I'll go downtown.'

'*And?*'

'And I'll… I'll…'

'You'll *what?*'

'I'll live there.'

'For an afternoon?'

'No… for longer. For *much* longer. For…'

'*For…?*'

'For a month!'

Ghita's father said nothing. He turned his back on the sofa, gazing out to the garden again.

'You don't even know where downtown is,' he said gently.

'Yes, I do… it's near the port… somewhere there, near all those ugly old streets.'

Omary had a flash of memory.

A young Berber kid playing soccer in the medina's filth. The other boys were taunting the first because his shoe had ripped open, and because his family came from down in the desert. The taunts led to a brawl, a brawl that ended with blood.

He turned round.

As he did so, Ghita stood up. She strode over to him. Her eyes were dark and serious, her breathing deep.

'I shall do it,' she said. 'I shall go and live downtown for a month without any luxury or funds. I swear on Mama's grave I shall do it.'

Twenty

A TIDAL WAVE of travellers swept out from the terminal building, the majority of them pilgrims newly returned from the hajj.

Many were clutching plastic containers, filled to their brims with precious Zamzam water from the sacred spring in Mecca. As soon as they reached the sun-drenched exterior of the terminal, they were engulfed by hordes of relatives. There was whooping and hugging, tears of joy, and exclamations of thanks to God.

Somewhere in the middle of the surge of humanity was Blaine, satchel and bin liner in one hand, Humphrey Bogart in the other. He was clothed in his grimy white macintosh, the trusty fedora balanced on his head.

The pilgrims soon gushed away, leaving him alone.

Blaine stood there, awed by the moment, the initial sense of apprehension gone. He smiled — a smile that led to laughter.

At last, he was home.

Twenty-one

AT OMARY'S MANSION, the sprinklers were at work again, rinsing away the footprints and the spilled champagne.

A gardener was planting new flowers around the edge of the lawn, on the instructions of Ghita. She had specified that they were to alternate in royal blue, red, and white, and that on no account was there ever to be any pink. A feng shui guru in Miami had informed her the week before that pink was her cursed colour, one that could bring nothing but ill fortune and despair.

In the house, Hicham Omary was stirring a cup of English breakfast tea, his mind on the night before. He rolled his eyes at the thought of high society, all too ready to parade in their jewels, and to take advantage of free entertainment.

His mind turned to the conversation after the party, the conversation that had ended in his daughter's promise. He jerked up straight, then grinned.

The maid entered with a fresh pot of tea.

'Meriem, would you please go and wake Ghita, and remind her of the conversation we had last night?' he said.

'Yes, sir. At once.'

An hour passed, the grandfather clock in the entrance struck nine times. There was the sound of leather slippers shuffling over polished parquet. Ghita entered, still in her pyjamas, texting a message as she came.

'Good morning, my dear,' said Omary brightly.

Ghita sent her text, leant down and kissed the crown of her father's head.

'Good morning, Baba. What a night that was!'

Omary cracked his knuckles.

'A fine morning,' he said. 'Looks as though you have good weather for it.'

'Good weather for what, Baba?'

'For your grand adventure.'

'Hmm?'

Ghita frowned sleepily and began typing another text.

'Surely you have not forgotten our conversation, and your promise?'

A moment or two passed, then a look of absolute horror descended like a curtain over Ghita's face. She murmured something unclear, a cross between supplication and apology.

An hour later, she was clothed in a lavender dress with matching shoes from Jimmy Choo. Around her neck was a double string of pearls, the diamond engagement ring weighing down her left hand. Behind her were three gigantic Louis Vuitton suitcases packed with accessories and clothes. They were so heavy that the butler had had to struggle getting them down the stairs.

Hicham Omary found his daughter standing beside the cases in the hallway. She was putting on lipstick, while a maid obediently held her iPhone to one ear. Blowing a kiss into the phone, she prepared to beg as much as was necessary to talk her father into seeing sense.

'I have been a fool, Baba,' she said unctuously, 'and have behaved shamefully.' Dabbing a lace handkerchief to her eye, she nestled her face in her father's shoulder, and muttered a rivulet of remorse.

Omary stepped back. He tapped his watch.

'Mehdi's waiting,' he said. 'He has instructions to take you down to Marché Central. And he will come back for you in thirty days.'

Ghita's nostrils flared with rage. She breathed in deep, felt her toes curl up in her lavender Jimmy Choos. She was about to say something when her father advanced a pace. Expecting to be hugged, to be told it was all a joke, Ghita breathed out in a sigh. The edge of her nose wrinkled as she smiled.

But Hicham Omary clicked his fingers.

Understanding the instruction, the butler strode up, a polished silver salver balanced upon his palm.

'For your protection I think it wise to relieve you of some of this,' Omary said.

Ghita was about to ask what he meant when her father unclasped the pearl necklace and placed it on the tray. Then, gently, he removed her earrings, her diamond-pavé Chopard and, lastly, her engagement ring. Before she could protest, Omary reached for her iPhone and placed it on the salver as well.

The butler disappeared.

When he was gone, Ghita's father motioned to the luggage.

'You can take one of them,' he said. 'And one alone.'

Ghita's cheeks darkened from plum red to dark maroon. Fuming like she had never fumed before, she was resigned to conceal the depth of her fury. She motioned to the largest case, a portmanteau. Before she could change her mind, it was whisked away to the car.

Any other girl might have got on her knees and begged a little more, but Ghita's pride was too strong. Seething, her stomach filled with bile, she pecked her father on the cheek and walked out to the black Maybach limousine.

A liveried chauffeur was holding open the door. He greeted Ghita but, as always, she ignored him as she got in.

Just before the vehicle moved away, Omary hurried out of the house to the driveway. Again, Ghita sighed and cursed him aloud, imagining that he was coming to call it all off.

She wound down the window and puckered her lips.

Her father held out his hand.

'I almost forgot,' he said. 'I think you'd better leave me your wallet for safekeeping. We wouldn't want you to get mugged down there, would we?'

Ghita would have burst into tears, but was too enraged to cry. All she could manage was a pained shriek that resembled the call of some exotic parakeet.

'What will I do without any money at all?!' she exclaimed.

Omary fumbled in his pocket. He pulled out a ten-dirham coin and passed it to her.

'That should get you started,' he said.

Twenty-two

HUMPHREY BOGART HAD been strapped to the roof of a dilapidated communal taxi — an old white Mercedes.

It was so full of people that the passengers had all melded together, making it impossible to say where one ended and the next began. Blaine was lodged on the back seat, pressed up between a pair of veiled women.

One of them had thrust her squalling baby onto his lap, as hers was occupied by an oversized wicker basket stuffed with live chickens.

All of a sudden, the baby threw up all over Blaine and began screaming ferociously. Terrified by the noise, the chickens began flapping wildly and became so animated that one of them broke free. In a frenzy of squawking and feathers, the bird flapped through the little empty space, wings fluttering against faces.

Embracing the adventure, Blaine savoured every moment.

An hour later and he was alone on the back seat.

His face pressed up against the window, he took in the gleaming streets of old Casablanca, and the hotchpotch of life that filled them.

There were wizened men pushing barrows laden with ripe pomegranates and twisted scrap metal; donkey carts, and blind beggars led through the gridlocked traffic by young boys. And there were street hawkers selling cigarettes one by one, pickpockets lurking in doorways, old women scrubbing down steps, businessmen in wide ties and nylon bell-bottoms, and the scent of diesel fumes thick on the ocean breeze.

Blaine wound down the window and breathed it all in.

He couldn't believe it — the *real* Casablanca, a destination of which he had dreamed night and day for as long as he could remember. He caught a flash of his grandfather's smile in half a glass of water, and rummaged in the band of his fedora for the ticket stub. It was still there, a trophy through whose magic the journey had all begun.

'I'm here, Grandpa,' Blaine whispered. 'I'm *really* here… in Casablanca!'

Twenty-three

UPHOLSTERED IN BEIGE calfskin, the Maybach 57 floated down the Corniche and passed the city's historic lighthouse. On a patch of communal ground opposite was the Italian circus, its elephants being scrubbed down by the clowns.

Ghita was too busy seething to take in the sights. Her expression was quite vacant, as if she had just been informed that a firing squad was to end her life at dawn. The limousine glided down past the great Mosque of Hassan II, through the underpass, and along the edge of the old medina. The ocean swell was heavy for the time of year, the waves crashing down against the barricades.

All Ghita could think was that her father was up to something, a ruse to hold a surprise party of some kind. She could feel it in her bones, that there was to be a high to counter the low. There would be a reception with laughter and more champagne, or a jaunt to Monte Carlo on the family's Gulfstream, or diamonds, or emeralds — a grand roll call of luxury and delight.

As the Maybach neared the Casa Port Railway Station, a uniformed officer flagged it down. Before the officer could deliver his much-practised line about exceeding the speed limit, the chauffeur lowered the window and slipped a crisp green fifty-dirham note into his glove. The whole operation took less than thirty seconds, and was executed as elegantly as a ballerina's pirouette.

The chauffeur turned right, away from the ocean, up a palm-lined avenue, towards the old art deco heart of Casablanca. The scent of calfskin, the faint hum of Mozart, and the silence of German engineering were a world apart from the harsh reality of the streets — streets which lay the thickness of a window-pane away.

Indicating left onto Boulevard Mohammed V, the limousine accelerated, then it slowed to no more than a crawl. Ghita felt a lump in her throat — a lump that was fast growing in size. She scanned the kerb for balloons, for well-wishers and old friends.

But all she could see was a tapestry of misery and neglect.

'What orders did my father give you, Mehdi?' she asked.

The chauffeur eased the car to a halt.

'To leave you here, Mademoiselle, by the side of Marché Central.'

Ghita smiled, then she grinned, her face tightening with angst.

'It's all a joke, isn't it?'

The chauffeur didn't reply. He opened his door, walked calmly around the car, and unloaded the Louis Vuitton portmanteau, wincing at its weight. Then he opened Ghita's door, back straight, staring into the middle distance as he had been instructed always to do.

Warily, a Jimmy Choo high heel stepped out onto the kerb.

As her body followed the foot, Ghita felt a pang of fear run down her spine. It was as though she were the last of an all but extinct race, about to be hunted by poachers in a hostile and unforgiving land. She began to sob, but the driver had been instructed not to fall for any tricks. Besides, he was revelling in her anguish. In a long career of driving the wealthy around town, he had never known a passenger more odiously pampered than Mr. Omary's daughter.

'What shall I do?' she asked him.

The chauffeur turned his palms upwards and shrugged. He strode back to his side of the car. Just before he got in, he touched the peak of his cap in respect.

'Good luck, Mademoiselle Omary,' he said.

Ten seconds later, the Maybach limousine was gone.

Twenty-four

A BURGUNDY-COLOURED TRAM rattled up Boulevard Mohammed V, once the main drag of art deco Casablanca, the greatest expression of French colonial might ever constructed outside France.

It was brand new and shiny, and almost empty of any passengers. The seats still had plastic covers on them from the factory. Part of the revival plan for a tired old beauty, it was a symbol of both past splendour and of glorious things to come.

Anxiously, Ghita stood on the kerb in the exact spot where the polished limousine had left her. She may have been born and raised in Casablanca, but all she knew were its wealthy quarters: Anfa, Marif and Californie. The secret haunts of the jet-set were what she knew best of all — in Paris, New York, and Monte Carlo. They were her real home — not the grim realities in the city of her birth. So she stood there, waiting for the balloons and for the brass band, waiting for the hugs and the cheers.

But they didn't come.

So Ghita sat down on her monogrammed portmanteau and she sobbed.

Quite a while passed, and nobody noticed her. After all, downtown Casablanca is a place of frenetic life. Commuters were hurrying through the bright morning light and the shadows, barking into mobile phones. Waiters were criss-crossing the tram tracks, miniature trays bearing glasses of *café noir* in their hands. Magazine sellers were laying out their stock on the pavement; postmen were riffling through their wads of mail; and street sweepers were doing their best to bring order to the grime.

The listing, clumsy silhouette of a bulky man to-ed and fro-ed against the yellow winter light, moving in the direction of Ghita and her enormous piece of Louis Vuitton. His movements were erratic, a consequence of mania and drink.

Lurching, fumbling, ranting, he covered the last few feet by leaping. Then, in a display of inner torture and bizarre affliction, he pointed to his open mouth and rubbed his shirtless stomach both at once.

Ghita screamed and screamed.

She waved her hands, beseeching him to leave her alone. But the man didn't agree. Instead, he became all the more aroused by having elicited a dramatic reaction in such a prim young lady. He began to gyrate wildly.

Then he dropped his trousers.

Clutching the handle of her case, struggling on her heels, Ghita dragged it down the grand boulevard as fast as she could go. Weighed down and hobbled, she wasn't able to move forwards in anything more than slow motion, the inebriated aggressor floundering close behind.

The curious sight of a trouserless figure pursuing a well-coutured young woman, pristine in lavender and matching Jimmy Choos, went quite unnoticed. It was just part of another morning's bustle down on Boulevard Mohammed V.

Jerking, the gears grinding, a decrepit and weatherworn communal white Mercedes took the corner onto the broad thoroughfare. Wide-eyed, his face pressed up against the grimy window, Blaine drank it all in — the buildings, the chaos, and the lives unhindered by welfare, mass employment, and social safety nets.

He caught a glimpse of fine clothes, delicate skin, and a large, square portmanteau gathering speed, and of a blur of naked flesh gaining ground.

A stone's throw from the central market, the taxi slammed on its brakes and Blaine recoiled from whiplash. The engine was overheating, and its driver was in need of strong coffee and a packet of Marquise cigarettes.

Humphrey Bogart was unstrapped from the roof and lowered down. Blaine gave thanks in English, smiled a great deal, and found himself on the kerb. And again he gave thanks. This time it was to his New York life for having dumped him so conclusively, and to the door that had opened — a door into another world.

His heels tight together, Casablanca's newest arrival stared up at the grandeur and the detail — the rococo curls and the once-gilded domes, the exquisite wrought-iron balconies, the Carrera marble, and the angular signage from a distant time. Shuffling clockwise, Blaine turned through three-sixty, mouth open wide, hands outstretched in awe of it all.

Adjacent to where he was standing was the Marché Central — a French market constructed in high colonial arabesque. Across from it, no more than a ramshackle shell held up by scaffolding, were the remnants of the Bessonneau apartment building, once a landmark visible across the city.

As his heels completed their rotation, Blaine caught sight of the simple, unpretentious facade of Hotel Marrakech.

Holding Bogart up to eye level, he winked.

The next thing he knew, he was lying on the ground, felled by a slim figure in lavender. The tip of a stiletto jabbed his ankle, and the edge of a voluminous leather portmanteau struck the side of his head.

Dazed, the American struggled to work out what had happened. As he did so, the lavender figure rose up like a cobra about to strike.

'How dare you bump into me!' she hissed, stumbling to get vertical, back up onto her Jimmy Choos.

'Excuse me, but it was you who bumped into me,' said Blaine.

Ghita glanced back, relieved.

'He's gone,' she said. 'Thank God for that. He was chasing me... hunting me.'

'Who was?'

'That... that... *that fiend!*'

Blaine dusted himself off and picked up Bogart.

'I've just arrived,' he said. 'Right off the red-eye from JFK. D'you know if this hotel's any good?'

Ghita looked at the American incredulously.

'Which hotel?'

'That one. The Marrakech.'

A homeless man pushed past and relieved himself on the exterior wall. The trickle of warm liquid soon seeped in between the cracked paving tiles. Ghita coughed forcefully into her lace handkerchief, then gagged. She whipped out a miniature bottle of hand sanitizer and disinfected her palms.

'I'd say it was a hellhole,' she replied curtly.

'And I'd say it was gritty and great,' said Blaine, giving an enthusiastic thumbs up.

He glanced down at her luggage.

'You new in town as well?'

Ghita froze.

CASABLANCA BLUES

'Er, um. Well, no… no, I live here. It's just my home is… is… is being redecorated. I'm going to the…' she faltered, glancing left and right. 'To the Hyatt. It's just down there at the end of the boulevard.'

Blaine touched a hand to his injured ankle.

'Well, have a good day,' he said, striding towards the portico of the Hotel Marrakech.

A little red taxi pulled up. The driver got out. With tremendous difficulty he hoisted the Louis Vuitton onto the roof-rack. Ghita motioned to the distance, in the direction from which she had come.

'To the Hyatt,' she said.

The unshaven driver flinched.

'You could walk that.'

Ghita gave him the look of death.

'Not in these heels.'

She clambered in, the passenger door slammed, the wheels moved, and within less than a minute, brakes were applied.

The cab driver's hand came off the gear stick and waited for payment. Fishing for her purse, Ghita remembered that she had been banished without funds. Then her fingers touched something circular and worn at the bottom of her pocket. The ten-dirham coin her father had given her. She looked at it, almost marvelling, unable to remember the last time she had actually taken notice of a coin.

'Here you are,' she said. 'You can keep the change.'

The Louis Vuitton was loaded onto the porter's trolley, domed in polished brass. The great mahogany doors of

51

the Hyatt were pulled open from inside, and a multitude of fawning bellboys bowed, scraped, and welcomed. There was the calming scent of lemongrass, and the sound of water spilling out from symmetrical fountains.

Digging her heels into the marble, Ghita made a beeline for the reception desk. She sashayed with the confidence and swagger of someone accustomed to comfort.

The duty manager looked up, caught eye contact, and smiled.

'Good morning to you, Mademoiselle. How are you?'

'I am all the better for being at the Hyatt,' she said. 'I won't bore you with the details of my morning, but it's been horrifying to say the least.'

'And what may I do for you?'

'A room. I would like a room,' Ghita paused. 'Actually, I would like a suite. Something big, with a view… a view away from the city.'

'Of course, Mademoiselle. And how long will you be staying with us?'

Ghita Omary glanced at the calendar behind the reception desk.

'For a month,' she said.

The manager's fingertips tapped away at a keyboard.

'We have an Ambassador Suite available, Mademoiselle. It has a fine view over the port, and complimentary breakfast. The price is one thousand and twenty-six euros per night, including tax. A total of thirty thousand, seven hundred and eighty euros.'

'That's fine, I'll take it.'

'We shall need your credit card to make the confirmation.'

Ghita delved into her handbag, a limited-edition Versace.

At the very bottom, below the compact, the lipstick, the silk scarf, and the leather-bound notebook from Coach, was a secret compartment. Unzipping it, she pulled out a Black American Express card.

Smugly, she passed it to the clerk.

After all, no top-notch shopaholic would go out without emergency plastic.

The card was swiped. The manager squinted at the computer display.

'I am so sorry, Miss Omary,' he said, 'but this card appears to have been cancelled. Do you have another we could try?'

Ghita felt her back warming with anger. Snatching the card, she snarled:

'Damn him! Damn him! How dare he subject me to this!'

The manager took a step back.

'My father,' Ghita said, straining to regain her composure, 'he seems to be having a little amusement at my expense. I'll just check into the room now, and give you another card later.'

The manager held up a finger.

'I am afraid to inform you that hotel policy insists that we take a valid credit card in advance.'

Ghita Omary calmed herself. She moved forward into the light, so that the duty manager could see the depth of the displeasure exhibited in her eyes.

'Do you have any idea who my father is?' she said. 'He's Hicham Omary, owner of Globalcom! If you don't give me a suite right now, I'll have you fired and then publicly disgraced! You'll be down in the Sahara by nightfall!'

The duty manager didn't respond. Calmly, he took back the credit card.

'Alas, it seems as though the card is stolen,' he said. 'There is a message in the system asking merchants to destroy it if located.'

Taking a pair of scissors from a drawer, he snipped the Centurion card in half.

'A very good day to you, Mademoiselle Omary,' he said.

Twenty-five

A LITTLE LATER, the Maybach limousine cruised through Anfa's palm-lined streets. Hicham Omary was reclining in the back. He had been going through the morning's news schedule on the phone, the leather seat strewn with papers.

Looking out at the traffic lights of the Boulevard Gandhi intersection, he noticed a commotion. A policeman had pulled up a truck piled with crates of oranges from Agadir. The officer was going over the driver's documents, all part of a ballet designed to end in a bribe.

Omary got another burst of childhood memory: a sun-drenched lane in the country and bare, swollen feet. He had picked citrus fruit near Tafroute after leaving school at the age of twelve. It was there that his family had herded sheep and raised crops for fifteen centuries and more. The sweet scent of oranges brought back memories of the endless citrus groves, and of his uncle, a wily old farmer who was bitter to the core.

Running a hand over his face, Omary watched as the truck's driver slipped over the neatly folded bill, before his ramshackle vehicle was waved on.

The lights changed and the Maybach rolled away down Boulevard Gandhi.

Omary's mind turned to his daughter.

A pang of guilt, even remorse, hit him. It was tempered by a sense of anger, anger at himself. He had been far too lenient, and his lenience had created a brat — the kind he had so despised on his way up through the ranks from the orange groves to the boardroom.

The limousine glided to the end of the boulevard and on towards Californie, where the most pretentious of the *nouveau riche* were to be found. They were lured there by the exotic name of the suburb, and by the size of the villas, grand enough to wow even the most blasé of socialites.

The old houses were few and far between these days. Most had been torn down and replaced by concrete monstrosities, wedding-cake homes like his own. The old ones from the French era had been studies in serene perfection, leftovers from an era dedicated to good breeding and to style.

On one corner there stood the finest of all — a villa that was almost a century old. It was absolutely perfect. Symmetrical in form and art nouveau in style, there was an almost enchanted quality about it, a sense that it had been conjured through an architectural alchemy.

Omary always looked out for it as he approached. He could feel it drawing near, and was energized by the mere thought of being in its presence.

But on that particular morning, something was wrong.

Outside the villa there stood a line of parked trucks, a battery of workmen attending each one. Every man was wearing a yellow helmet and was clutching a pickaxe, as if he were heading down a mineshaft.

The limousine slowed in the traffic, and Hicham Omary watched in horror at what was going on. The workmen were demolishing the villa, the jewel of jewels — smashing, crushing, slamming. It was an execution.

Omary asked the chauffeur to pull over.

He got out. Reeling in revulsion and shame, he strode over to the ruins.

An aged guardian was squatting on the sidelines. He was grizzled and half blind, his eyes frosted by cataracts. Omary approached him, squatting down as well. He gave greeting, and said:

'Tell me, brother, what is happening here?'

The guardian whispered a line of greeting in return, waved a hand at the rubble and the dust.

'They're breaking it up,' he said very slowly. 'I've worked here all my life, keeping it safe. And now this… the end of a life.'

'How can they get permission to tear down such a treasure?'

The old man rubbed the side of his hand to his eye.

'They can do anything they like,' he said.

'But it's against the law.'

'Law, *what law*?'

'The law of the city, the law of the land!'

The guardian rubbed a thumb and index finger together.

'Pay the bribe to the right people and you can do anything you like,' he said.

Twenty-six

EXPELLED FROM THE Hyatt, Ghita had taken refuge at a tumbledown kiosk opposite the Marché Central.

It sold cheap cigarettes and lighter fuel, chewing gum and glue. On the journey back down the main boulevard she had run the full gamut of emotion, ranging from bizarre euphoria to despair and rage.

She had dragged the portmanteau behind her, leaving its underside battered and scarred. Had she not been so extremely attached to its contents, she would have abandoned it.

Instantly grasping from her clothes and her luggage that she was out of place, the kiosk's owner slid over a telephone.

Snatching the receiver, Ghita wiped it with lace, and dialled. There was a pause, then a woman's voice, shrill and excitable.

'Aicha, darling, it's me, it's Ghita. I'm having an awful time. Thank God I remembered your number. Baba's being beastly...'

'Ghita, darling, it's early for you, especially after a night like that.'

'I swear I'm still dreaming… but it's no dream — it's a nightmare. You have to help me!'

'But dearest, I'm en route to the airport, going to Gstaad for the weekend. Last skiing of the season. It's Malik's little treat.'

Ghita broke down again.

'I need help,' she repeated. 'I am in danger!'

Aicha's voice crackled and faded away as the line went dead.

Slamming down the receiver, Ghita spat out a line of expletives. Then she stormed across the road to Hotel Marrakech, dragging the Louis Vuitton behind her.

Outside it, a young man was touting stolen phones from a scruffy old shoebox. His accomplice was on the lookout for possible customers and for the cops. Spotting a well-dressed woman in lavender heels, the pair made a beeline for her.

'Need a phone?' they both said at once. 'Got some nice ones here.'

Ghita peered into the box. One of the mobiles was buzzing. Another was chiming 'Yankee Doodle Dandy'. She spotted the familiar outline of an iPhone.

'How much is that?'

'Four hundred dirhams.'

Ghita unclasped her brooch. It was gold, fashioned in the shape of a dolphin, and had been a gift from the mayor of Paris.

'I'll swap it for this, and only because I'm desperate.'

The young man snatched the brooch, furled it away, and handed over the iPhone. Wasting no time, Ghita tried Aicha again. Unable to reach her, she sent a text.

There was no reply.

Cursing, Ghita shook her fists and stamped her stilettos as angrily as she could. Then, crushed, she climbed the steps up to the Hotel Marrakech, dragging the portmanteau up behind her.

The lobby was dark, caked in dirt, and decidedly unappealing. It was decorated with ashtrays, tattered old airline posters, and third-rate plastic plants. Every surface seemed to be a perch for a cat. There were dozens of them — tabbies, tortoiseshells, anxious Siamese, and sleek Burmese.

Having pushed the door open, Ghita stood in its frame, somehow unable to summon the courage for the final step. She had never witnessed such vile accommodation. Just as she prepared to retreat into the street, something goaded her forward.

The thought of proving her father wrong.

In the middle of the lobby, the clerk was asleep on a flea-infested sofa, its once ivory-coloured upholstery matted sludge-brown with dirt. Opening an eye, he swished a nest of kittens off his chest and welcomed Ghita in.

'I would like a room,' she said frostily.

The clerk lit a cigarette and sneezed, twice. His chest was covered in cat fur. Before attending to the newly arrived guest, he poured a large bowl of milk. Instantly, a kaleidoscope of cats darted to it from every corner of the room, miaowing and purring as they came.

'Do you have a reservation?' said the clerk in his own time.

Ghita balked.

'What kind of low-life vagrant would make a reservation to stay in a place like this?'

The clerk put down the milk carton and shuffled over to the reservation book. His fingers moved through many weeks of blank pages, the cigarette clenched between his teeth.

'I think I have something free, up on the second floor,' he said. 'Room thirteen. It's seventy dirhams a night.'

'I'm waiting for my money to come through,' Ghita replied, her voice a little meek. 'I'll pay you as soon as I can.'

The clerk nodded sympathetically, as though prompt payment was unknown at the Hotel Marrakech. He slid a key across the desk — the key to room thirteen.

Ghita took it, turned, and found herself face to face with the American from the street. His hair was damp from the shower, his face scrubbed clean. There were dimples in his cheeks.

'Hello again,' he said.

'Hello.'

Blaine grinned.

'Wasn't the Hyatt to your liking?'

Ghita waved a hand through the air and found herself peering down at the feline sea.

'It was too obvious,' she said.

'Too obvious?'

'You know — one Hyatt's just like another. There's no soul.'

'Well, it sounds as though you've come to the right place,' said Blaine.

Twenty-seven

THE HEADQUARTERS OF Globalcom were forged from black glass and steel, a towering expression of corporate power that rose forty storeys into the North African sky.

The building's roof was paved in giant satellite dishes and television masts. The only zone clear of them was marked with an enormous letter 'H', and was reserved for the Globalcom Eurocopter EC135, finished in metallic blue.

Every few minutes a satellite truck would arrive or leave through the main security gate on the north side of the perimeter fence. The only vehicle permitted to enter by the other, smaller entrance, was the chairman's black Maybach 57.

The barrier rose as the car approached, the duty guards saluting in unison. A moment before the vehicle had reached the building, a cluster of staff hurried out. They fell into line and stood to attention as the tyres drew to a halt.

At the head of the line was Patricia Ross. A tall redhead, she was dressed in a tailored business suit, her hair tied up in a bun. Omary regarded her as a confidante and a friend, and entrusted her with far more than the duties of an ordinary PA.

'Cancel all my meetings,' he said, as he strode fast towards the great revolving door. 'And assemble my senior policy unit in the boardroom. I want them there in...' Omary glanced at his wristwatch. 'On the hour.' He paused, thought for a moment, and added: 'Oh, and make sure you get security to sweep it first.'

'Very good, sir.'

'Is there anything on the agenda that can't wait?'

Ross touched a hand to her hair as they walked to the elevator.

'Just a lunch meeting.'

'With whom?'

'The Portuguese prime minister. He's here with a trade delegation.'

'Oh God. Where's he staying?'

'At the Hyatt.'

'Send my sincerest apologies. The usual excuses. An international crisis. Something like that. Send a huge bouquet... and a case of Dom Pérignon from my private cellar.'

'Right away, sir.'

Twenty-eight

A LINE OF conical tagines was bubbling with steam at the Marché Central.

Nearby, in the covered area, a horse butcher was cleaving a steak for an elderly French client, one of the last of the *pied noir*. Weighing the meat in his hand, he slapped it on the scale and grunted a price. Across from him, the oyster stall was doing brisk business, the shells served up with a lemon wedge and a sprinkle of salt.

Blaine strolled through the arcades, taking in the bustle. His old life in Brooklyn seemed like a million miles away. As he took it all in, he became absorbed by the vibrant cultural colour and found himself overlaying what he saw on the black-and-white scenes of his own obsession. *Casablanca* may have been filmed entirely on a Hollywood back lot, but to Blaine it was inseparable from the actual city that bore its name.

Strolling out from the market, the American gazed up at the buildings, all crumbling and worn. The peeling paint gave a sense of faded grandeur, as if the old Casablanca, the one from the movie, was lying just below the surface, waiting to be discovered.

At the end of a narrow street, just past the little Garage de la Bourse, Blaine came to a cinema, the Rialto. Peering up at the facade was like setting eyes on a lost sweetheart.

Without hesitating, he stepped inside.

The swing doors were shut, light flickering under them. At the booth he bought a ticket — spewed from the same machine that had been used in New York on premiere night.

And then, in a moment touched by magic, Blaine pushed through the swing doors, half imagining he was in a dream.

Alive on the screen before him was the smoke-filled scene of Rick's Café Américain. Waiters in starched white jackets were weaving between the tables with cocktails and cigarettes. A croupier was spinning the wheel and dealing cards and, in pride of place at the upright piano, was Sam.

Twenty-nine

UP IN NUMBER thirteen, perched fearfully on the edge of the bed, Ghita coaxed herself to be brave.

Her gaze moved fitfully across the room, from the soiled walls to the cracked pane of glass in the window, then to the spatter of dried blood sprayed over the wardrobe doors. And then, cautiously, she pressed a hand down onto the mattress, its blanket peppered with cigarette burns and stray hairs.

Strewn out from the Louis Vuitton case was a swirl of designer clothing and assorted accoutrements, packed and unpacked with equal speed. There were belts and shoes, dresses and underwear, makeup pouches and lace gloves. Many of the items had never been used, and still had the price tags hanging from them.

Ghita reached for a Ferragamo scarf in fuchsia silk and pressed it to her face. As she did so, the stolen iPhone she had bought began to ring.

'Hello?'

A man's voice was on the other end, a voice she recognized.

'Mustapha, *chéri*, how did you get this number?'

'From Aicha. She said you texted her from it. I didn't know you had a new number. Where are you? Want to have dinner tonight?'

Ghita blinked hard. She let out a squeal.

'No, no, dearest, not tonight. I'm busy tonight.'

'Then tomorrow?'

'Er, no, busy then as well.'

'Ghita, my love, is there anything wrong?'

'No, not at all. It's just that I'm out of town in... *Mmmmm...*'

'In Marrakech?'

'No... in... Monte Carlo.'

'That's a surprise! I didn't know you were travelling!'

'Oh, it was a last-minute girls' thing... an engagement shower.'

'How long will you be away, my darling?'

Ghita bit her knuckle in thought.

'For a month,' she said.

Thirty

THE FAR WALL of Hicham Omary's expansive office at Globalcom was tiled with flatscreen TVs. There were eighteen of them, each one playing a different channel — a jumble of soap operas and rolling news, documentaries and sport.

A long walnut veneer desk ran down the far side, with a view towards the city far below. Its surface was cluttered with files and computer screens. On another small table lay a cluster of photographs, each one in a solid silver frame. The largest was of Omary and his wife Fatym on their wedding day; the others were all of Ghita arranged in order of age.

Omary swept into the office. He logged on at the central computer as an assistant came in with newspapers and espresso. She was waved politely aside.

'No time for that. Get me Abdallah right away.'

Less than a minute later, Abdallah Smiri, Globalcom's head of news, was on the bank of TV screens. Omary looked up.

'Hi Abdallah. I need a favour. Hold the prime slot at six. What are you leading on right now?'

'On a massive car bomb in Baghdad.'

'Put it in at number two.' Omary pinched the end of his nose and sniffed hard. 'I've got a new lead.'

'Yes, sir.'

'Send me your chief reporter up here and a crew.'

The screens jerked back to their various channels. Omary picked up a landline on his desk and hit a speed dial.

'Good morning, Governor. This is Hicham Omary. Sorry for the disturbance. I'll be brief as I know how busy you are. There's something I'm putting out on the evening bulletin. It may tread on a few toes and so I just wanted you to have a head's up.'

Thirty-one

THE BRIGHT WINTER sunshine threw long shadows in the late afternoon as Blaine strolled down the length of the grand Boulevard Mohammed V. He was walking on air, having been serenaded by Bergman and Bogart at the Rialto.

As he glanced into the shop windows and took in the random features of the street and of life, he thought about the world he had left behind. It had been a sham, one detached from reality.

Three blocks from the end of the boulevard, Blaine noticed a scruffy shopfront. The sign had fallen away decades before, but the window display hinted at treasures within.

He forced open the door.

Inside lay an Aladdin's den of oddities and accessories from the days of the French Protectorate. There were old postcards in black and white, threadbare furniture with rounded legs, cut crystal glasses and cocktail shakers, gramophones, empty jeroboams of Moët, aspidistra stands, and crates of scratched old 78s.

Against one wall, a dark mahogany cabinet was packed with all sorts of odds and ends. In the middle of it all was a photograph — a large, signed studio shot of Humphrey Bogart, cigarette smouldering in his hand.

A figure was slumped in one corner. He was so still that Blaine didn't notice him at first. His name was Adam Raffi. Wizened with great age, he had a lazy eye, and a shirt-front speckled with gravy from his lunch. He had been dozing, but was wakened by the sound of the door, which was warped at the top.

'*Bonjour Monsieur*,' he said, pushing his shoulders back and fumbling for his spectacles.

'*Bonjour*,' Blaine replied, as he looked into the cabinet.

'Is there something you are searching for?'

'That picture… how much are you asking?'

The shopkeeper gazed out at the street.

'It's not for sale,' he said.

'That's a great pity. It's a nice one.'

'It's special to me. You see, he gave it to me.'

'Bogart did? He was here... in Casablanca?'

Monsieur Raffi blinked a yes.

'When?'

'During the war. He was here with his wife, the drunkard. They were entertaining the troops.'

Blaine stepped into the light. He caught the lilting sound of the call to prayer streaming out from the old medina, and the clip-clop of horses' hooves closer by.

'I take it you are an admirer as well,' he said.

The shopkeeper looked at the American hard, his good eye sharp as steel.

'Aren't we all?' he replied.

'Did you get to speak to Bogart?'

Monsieur Raffi stood up and staggered over to the cabinet. His face was wrinkled like elephant hide; his old hands speckled with liver spots.

'To say we spoke together much would be misleading,' he said. 'But we passed many hours together, hours in another kind of conversation.'

Blaine didn't understand.

'Conversation without words?'

Raffi nodded slowly.

'Yes, yes, conversation without words,' he said. 'A conversation played in chess.'

Thirty-two

FIFTEEN WELL-GROOMED MEN and women were seated around an oval conference table, miniature bottles of mineral water and pencils laid before each one.

As they sat in silence, wondering what could be so important as to change the running order, Omary entered. He was composed, calm, and was followed by Patricia Ross.

Pulling off his jacket, he rolled up his sleeves and loosened his tie.

'Has security been in here yet?' he asked.

'It's all clean,' said Ross.

'Good.'

Omary slipped down onto the chairman's seat at the head of the table. Wringing his hands together, he took a deep breath.

'My friends, there's a terrible threat hanging over us all,' he said. 'It's invisible and more deadly than anything we have encountered before. It is far more treacherous than our most scheming competitor and, if gone unchecked, it will bring this great company and many more like it crashing into the ground!'

The policy team listened attentively.

'Yet this opponent,' Omary went on, 'is regarded by most of us as a harmless irritation, something we endure in all our daily lives. In actual fact it's a killer, an exterminator of justice and of truth! And so I have decided that I shall wage a war against it, and direct every resource I have at my disposal to destroy it.'

The chairman got up from the table and smoothed a hand down over the side of his face.

'I can hear you asking what is it — this enemy?' he said. 'And so I shall tell you. It is CORRUPTION!'

An uneasy wave of whispering rippled through the room.

Seated at the far end of the table, Hamza Harass spoke up:

'With respect, Mr. Chairman,' he said, 'how do you propose to destroy something that is so endemic in society? It would be like trying to wipe out the common cold.'

Hicham Omary cleared his throat.

'From this moment we shall no longer pay bribes of any kind,' he said. 'Whether it be five dirhams to a parking guardian on a street corner, or fifty to a cop for an invented traffic violation… or bribes to judges, politicians, or anyone else. No longer shall we live in fear. And gradually, if we survive, others will regard us as pioneers and they will follow our example.'

Omary paused. He took a sip of water and stared down the conference table.

'I shall give an interview for the evening news,' he said, 'a rallying cry for the new order. But before that, I am sending out a memo, to all personnel at Globalcom. From now on, anyone found paying bribes or being involved in corruption of any kind shall be immediately dismissed.'

Thirty-three

A STRING OF street vendors were touting used clothing and junk on the western side of Boulevard Mohammed V.

Most were dressed in heavy woollen jelabas — the kind that keep out the Atlantic winter cold. A few were crouched down, rearranging their wares, calling out to anyone who might listen.

One was eager to draw attention to a cluster of dirty wooden spoons, a pile of German paperbacks, and an ashtray stolen from the Hotel Negresco in Nice. Another had a bundle of coat hangers laid out on a mat, half a dozen screwdrivers, and what looked like the back end of a vintage vacuum cleaner.

Rather out of place between them was an open Louis Vuitton portmanteau, overflowing with designer garments and accessories.

Standing beside it, a little awkward and a little cold, was Ghita.

From time to time burly women would sidle up, root through the clothes, and wander away.

One of them lingered longer than the rest.

'*Bonjour, Madame,*' Ghita said politely. 'What about this, it's Dior, and has never been worn? Or how about this belt — it's Lagerfeld, this summer's collection?'

The large, meaty woman picked out a crimson cocktail dress and held it to her chest. Ghita exhaled in a sigh.

'It's Valentino,' she said. 'A limited edition, one of only six.'

'I'll give you twenty dirhams.'

'You must be out of your mind! It cost twelve hundred euros!'

The woman held out a banknote so worn that it felt like cloth. Gritting her teeth, Ghita snatched it and stuffed it in her bag. She was about to curse her father again when she saw a familiar outline cruising down the boulevard. It was low to the ground and scarlet, and was driven by Mustapha.

He paused at the lights, easing on the accelerator as they changed. Through the corner of his eye he noticed a slim figure in lavender with matching heels. She had a hand to her face and what looked like an open leather case in front of her. He almost frowned.

It looked like his fiancée.

But how could it be her, in such a shabby part of town? It couldn't be Ghita. She was living it up in Monte Carlo.

Thirty-four

THE TELEVISION ON the back wall of Baba Cool was mounted high, to prevent the clientele who packed the café from morning to night from changing the channels.

A moody, smoke-filled haunt, it was patronized by the legions of local men who were taking it easy and hiding from their wives.

No one could remember the last time a woman had ever dared to enter Baba Cool. It wasn't that women weren't welcome, rather that they stayed away, alarmed by what they regarded as an atmosphere of shameful iniquity.

The waiter zigzagged between the tables, serving up miniature glasses of the ubiquitous *café noir*. The beverage was slapped down whether you ordered it or not, as were the ashtrays. They came two at a time. After all, in Morocco there's nothing quite so honourable than for a man to put in the hours at his local café, knocking back bitter coffee and chain-smoking Marquise cigarettes.

On the back wall, a prim female newsreader was serving up the headlines:

'Mr. Hicham Omary, the CEO of the Globalcom media empire, has announced today that he will, quote "dedicate his life to eradicating every form of corruption in the kingdom". He began his crusade without warning, and the first high-profile head has just rolled — that of Casablanca's governor. The official was caught red-handed by Globalcom reporters for taking millions of dirhams in illicit "donations". While we cannot be sure how many other leading officials Mr. Omary has in his sights, we can be certain that he is going to make himself plenty of enemies.'

The waiter glanced up at the TV on his way to the door, where a uniformed silhouette was waiting, his back against the light. Without a thought, the waiter's hand fished down into the pocket of his apron, pulled out a hundred-dirham note. Folding it in half, then in quarters, he slipped it over to the policeman, who ambled away without a word.

Thirty-five

Two full days had passed since Ghita had left home.

She felt disorientated and unloved, and was filled with loathing and self-pity. It had taken her all afternoon to make enough money for a bowl of soup and a chunk of bread at one of the stalls in the Marché Central. In that time she had been relieved of a small fortune in couture garments by her bargain-hungry clientele.

As she sat there, her belly stinging with hunger for the first time in her life, the stolen iPhone began to buzz. Squinting at the display, she thanked God.

'My dearest Aicha!' she exclaimed.

'We touched down just this moment. Gstaad was sublime. How was your weekend, dearest?'

'It was abhorrent!'

'Oh, you poor baby! Where are you?'

'Staying downtown… in a hotel.'

'The Hyatt?'

Ghita's expression glazed over. She bit her upper lip.

'No, no, in a little boutique place. I don't have a car. Can you come meet me right away?'

Within the hour, a magnolia-coloured Bentley pulled up outside Hotel Marrakech. The chauffeur stepped out and opened the passenger door, kicking away a dead rat with his heel. There was a long pause.

Then, very slowly, an impeccably dressed woman got down.

Her eyes hidden beneath enormous Jackie O sunglasses, she was dressed from head to toe in pink Prada mink. She didn't walk so much as waft, making her way between a pair of drunks lying outstretched on the pavement, leaving a vapour trail of rare perfume behind her.

Tugging a silk scarf from her Hermès Birkin like a magician in the middle of a trick, she used it to push open the door.

The lair of hungry cats was awaiting her inside.

In a deep, hash-induced sleep on the sofa lay the clerk. Like his pets, he was unused to high society. Opening an eye, he struggled drowsily to sit upright, as the scent and silhouette of Ghita's best friend approached.

Before she knew it, Aicha was standing outside room thirteen. She knocked.

The door opened inwards.

As soon as she saw her friend, Ghita burst into a flood of tears. She was inconsolable.

'I can never forgive him!' she sobbed. 'Baba's cruelty knows no bounds.'

'But my dear Ghita, why are you here?'

'Baba thinks I can't survive in the real world. He thinks I'm incompetent, that I'm lazy.'

'My darling, this is not reality. It's hell,' Aicha said, pulling Ghita's reddened cheek to her mink-covered breast, the tears soaked up by the fur.

'What horror! What absolute horror! Get your things and come with me at once! The Bentley's waiting downstairs. Come and stay with me for as long as you wish.'

Collapsing onto the bed, Ghita waved a finger left and right.

'I'm going to break him,' she snarled. 'He's a beast, but there's no way I'll let him win!'

'But now that you've proved him wrong, surely you can go home.'

'No, I can't.'

'Why not?'

Ghita wiped a tear from her chin.

'I said I would support myself for a month.'

'*A month*? That's ridiculous!'

'No, it's not. I have to prove to him that I'm as capable as anyone else… and I'm certainly as capable as any of those goons he employs. He regards me as useless as a little toy poodle, but I'm going to show him! Besides, he's sure to have his spies out checking up on me. You know how he is.'

Aicha reached out, her mink cuff brushing over her friend's shoulder.

'There's danger in this,' she said. 'It may be a matter of honour for you, but what if they find out?'

'*They*?'

'Mustapha… our friends… *society*!'

Swallowing hard, Ghita's eyes welled with tears.

'This is more important to me than anything else,' she said.

'More than losing your fiancé? Don't be so stubborn. Come with me now.'

'I can't. I really can't. I just ask that you give me some time and,' Ghita swallowed again, 'and that you lend me some money to buy a proper meal.'

Reaching into her Birkin, Aicha removed a brick of bank notes. It was two inches thick.

'Here's some change,' she said.

Ghita reached out in a hug.

'Please promise me that you won't tell Baba that you saw me, or that you lent me this,' she said. 'I want him to think I'm suffering. I know that with a little time he'll come crawling to me on his knees.'

Thirty-six

A WATER SELLER was chiming his great brass bell outside the Marrakech Gate — the main entrance to Casablanca's old medina.

He was dressed in traditional red robes and straw hat decorated with pompoms, his chest criss-crossed with water-skins. Spotting a foreigner, he made a beeline across the flagstones. But Blaine waved him aside and pushed his way through the arch.

Lost in the shadows of late morning, there were storytellers huddled in circles, and all manner of services and wares — shoe-shiners and lizard sellers, rat-catchers, letter writers, and stalls selling everything from underpants to imitation Rolexes, and from Reeboks to freshly stolen phones.

Blaine's attention was drawn in all directions.

He paused to watch a snake charmer, flute in hand, the cobra's hood jerking back and forth as if about to strike.

Nearby, lamb kebabs were roasting on a makeshift brazier, the heavy, oily smoke hanging like a curtain in the bright sunlight. A group of acrobatic dwarfs were tumbling from each other's shoulders. As he pushed through the crowd to watch them, Blaine felt someone nudge up hard against him.

Fumbling a hand into his pocket, he cursed. His money clip was gone. Scanning left, right, forwards, back, he caught sight of a young man in a red hooded jacket darting through the crowd. He gave chase.

But suddenly, he was gone.

Then he noticed a policeman at the end of the street. Dressed in a navy-blue uniform, a white holster at his side, he was doing the rounds, taking favours in cigarettes and tea. Blaine rushed up.

'I've just been robbed. A thief stole my money clip.'

'*Quoi?*'

Acting out a hand slipping into his pocket, Blaine half expected the officer to give chase.

'*Un voleur…?*'

'Yes, I mean, *oui, oui, un voleur…* a thief!'

The policeman shrugged.

'*C'est la vie,*' he said.

'Aren't you gonna do something?'

Again, the officer shrugged, a little more incredulously than before.

Standing there, wondering what to do, Blaine heard a young, scratchy voice in English:

'You must help him. Then he will help you.'

With a stream of people pushing by, Blaine peered downwards.

A boy in his early teens was squatting on a stool, a shoeshine box gripped between his knees.

'Excuse me... You talking to me?'

'Give him something. Then he will help you.'

'Huh?'

'You saw the thief?'

'Yeah... a young guy... he was like twenty... medium height with kind of a beard and a red jacket with a hood.'

The boy pointed to an upper window of the building opposite, where a man of the same description was leaning out.

'*Him?*'

Blaine nodded energetically.

'Yes, yes, that's him!'

Picking up his shoeshine box, the boy edged over to the cop and explained the situation in Arabic. But still the officer showed no interest. The boy rubbed thumb and forefinger together, then he winked.

Only then did the officer stir into action.

He hammered on the door, barged in, ran up the stairs, grabbed the thief, recovered the money, and was back on the street — all within a minute.

The money clip was handed back to Blaine. He counted it.

'It's all there,' he said.

'Give him something... for his time,' said the shoeshine boy.

'How much?'

'Fifty dirhams.'

Blaine handed over the tip and the officer ambled away.

'I've never given a bribe before,' he said.

The shoeshine boy greased a comb back through his hair with a smile.

'It's not *baksheesh*,' he said. 'Just a way of saying thank you.'

'How come you speak such good English?' asked Blaine.

The boy thought for a moment.

'Because of *Dirty Harry*,' he said.

Thirty-seven

ON THE WESTERN edge of Casablanca, not far from the fashionable Corniche promenade, stood an ancient-looking outcrop of low white buildings — the shrine of Sidi Abdur Rahman. Clustered together like barnacles on a sea wall, they were remote, haunting, and only easily reached from the mainland at low tide.

A figure moved across the beach towards them, stumbling and off-balance on impossibly high heels. Wrapped in a jet-black cashmere scarf, she reached the rocks and found a barrier of water ebbing and swirling.

A fisherman appeared from nowhere, a giant rubber inner-tube his one-man ferry service to the islet. After a short and clumsy voyage on which she was soaked through, Ghita made landfall. Clambering out, she ascended a steep set of steps and made her way hesitantly to a whitewashed shed on the right side of the tomb.

The door was open and she went inside.

A crone was sitting cross-legged in the corner beside a brazier. Murmuring incantations, she held a lump of burning incense between finger and thumb. Her eyes were closed and she seemed to be barely conscious.

'Did you not receive your prince, my daughter?' she asked, without opening her eyes.

'Peace be upon you, Hajja,' Ghita responded. 'Yes, yes, I did, but I am here with another request.'

The *sehura* moved the incense in a circle around her head. She appeared agitated, her eyelids quivering, her breathing shallow.

'Your father,' she said.

'Yes…'

'I am sensing that he has wronged you…'

'Yes… yes, he has…'

'Sit down on the floor.'

Ghita sat. The sorceress took her hand and felt the knuckles one by one.

'I want revenge,' Ghita said, her voice charged with emotion.

The old woman's expression soured.

'The flames of revenge burn as a wildfire,' she said. 'Once alight they cannot be tamed.'

'But I've already been burned.'

'Are you prepared to face the consequences?'

'Yes. I am more than prepared.'

The witch opened her eyes. She rooted about in a small wooden box and took out some scarlet thread. Winding a piece of the thread around Ghita's thumb, she tied a second strand around a lump of coal. Then she threw the coal onto the brazier and spat out a spell.

After that, she melted a strip of lead foil in a little porcelain crucible and poured the silvery liquid into a cup of cool seawater. Fizzing, it sank to the bottom. The sorceress fished it out and inspected its contorted form.

'Your father will taste the pain he has brought to you,' she said. 'But for this to take place, there must be blood.'

Ghita put a hand over her mouth.

'*Blood?*'

'You must make a sacrifice.'

Outside in the lane, the *sehura* presented to Ghita a live chicken by the feet. It was flustered and fretting.

'Kill it,' she said.

'But I don't know how.'

'You must break its neck. Only then can you hope for true revenge.'

Grimacing and gasping, Ghita fumbled for the bird's neck. Holding it between her hands, she snapped. A great deal of flapping followed.

Hunched there in sodden clothes, her back to the city, her face to the Atlantic horizon, and with death on her hands, Ghita felt powerful in a way she had not experienced before.

'When will I have my revenge?' she asked, the words blown out to sea.

The sorceress closed her eyes and touched a hand to her brow.

'Immediately,' she said.

Thirty-eight

AFTER MUCH AGITATION and the purring of cats, Blaine managed to get through to the international operator from the lobby of Hotel Marrakech.

Having smoked himself into a delirium with a fresh supply of *kif*, the clerk was lying outstretched on the floor, his head nudged up against the bowl of milk.

'Hello, operator, I'll repeat the number, a little slower this time...' said Blaine, enunciating.

There was a click, then a shrill whistling sound.

'Hello? Charlie? That you?'

'Blaine? Where the hell are you, man?'

'I've had a change of scene. Got thrown out of my apartment... *and* I lost my job. No, no... I don't need a bed... Why not?' Blaine paused, relishing the moment, his grin sliding into rapturous laughter. 'Because I'm in frigging Casablanca, that's why!'

Thirty-nine

THE NEWS CONTROLLER was up in the news gallery feeding instructions to the cameraman when Hicham Omary entered. It was unknown for senior managers, let alone the owner of Globalcom, to ever bother with the gallery. The editors jerked to attention in their seats.

'How long before we go on air?' Omary asked.

'Three minutes, sir.'

'OK. Then I have just enough time to brief you,' he said, sitting on the edge of the desk. 'I want as many reporters as we can spare on this story, day and night. They're to get footage of bribes being dealt — covert stuff if needed. Within a week I want this city shaking. You take care of the small fish, and I'll go after the big ones…'

Omary's mobile rang. He glanced at the display.

'Hello, Governor,' he said coolly. 'I'm so glad you caught our bulletins. Now, now, that's not entirely fair. I did call you to warn you of our little crusade.'

On the other end, the governor of Casablanca was fuming, his voice trembling with rage:

'Listen to me, Omary, I don't know if you want a firestorm, but you're about to unleash one. And you and your organization are going to be the only casualties, do you understand?'

Omary moved the phone away from his ear and smiled.

'I'm sensing that I've touched a nerve,' he said calmly.

The line went dead. As it did so, Patricia Ross entered.

'Mr. Harass is waiting for you downstairs, sir.'

'OK. I'll be right down.'

A few minutes later, Omary strode into his office, where he found his friend sitting on a plush Scandinavian sofa beneath a large blue abstract by Picasso.

'I'm so sorry, I've become rather absorbed with a little campaign,' he said.

Harass got to his feet.

'News of it is on a great many lips.'

'Is that so? Excellent! I was hoping it would catch on.'

'I'd say there is little chance of that.'

'Oh… why not?'

Harass pressed his hands together.

'Hicham, I am here as your old friend… here to warn you.'

'Against what?'

'Against behaving with a foolishness that could get you in a great deal of trouble.'

Omary sighed. He stepped forward and put an arm around his friend's shoulder.

'Hamza, you know me well. And you know that when I feel passionately about something, I act on it… and that nothing can change my mind. I'm not going to stand by and watch the country I love disintegrate because of greed and corruption.'

'Would you risk all this?'

'Yes, I would. I would risk *everything.*'

Omary stepped forward to the window and stared out at Casablanca, an ocean of white buildings stretching far into the distance.

'You forget that I came from nothing,' he said in a soft voice. 'I am proud of my achievements, but far prouder of the simple values my father planted in me. The first of which was to keep my feet on the ground.'

'And what of Ghita?'

Omary sighed again.

'I know… she's out of control. There's no chance of her feet being on the ground because her head is in the clouds. I've indulged her and I take responsibility for that.'

'I don't mean that. I mean your crusade. What harm will it do to her?'

Hicham Omary looked out at the city. He pinched the end of his nose and sniffed.

'I have a feeling it will do her a lot of good,' he said.

Forty

FOLLOWING THE CALL to his best friend, Blaine was hit with an adrenalin rush. It came from the sense of danger and from breaking free — free from the bedrock of hysteria he had inhabited with every other schmuck New Yorker.

As he stood in the hotel's small lobby, cats circling round his ankles expectant of milk, he caught the scent of expensive perfume. It wafted down the staircase and was accompanied by the sound of high heels negotiating steps one by one.

The American turned and found himself captivated by the sight of an elegant young woman, dressed in a bright orange slip, a feather boa furled around her neck. He recognized her at once as the owner of the stiletto that had injured his ankle.

'Hello, again,' he said. 'How are you enjoying Hotel Marrakech?'

Ghita stopped in her tracks, glanced round, and struggled to look condescending.

'To be a trend-setter one must sometimes endure a little hardship,' she replied.

Across Rue Colbert, the Marché Central's fishmongers were lining up the catch, shooing away the droves of feral cats that prowled the green tiled roofs. They were doing brisk business due to the fact that an Italian cruise ship had docked at the port, and the head chef was demanding fresh langoustines for a thousand hungry mouths.

Blaine strolled through the market, taking in the fruit stalls and the ones from which the beekeepers sold their honey in used jam jars. He was still thinking about breaking free, about cashing in a tired old life for a new one, when he spotted Baba Cool.

There was something gloriously sordid about it, something reprehensible, something only understood by men. Drawn forward by an almost magnetic force, he crossed the street and took a seat on the slender terrace.

Listlessly, the waiter meandered over. He slapped down a pair of ashtrays and a glass of tar-like *café noir*, a miniature mound of sugar lumps at the side.

From time to time, when the smoke saturation inside reached a peak, a cloud of dense cigarette smoke was belched out through the windows. The muffled sounds of an Egyptian soap opera could be heard emanating from the back wall. It was punctuated by indistinct conversation and coughing, and by men moaning about their wives.

Blaine sipped the coffee and winced. This is the real thing, he thought, the real gritty Casablanca, the one worthy of Humphrey Bogart.

All of a sudden he heard a voice, a child's voice, loud and guttural.

'Go ahead, punk, make my day!'

The American glanced out at the street. The shoeshine boy from the medina was standing there with his box.

'Hello, Dirty Harry,' Blaine said.

Before he could object, the boy squatted down under the table and got to work on his left shoe, polishing vigorously.

'You like Clint Eastwood, too?' he asked.

'Yeah, I do.'

'I learnt English from his movies.'

'Shouldn't you be in school?'

'School fills your head with worms,' said the boy. 'And I don't want worms in my head.'

'How are you gonna get a job if you don't know how to read or write?'

'I have a job.'

'A *better* job. One with prospects.'

The boy moved on to the right shoe.

'*Prospects?*'

'A future.'

'I have a future. A big one.'

'How's it gonna be?'

The boy stopped brushing and stood up. He was about to say something when a stylish woman in orange strode purposefully across the street, a feather boa around her neck.

'Casa Trash,' he said.

'Casa what?'

'Trash. *Le snob.*'

Blaine called out.

'Hey! Hi… Wanna join me for a coffee?'

Sweeping her feathers to the side, Ghita squinted at the café with a look of utter horror.

'*In there*? At Baba...'

'*Cool*. It's called Baba Cool.'

'No woman in her right mind would be seen dead in there!'

Blaine stood up, pulled out a chair.

'Why don't you make a break with tradition?' he said.

Dripping in self-importance, Ghita sat down.

The American held out a hand.

'I'm Blaine,' he said.

'And I am Ghita Omary,' said Ghita, without offering her hand in return.

'And this... this is Dirty Harry,' Blaine added.

'Saed,' said the boy. He jabbed a knuckle down at the stilettos. 'Clean those?'

Holding up her hands in horror, Ghita managed a sneer.

'Keep away from me, you dirty little rat!'

Another pair of ashtrays and *cafés noirs* were slid down onto the worn Formica tabletop, and the waiter slalomed back into the smoke.

Then, from nowhere, a burly figure armed with a meat cleaver charged onto the terrace, swinging the weapon in Saed's direction. Grabbing his shoeshine box, the boy darted out into the light.

'I wonder what that was about!' Blaine said in a shocked voice.

Ghita raised the glass to her nostrils, sniffed the coffee. She glowered and put it down.

'Thievery, no doubt,' she said. 'Boys like that are all thieves. It's in their blood.'

'He seemed nice, I thought.'

Stroking a hand through the feathers, Ghita replied:

'The first thing you must learn about our country is that the lower classes are not to be trusted. They're thieves.'

'All of them?'

'Oh yes, *all* of them.'

Blaine swished away a dark cloud of cigarette smoke that had billowed out from the café.

'So what do you do?' he asked.

'*Do*?'

'Your line of work.'

Ghita frowned.

'I don't *do* anything.'

'You don't work?'

'*Work*? No, of course I don't work.'

'Well, how do you fund an outfit like that?'

'I come from a wealthy family.'

'Have they always been wealthy?'

Clearing her throat, Ghita looked across at the American.

'I am aware that you come from a place where there is an overwhelming need to fill silence with speech,' she said coldly. 'But you would do well to know that here in Morocco we regard silence as something golden, something precious... at least to the upper classes it is.'

Blaine struggled to remain composed.

'Well, forgive me for intruding into your precious golden silence,' he replied, 'but I can't remember the last time I met such an opinionated, conceited, self-infatuated misfortunate as yourself.'

Ghita pushed back her chair and stood up.

'How dare you speak to me like that!'

'How dare I? Well, I dare very easily, thank you!'

'I'm going back to the hotel now and I hope very sincerely that our paths do not cross again,' Ghita snarled, as she stormed away.

Blaine cupped a hand to his mouth.

'I couldn't agree more!' he yelled.

Forty-one

FIVE MINUTES BEFORE midnight, a dozen armoured police vehicles screeched through the narrow streets of Anfa and braked hard outside the Omary mansion.

With sirens blaring and the sapphire lights whirling against a moonless night, fifty officers charged out of the vehicles and over to the house. Forcing apart the great arabesque gates, they surrounded the building and set about battering open the main door.

Roused by the noise, Hicham Omary clambered out of bed and paced over to the window. Five minutes later, still wearing pyjamas, he was standing in the garden, in handcuffs.

'What's going on?'

'Shut up and stay quiet!' shouted the chief officer.

Just then, a sergeant hurried out of the building, a kilo-bag of fine white powder in his hand. His superior grinned.

'You are under arrest,' he said.

Forty-two

A HAGGARD LANDLORD led the way through the long, curved corridor of a dilapidated art deco apartment building, a stone's throw from Baba Cool. It was so dark that he guided himself down the wall, running a thumb along the grooved line halfway between the ceiling and the floor.

Inching after him was Ghita.

'It's a good place,' the landlord said deliberately. 'Sometimes a little noisy at night, but well built.'

'How much is it?'

'Eight hundred dirhams a month.'

'How many rooms?'

'Four. Five if you include the bathroom.'

'I'll take it,' Ghita affirmed.

'But you haven't seen it yet.'

Ghita took out some money and handed it over.

'You heard me,' she said.

Forty-three

THAT AFTERNOON, SIX large delivery trucks pulled up outside the apartment building, and a stream of personnel staggered inside, laden with equipment and supplies.

Across the street at Baba Cool, Blaine was sitting at the same table as before, sipping a miniature glass of coffee. He was pondering his circumstances, wondering whether he could ever fit back in to American life.

Inside the café, the television was reporting breaking news:

'Our lead story today is that Mr. Hicham Omary, the well-known and charismatic CEO of Globalcom, was arrested by armed officers, and charged for being in possession of a massive narcotics stash. The haul, described by police as "monumental", was taken away for examination, while Mr. Omary was refused bail. Speaking a short time ago, the governor of Casablanca said that he was saddened by the news, that such a respected pillar of society should be involved in such illicit activities.'

Blaine blinked, and found Saed crouching beneath the table on his box.

'Shoeshine?'

'What, again? No, don't need one. Anyway, what was all that about with the meat cleaver?'

'He was looking for my cousin.'

'From where I was sitting he looked like he wanted *you*.'

'My cousin... he looks like me.'

Blaine pushed out a chair.

'Have a seat,' he said.

'Why don't you go to Marrakech… all tourists, they go to Marrakech?' Saed asked.

'Because it's Casablanca that I like.'

'But no one likes Casa.'

'Why not?'

'They say it's dirty, that it's not beautiful.'

'Well, I like it,' Blaine replied. 'Sure, it's a little worn in. But you know what they say about beauty?'

'No.'

'That it's in the eye of the beholder.'

Blaine's attention moved from Saed over to the building opposite, where the delivery trucks were moving away. He thought he saw Ghita coming out, but wasn't sure.

'Where is your Casa Trash friend today?' asked Saed, reading his thoughts.

'She's no friend of mine! She's awful!'

The shoeshine boy let out a shrill laugh.

'I think you like her,' he said.

Forty-four

A PAIR OF officers was standing guard outside Cell No. 5 at the imposing Central Police Station on Boulevard Zerktouni. Tucked away at the end of a whitewashed corridor two levels underground, it stank of urine and fear.

Still in his pyjamas, Hicham Omary was sitting in the far corner. He was biding his time.

All of a sudden, there came the sound of hobnailed boots on stone, and a trail of cigarette smoke. Omary listened as the guards snapped to attention, greeting an officer of rank.

There was a rattling sound, and then a small oval inspection window slid back, throwing an angular shaft of light through the cell.

'Stand up!' the guard ordered.

Hicham Omary didn't move.

'Get up or I'll beat you!' the voice commanded.

Slowly, Omary got to his feet. As he did so, the key turned in the lock. A moment later, the door was open.

'Stand back!' the guard roared, as a short, angry-looking police chief advanced into the doorway. Drawing hard on his cigarette, an imported one, he blew the smoke in Omary's direction.

'I would have expected a man like you to be wiser than this,' he said.

The prisoner smoothed back his hair with a hand.

'I expected to ruffle a few feathers,' he replied.

'You have succeeded in doing that… You've ruffled a lot more feathers. The governor is apoplectic. And the police force isn't exactly flushed with joy at your campaign.'

Hicham Omary leaned back against the wall.

'A trapped cat is all fangs and claws,' he said. 'Nothing more than that.'

The chief held up a clipboard and squinted to make sense of the scribble written across it.

'What a great shame you were found with the narcotics. What was it — *heroin*?'

'You tell me.'

'Says here they found ten kilos in all, stashed under the floorboards in your home. Ten kilos… you know what that means?'

Omary didn't answer.

'It means they're going to lock you up for good.'

Forty-five

MONSIEUR RAFFI WAS asleep in the pool of sunlight at the front of his shop.

He was reclining in a rounded art deco chair upholstered in faded red satin, his feet resting up on an ancient stack of *Paris Match*. In the habit of taking a long siesta in the afternoon, he always dreamt the same dream. It was of the glory days of his youth, days unhindered by the complexities of modern life and advanced age.

Raffi rarely sold anything of any value, but the shop gave him a purpose, and the occasional chance for an interesting conversation.

Feeling a draught of cool air on his hands, he stirred from his doze and opened an eye.

'*Bonjour, Monsieur Américain,*' he said.

Blaine shut the door behind him.

'Good afternoon. I hope you don't mind, but I couldn't resist.'

The shopkeeper sat up and searched for his glasses.

'I am sure you didn't come here for advice,' he said. 'But as an old man, I feel it my duty to impart some to anyone who might listen.'

Blaine looked round into the light.

'I'd be happy for any advice on offer,' he replied.

Monsieur Raffi touched a hand to his knee.

'I'm as old as time itself,' he said, 'and I ache from my eyebrows to my toenails... my advice is to seize every day you're given, while you're still young enough to appreciate it all.'

'That's exactly why I'm here in Casablanca,' Blaine said.

He stepped forward to the cabinet and began inspecting the objects through the glass.

'My grandfather taught me to follow my dreams,' he said, 'and told me never to listen to anyone who tried to hold me back.'

'He must be a wise man, your grandfather.'

'He *was*... and he would have loved it in here, that's for sure.'

Monsieur Raffi looked out at the street, no more than a glance, but long enough. 'I have to take my pills,' he said. 'They keep me alive.'

Blaine wasn't quite listening.

'It's as though your shop, your objects... they're a missing link,' he said, 'as though they help me see *my* Casablanca... how it all once was — you know, in the movie.'

Raffi knocked six small pills onto his palm, counted them once, then again, and swallowed them with a cough. He took a sip of water from a jug by his chair, then belched.

'You need imagination these days,' he said, rearranging himself. 'The old Casablanca isn't as obvious as you might think. You have to search for it. But it's out there, lurking in the shadows and the mess... not on the surface, but deep underground.'

'Do you remember how Casablanca was?' Blaine asked.

The shopkeeper closed his eyes.

'It was like something from a child's fantasy,' he replied very slowly. 'The streets were paved in the finest stone, so clean you could have eaten your dinner off them. The buildings were dazzling, like cut crystal, each one more marvellous than the last, and each one a symbol of colonial power.'

Monsieur Raffi paused to take another sip of water. He knocked a hand to the back of his neck and cleared his throat.

'The women walked on heels from Paris,' he said, 'and the men dressed impeccably in pinstripe suits and hats. They were prosperous and handsome. There was a sense of invincibility, as though the world was our oyster, that there wasn't anything we couldn't achieve.'

'So what happened?'

'The French left, that's what happened. This was their city, their obsession, their fantasy. Forget what you know from the movies — Casablanca was a French invention, not a Moroccan one.'

Blaine picked up an old silver ice bucket and weighed it in his hands.

'I can feel them here,' he said, 'just like in *Casablanca*, the officers of the despised Vichy rule... the danger... the secrecy.'

Struggling to his feet, Monsieur Raffi plodded over to the cabinet. Blaine and he were inches from one another, their faces reflected in the same small sheet of glass.

'Will you tell me about Bogart?' said the American. 'What was he like?'

Raffi breathed in, then exhaled hard in a sigh.

'He was no angel,' he said. 'He drank and smoked himself to an early grave. No one could keep up with him, no one except for Mayo.'

'Mayo Methot?'

'That's right. She was his third wife. Think of it… married three times by the age of thirty-eight.'

'And four by forty-five.'

The shopkeeper blew his nose on a square of rag.

'That's right. But of them all, Mayo was the most wanton. In her appreciation for liquor she was more than his match. She liked cheap cognac. A horror of a woman,' he sighed again. 'She stabbed him once, with a butcher's knife. Did you know that?'

Blaine shook his head.

'No, but it doesn't surprise me. Was she here with him in Morocco?'

The shopkeeper went back to his red art deco chair and slumped down like a tired old cat.

'Yes of course. She followed him like a shadow. Didn't trust him for a moment, after all…' Raffi stopped mid-sentence, as though he had lost his train of thought. 'I'll tell you something,' he said all of a sudden. 'I may be an old man, and not a very wise one at that. But I know Bogart's secret, the one he kept hidden from everyone — even his wife. And it's waiting for a bright young spark to root it out.'

'What is it, the secret?' Blaine asked.

Raffi shook a finger at the American's chest.

'There's no value in being told something when you can work it out for yourself,' he said.

'Will you start me off with a clue?'

The aged shopkeeper lifted his feet back onto the stack of *Paris Match.*

'Sometimes the best way to find something,' he said, 'is not to search for it at all.'

Forty-six

THAT AFTERNOON, AS he left Baba Cool, Blaine caught sight of Ghita going into the apartment building opposite. There was something different about her, less of the peacock and more of a snipe, as though she was struggling not to be recognized.

A pair of oversized sunglasses were pulled down over her eyes, her hair furled up in a patterned silk scarf and her slim form wrapped in a voluminous coat. It was the heels that gave her away, though. They were four inches high and were monogrammed fox fur.

Unable to resist, Blaine followed.

Leaving the street, he stepped into the gloomy building, where an old woman was down on her knees mopping the floor tiles with a cloth. Without even being asked, she held up four fingers, then jerked her head back towards the stairs.

Blaine climbed, the wide sweeping staircase spiralling upward in darkness like a snail's shell.

By the fourth floor, he was wheezing from the ascent and the dust, and felt as though he was back in Mr. Rogers's walk-up. Then he sneezed and, as his nose cleared, he caught the smell of fresh paint.

Peering to the left, and then right, he realized there was only one door on that level. Lightly curved, it was teak, the brass fittings long since sold. From beneath it there radiated a trace of bright yellow light.

Blaine knocked hard. He waited. There was no reply. He knocked again, and was about to leave, when the door opened no more than a crack.

'Yes?' said a woman's voice, an eye straining to focus. It was Ghita. She seemed flustered. '*You!*' she exclaimed.

'I saw you from across the street and I... I couldn't resist...'

'Following me?'

'No... well, I guess so... Aren't you staying at Hotel Marrakech any more?'

'No. I've rented this little room instead.'

Blaine looked down at his feet, then up into Ghita's eyes.

'Look, I think we got off to a bad start,' he said. 'I thought you were an arrogant princess...'

'And I thought you were a stupid American.'

'Shall we try again?'

Blaine held out his hand. This time Ghita shook it.

'Come inside,' she said. 'It's not very fancy, but it's my home, for the moment at least.'

The apartment's sitting room was just fifteen feet square, with a large cupboard on the wall adjacent to the door. There was a terrible stench of damp and possibly even death. In one corner there lay a pile of dead cockroaches. Above it on the wall was an alarming damp patch — a patch that seemed to be spreading.

There were no windows.

Except for the wardrobe, the only piece of furniture was a mattress spattered with vomit and blood.

'It's... it's... it's nice,' said Blaine, lying.

'I like to think of it as home,' Ghita replied humbly.

Blaine felt that he ought to sit, to give the sense he was comfortable there. But there was no chair, so he stood.

'I have to tell you something,' he said.

'What?'

'Well, I came to Casablanca because of a love affair.'

'With a woman?'

Blaine smiled.

'With a movie,' he said. '*Casablanca*. It's the most important thing in my life, something of an obsession. I came here on kind of a pilgrimage, expecting to find a city brimming with intrigue and mystery... and until now you are the only mysterious person I've met.'

'Mysterious?' Ghita pushed back her hair. 'How ever am I mysterious?' she asked.

'Well, it doesn't add up. *You* don't add up.'

'What do you mean?'

'Well, forgive me for saying it, but you reek of wealth and sophistication, and you're living here like this.'

Ghita looked at the American coldly.

'Do you always speak so plainly?' she said.

'Well, I don't believe in beating around the bush.'

'Beating…?'

'*Around the bush*. It's an expression.'

'I am here because of circumstances.'

'What circumstances?'

'I'm proving a point to my father.'

'Huh?'

'He doesn't believe that I can survive without the finer things in life.'

'Can you?'

Ghita fluttered a hand towards the mattress.

'Well, it appears that I am doing quite well,' she said.

'And what's the point… the point of proving your point?'

'Respect.'

'From your friends?'

'No, no… from my father. My friends must never know I stayed down here like, this… like a pauper.'

'Why not?'

'Because I'd die of shame.'

Blaine took a step backwards, towards the damp.

'Let me get this right,' he said. 'You're here pretending to be poor to win some kind of a bet with your dad?'

'He's going to regret pushing me to this,' Ghita declared, knotting her fingers together.

'You're doing it all to make him feel bad?' Blaine asked, frowning.

'My reasons are none of your business!'

'Excuse me, but it sounds as if you're one decidedly unhinged young lady.'

Ghita's fingers unknotted.

'And you… you're the most stupid American I've ever met, and the one person I hoped I wouldn't ever encounter again!'

Blaine stepped out into the corridor.

And the door slammed hard behind him.

Forty-seven

AT CASA VOYAGEURS, Mortimer Wu climbed down from the Marrakech train, amid the heaving frenzy of luggage and confusion that accompanies the major stops.

He had horn-rimmed glasses, a spike of jet-black hair, and a week's growth of stubble on his cheeks. Wu was like any other backpacker — scruffy, lost, and in need of a good hot meal and a bath.

Exiting the station, he pushed through the droves of taxi drivers touting for a fare and made his way to the café across the street.

In his left hand was a rolled-up newspaper, that morning's *Le Matin*, and in his right was a soft pack of Marlboro, even though he didn't smoke. He took a seat with his back to the road, ordered a *nous-nous* — coffee mixed with milk — and he waited as he had been instructed.

An hour passed, and then another.

Wu felt certain he had missed the contact, or that he had got the wrong café, when a man in a tweed jacket and matching cap rushed in and sat down.

'There was a problem with the supplier,' he said, helping himself to a cigarette. 'I have the documents now.' He slipped a brown manila envelope into the folded newspaper and lit the cigarette.

'Once I've done this, I'm free to go, right?' said Wu anxiously.

'Do the job right and you'll be notified, do you understand?'

The contact took a long, hard drag, breathed out, and disappeared behind the smoke.

Mortimer Wu thought of his boyhood in Hong Kong, an elderly aunt leading him around the wet market in search of live turtles for soup. He picked up the newspaper and pulled out the envelope. It was thicker than he had expected. Stuffing it into the inside pocket of his fleece jacket, he left a coin for the coffee, and went out onto the street.

Forty-eight

GHITA WAS MAKING her way through Derb Omar, the cloth market, when she noticed a television shop opening its shutters after lunch. The only shop on the street that didn't sell textiles, it seemed rather out of place. But it wasn't the televisions that caught her eye.

It was what was on them.

Each one was tuned to the same channel — 2M. And, to Ghita's horror, each one was screening the same picture, of her father being led to a prison van in chains.

She rushed into the shop.

'Put up the volume at once!'

A salesman stepped from the shadows.

'Which unit would you like to be demonstrated, miss?'

'Any one… just turn up the volume!'

Frowning, the sales assistant shook his head.

'Excuse me, miss, this isn't a café, but a television shop.'

'All right, all right…' Ghita stammered, pointing to a large flatscreen model. 'That one. I'd like to hear the sound.'

The salesman pressed a button on the remote control.

'Omary is expected to be incarcerated without bail,' said the news anchor, 'due to the seriousness of his crime.'

'*Crime*? What crime?' Ghita exclaimed.

'As you can hear, miss, the sound on this model is particularly good.'

'*What*?'

'And the picture is exceptional.'

Regarding the salesman with a look of utter contempt, Ghita darted from the door and hailed a cab.

'Take me to Anfa, as quickly as you can!'

Forty-nine

THE IDEA OF Humphrey Bogart's lost treasure gnawed away at Blaine.

The more he tried to dismiss it as an idle daydream, the more it crept back into his thoughts. He felt a little bad at bothering Monsieur Raffi yet again, after all he had no spare funds for knick-knacks. But, as he reasoned it, the old shopkeeper valued conversation with a genuine *Casablanca* aficionado. And so, seeing the shutters up, Blaine crossed the street and shoved open the door.

The shopkeeper was asleep in his chair, a chipped china cup skewed on its saucer beside his left hand. He opened an eye, then the other, and pushed himself up.

'*Bonsoir Monsieur Américain*,' he said. 'I am hoping you have come with some answers and not more questions.'

Closing the door, Blaine smiled hard, his cheeks dimpling.

'I regret to say that I am here to bother you again with questions... questions to get an answer.

'An answer to the secret of Humphrey Bogart?'

'The very same.'

Monsieur Raffi got up, shuffled to the corner, and boiled a kettle on the gas ring.

'My sister used to bring me a special blend of tea from Lyon,' he said. 'She died last year, but thankfully she left me with enough packets to see me out. Wait till you taste it. There's nothing like it in the entire world.'

The American took a step forward.

'I have to explain something,' he said. 'You see, I'm one of the purists who regard it as the finest movie ever made. I know every line... every word.' He slapped his hands together hard. 'Hell, *Casablanca* is far more than an obsession,' he said. 'It's a way of life.'

The shopkeeper measured two spoons of his precious tea into the pot, added the water, and stirred.

'And why has that film had such an effect on your senses?'

'Because of the way it gets under the skin.'

Monsieur Raffi poured two cups of tea. It was straw-coloured and scented with ginger.

'You know the story. It wasn't ever expected to be anything more than a B-picture,' he said.

'And that's what it is...' Blaine replied. 'There's "B" stamped all over it! But it's the one B-movie that was better than any of the A-list.'

'You really think so?'

'Yes, I do.'

'Why?'

'Because of Bogart. His depth, his anger, his helplessness...'

'And why did he succeed where so many others had failed?'

Blaine peered into the mahogany cabinet and took in the studio shot.

'Because he didn't give a damn,' he murmured, then paused. 'Will you tell me the secret?' he said, his voice a little louder.

The shopkeeper tapped six of his little pills out of their bottle and gulped them back with his tea.

'If I was going to tell what I know, I would have done so long ago,' he said. 'You see, some secrets are better lost with time.'

'Is it about an affair? I heard that Mayo thought Bogart was sleeping with Ingrid Bergman.'

'Of course she did. After all, he was sleeping with half the known world,' said the shopkeeper, 'but this secret isn't about infidelity.'

'Then?'

'Then you have to work it out.'

'But I need a clue to start me off.'

Monsieur Raffi was about to say something when a group of Chinese tourists peered in the window, hands cupped to their eyes. They clicked a volley of photos and were gone. Raffi sunk down into his favourite chair, hands caressing the faded satin armrests.

He took another sip of tea.

'What will you give me in return for a clue that leads to the secret?' he asked quietly.

The American sensed his spine warming with resentment. Until that point he had liked the old French shopkeeper, but as a New Yorker he had a sixth sense for being taken for a ride.

'I don't have any cash,' he said. 'Just a mountain of goodwill.'

'I'm not talking about payment in money,' Monsieur Raffi said. 'I'm talking about detail. Give me a detail and I shall give you a clue.'

'What kind of detail?'

'One from your life.'

Blaine thought for a moment. He almost smiled.

'Any detail?'

Raffi blinked.

'OK. Let me think… When I was a child we lived for a while at Catskill, upstate New York. I used to go fishing in the river with my pals. We camped out in the summer beneath a full moon. And on those nights, when my buddies were asleep, I'd crawl out of my tent and sit on the rocks, watching the reflection of the moonlight on the water. It was silver… magical… like something from another world.'

'A detail of moonlight in exchange for a clue?'

Blaine nodded.

The shopkeeper drained his cup. The tea was cold, but he didn't care.

'Do you know why Bogart was here in North Africa?' he asked.

'To entertain the troops.'

'That's right. Or at least, that was the official story. It was, as you might say, the "cover".'

'Then what was the real reason?'

'The secret.'

Blaine cleared a chair of its magazines and sat down close to Raffi.

'We're going around in circles, aren't we?' he said.

'Well, the best way to arrive at a destination is by a circle, or a spiral.' The old man paused, then glanced at the floor. 'Tell me another detail. A detail about taste.'

Concentrating, the American closed his eyes.

'When I was eleven years old,' he said, 'my parents were out for the evening. My brother and I found the key to the drinks cabinet. We opened it and drank the bourbon — Jack Daniel's No. 7. It tasted like liquid fire. I can still remember it burning my mouth, then my throat, and my stomach.'

Monsieur Raffi blew his nose into a polka-dot handkerchief.

'The real reason Bogart was here in North Africa wasn't to entertain anyone,' he said. 'It was to collect something.'

'*What*?'

'A box. A very special box.'

'Couldn't it have been shipped to him?'

'No… no… not this box.'

'What was inside?'

Raffi winced.

'A secret.'

'Something valuable?'

'Perhaps.'

'Where is it now?'

'That's a secret, too.'

Blaine turned to look at the cabinet, and glimpsed Bogart framed in mahogany and glass.

'So many secrets,' he said.

'It went with the time.'

'With the war?'

'That's right.' Monsieur Raffi coughed hard into his hand. 'Bogart played chess by mail with a few GIs,' he said. 'The game was his greatest love — more precious to him than women or even drink. In one match, a GI stationed here in Morocco promised him something if he won. But the arrangement was that he would have to come and collect it himself.'

'A treasure?'

Raffi rubbed his eyes.

'A spoil of war.'

'So he won the game, and then came to collect his prize?'

'Something like that, yes.'

'It's a good story,' Blaine said.

'But it's far more than that… more than a story.'

The shopkeeper sat up. He looked at the clock. Almost time to close for lunch. He pressed a knuckle to his lips and thought for a good long time.

'I'll be dead soon,' he said suddenly. 'Not much life left in these bones. I have outlived my son, and my daughter has no interest in anything of substance. She's never shown any interest in the things I hold dear.'

'No interest in Bogart or Bergman?' asked Blaine.

'None at all.'

'A wasted life?'

Monsieur Raffi grinned. He looked at the American, old eyes mapping the young man's face. Then he pointed to a dresser to the right of the door. It was covered in junk acquired through decades of collecting.

'Open the third drawer,' he said, 'and inside you will find your clue.'

Blaine stood up, crossed the room, and gently eased the drawer open. He expected to find it packed with odds and ends, but there was only one thing inside.

A postcard.

It was a hand-coloured picture of a Casablanca street. The buildings were gleaming white, the pedestrians dressed in suits with hats. Blaine turned it over. It was blank on the back.

'What kind of clue's this?'

'Take it,' said Raffi. 'Turn what you see over in your head and...'

'*And?*'

'And let the spirit of Humphrey Bogart seep into your veins.'

Fifty

THERE WAS NOTHING the taxi driver disliked more than going to the ritzy neighbourhood of Anfa. Everyone there owned a car, and the journey meant he would most likely be returning empty.

He disliked the people too, regarding them as most locals did: as phoney Moroccans, the kind that were far more at home in France.

Jerking the wheel to the left after the Saudi Palace, the driver gritted his teeth. A sea of congestion stretched out in front of his car's bumper — most of them black Range Rovers and new German cars.

'The traffic's always bad here,' he said under his breath, 'because these stupid rich people don't know how to drive.'

Ghita wagged a finger aggressively.

'Don't you blame the wealthy!' she barked. 'They've got enough problems in life without fools like you giving your pathetic and unwanted opinion!' She threw down a note. 'This will do fine. I'll get out and walk from here.'

A minute later she reached the curled iron gates of the Omary mansion. They had been sealed with chains and the wax seal of the high court.

A pair of uniformed officers was standing to attention outside.

'Open these gates at once!' Ghita ordered.

'You can't go in,' said the first officer.

'No one can,' added the other.

'Well, I am Ghita Omary… I live here!'

'I don't care who you are,' said the first. 'If you don't leave I shall arrest you!'

Freezing the officer in a poisonous stare, Ghita turned and strode briskly down the street, passing half a dozen palatial villas. As she walked, she called Aicha on her stolen iPhone, her cheeks running with tears.

No one picked up and so she left a message:

'Aicha, darling, it's me. Look, I don't know what's happening. Baba has been arrested. The house has been seized! I'm panicking. I don't know who else to call. Call me as soon as you get this!'

Ghita stopped at an enormous house set back from the street. She marched up to the front gate and rang the bell. The security camera rotated clockwise, its red LED light flashing as it did so.

'Yes?' said a voice from a speaker on the wall.

'This is Ghita Omary. I want to see Mustapha, at once.'

The gates clicked opened electronically, and Ghita paced purposefully across to the house. A butler opened the front door as she approached. He escorted her through into the main hallway, the walls hung in antique yellow silk, and down a long corridor adorned in Warhol's *Soup Cans.*

A minute later, Ghita found herself seated in the library on a suede sofa, the wooden parquet overlaid with Persian rugs. The shelves were lined with a multitude of books, each of them bound in identical red leather, gilt lettering down the spines.

On the mantel, a clock with ormolu fittings chimed the hour and, as it did so, the door opened.

Mustapha's father came in.

'Ghita, my dear,' he said, kissing her cheeks, 'I am so happy to see you.'

'And I you, Mr. Harass. Please forgive my intrusion but I was hoping to find Mustapha. He's not picking up his phone.'

'Did he not tell you? He had to leave town for work.'

Ghita frowned.

'No, I didn't know. But I was unreachable myself.' She paused, touched a hand to her lips. 'I just found out about my father. I'm confused, and so worried.'

'My dearest Ghita, I am sincerely sorry about what has happened,' Harass replied. 'I warned him that he was placing himself in terrible danger.'

'What do you mean?'

'He embarked on a mission, a crusade, an exposé of corruption. Going on national television and unmasking high-level officials, publicly shaming them... well, it's a hazardous sport.'

'Is it a crime to stand up for what you believe in?' Ghita said, her eyes welling with tears.

Harass stepped over to the window. He removed a book at random, a first edition of Victor Hugo's *Les Misérables*, Volume Three. Glancing at it vacantly, he laid it down and turned to face Ghita.

'Is it a crime?' he asked. 'Well, I shall tell you. A great many powerful people have been landed in hot water... *boiling* hot water... and they don't like it, not one little bit. So what you see is them — and the system they control — biting back.'

'Where have they taken my father? I want to be with him.'

'I understand he's been taken to a central jail, just for now. I have spoken to Driss Senbel, who's acting for him as you would expect. But the charges are so severe he's not been permitted to see anyone at all, not for the moment.'

Ghita crossed the carpet and moved towards the shelves. Grasping Harass's hand in hers, she lowered her head.

'You are our family's oldest and most trusted friend,' she said. 'I am begging you to help us in our moment of need. If Baba goes to prison, he'll be eaten alive — you know he will.'

Hamza Harass took half a step backwards, the leather sole of his right shoe intruding on the carpet's geometric design. The shoe was handmade by Lobb of St. James's, fashioned from indigo ostrich leather. Ghita couldn't help but wonder why a man of such wealth should have such abysmal taste. She looked at him, and he at her, his eyes cold and his jaw clenched.

'I am afraid that there is nothing I can do for you,' he said.

Fifty-one

FOR THE REST of the afternoon, Ghita tried calling her friends.

Each one in turn hung up as soon as they heard her voice. It was as though an invisible enemy was conspiring to gain the perfect revenge. Confused and tearful, Ghita took a taxi back to the apartment building and made her way up the dim stairwell.

The dirt and stink were almost too much to take. But at that moment, it seemed the one safe place, a refuge from which she could make sense of what was going on, and struggle to make a plan.

On the fourth floor Ghita poked the key into the lock, opened the door to her apartment, closed it, and peered out through the spy hole.

Only when certain that the coast was clear, she pulled open the doors to the voluminous wardrobe and stepped inside.

Closing them behind her, she slid away a secret hatch at the back and climbed through…

…into a fabulously bright apartment.

The walls were painted taupe, hung with original artwork from Japan, the furnishings upholstered in ivory white, and the floors scattered with exquisite Turkish kilims.

The sitting room was dominated by a white leather canapé, its matching ottoman strewn with designer catalogues and magazines. Standing between it and an open kitchen area on the left was a great wrought-iron birdcage, suspended from a brass hook mounted on the ceiling. In the cage was a parrot, its lime-coloured plumage bringing out subtly the green accents of the room.

Shuffling into a pair of Thai slippers, Ghita lay back on the sofa. She took a deep breath, kicked the magazines off the stool, and hit a speed dial on her phone.

After much ringing, a voice came on the other end.

'Hello? Aicha, sweetie, it's me! I've been trying you all day!'

Silence prevailed. Ghita assumed the call had been lost. Just before she redialled, Aicha spoke:

'Ghita, you are never to call me again,' she said in a low, bitter tone. 'Do you understand? We are no longer friends.'

'Aicha, what are you saying? It's me! I'm your best friend!'

'Your father has betrayed us all!'

'Darling, listen... I don't know what's happening, but he's been taken away in handcuffs!'

'So has mine, and Bouchra's and Hamid's as well!'

'But why is this happening?'

'Because your damned father began exposing people, that's why!'

'I'm so confused. I just don't understand.'

Aicha's voice was now charged with emotion, the words delivered one at a time:

'Listen to me, Ghita! You will never call me again! In my eyes you are dead!'

Fifty-two

THE ROOF OF Hotel Marrakech was flat, tiled in red bricks, and covered in a spider's web of junk.

There were rusting old bicycle frames and rotting bamboo deckchairs, crates of empty gin bottles, strands of lead piping, threadbare furniture, and a line of refrigerators from the days when home appliances were the size of family cars.

On the south side of the roof there was a small area free from clutter. It was just big enough for a wrought-iron table and chair, and an ice bucket arranged on a stand that doubled as an ashtray.

Blaine sat there all afternoon, his gaze locked on the postcard, his mind conjuring fantasies of a lifetime ago.

As his concentration strayed, he found himself wandering the streets of wartime Casablanca. He could picture himself clearly, strolling down the grand boulevard — what was then Avenue de France. The dazzling winter light bathed it all, reflecting off the gleaming art deco apartment blocks, the shops below them emporiums of wonder and delight.

And he could picture Bogart passing him, cigarette in hand, grey fedora tipped down low on his brow.

Blaine peered down to the street below and closed his eyes.

He wished he could wind back the clock's hands, slip into the black-and-white postcard world, a realm of unending possibility.

By the end of the afternoon, he knew every detail of the picture — every shadow, every straight line and curve. He admonished himself for falling victim to an old man's story. Then, slipping the card into his shirt pocket, he went down to Cinema Rialto, where the early evening screening of *Casablanca* was about to begin.

Fifty-three

HIS BACK WARMED by the walk, Mortimer Wu arrived at the Marché Central, where he treated himself to a bowl of fish broth and a stale chocolate croissant. He wasn't in the best of spirits, and hadn't been for days, not since the bad business in Marrakech.

As he spooned the thin soup to his lips, holding the bowl in his right hand, he wished he were home in Hong Kong, away from the trouble that had overrun his life.

'Want a shoeshine?' said a voice.

Saed sauntered up to the table with his box.

'I'm wearing sneakers,' Wu replied, 'don't think you'd get much of a shine on them.' He struggled a smile. 'Want half a croissant?'

Leaning forward, as if only half trusting, Saed took the pastry.

'You are new... new to Casablanca, no?'

'How did you guess?'

'Your shoes... they are dusty. Marrakech dust.'

Mortimer Wu slurped the broth. He motioned to the waiter.

'My little friend here is joining me. Bring another bowl of soup.'

Saed sat down and was soon slurping as well.

'Which hotel you staying?'

'Not sure. I'm travelling to Tangier tomorrow. D'you know anywhere cheap and good?'

The shoeshine boy jerked a thumb behind him.

'Hotel Marrakech,' he said. 'If you don't mind cats.'

Fifty-four

At seven forty-five, Blaine left the Rialto.

He was still glowing from the final sequence, and was mumbling the dialogue as he went. Drifting through the empty streets on his way to Baba Cool, he noticed a light in Monsieur Raffi's shop.

Without thinking, he crossed the street and rapped gently on the window.

Raffi unbolted the door.

'Come on in, my American friend,' he said. 'I have been sitting here waiting for you.'

'But we hadn't planned to meet.'

The shopkeeper locked the door once Blaine was inside.

'Of course we had — you just didn't know it,' he said, slumping down in his tattered satin chair. 'Now, tell me, how are you getting on with the clue?'

Blaine pulled out the postcard.

'I've spent the afternoon staring at it.'

'And what have you seen?'

'Old Casablanca in a time before the rot set in.'

'That's good,' Raffi said, 'but you are missing the details. And the world depends on details.'

'Believe me, I've seen them all.'

Monsieur Raffi shuddered.

'Seeing is not the same as understanding,' he said.

'Seeing what?'

'The real picture.'

The American frowned. He held the card up to the light and turned it slowly.

'What am I missing?'

'*Everything.*'

Again Blaine turned it, slower this time. As he turned, he noticed the edge gleam very slightly, as if it had been glued flat. He assumed it was part of the printing process. But, as he turned it again, he saw that the glue had been added later.

With great care, he pushed his thumbnail into the space where the picture was pasted onto the card. The two sheets separated easily, as if they were supposed to be pulled apart.

Working his way around the entire edge, Blaine found himself staring at the side of the card that had been glued to the image.

The left side was covered in writing, made in a small, neat hand. It looked like a series of directions — directions through Casablanca. The right side was devoted to a very rough hand-sketched map. It featured what appeared to be a main street, with bars, cafés, and cinemas, all of them crudely marked.

Blaine's mouth opened but no words came out at first. Then, as if in a daze, he said:

'This is Bogart's handwriting. I'd know it anywhere.'

Monsieur Raffi coughed hard, then blew his nose.

'Now you have the clue, you can begin to unlock the secret,' he said.

Fifty-five

A GLEAMING GLASS elevator ascended through a sumptuous office building, the floors and walls clad in pallid grey granite, the fittings all polished steel.

Ghita Omary stepped out at the fifteenth floor. Dressed more conservatively than usual, she moved with uncharacteristic urgency.

Striding up to the reception, she tapped a manicured fingernail on the desk. The receptionist, who was talking to her boyfriend on the phone, glanced up.

'I will be with you in a moment,' she said tersely.

'Please tell Mr. Senbel that Ghita Omary is here to see him.'

The receptionist covered the receiver with her hand.

'Would you wait? Mr. Senbel is very busy indeed.'

Turning, Ghita pushed her way fast down the corridor and began searching for the largest office. She had not visited the lawyer before, but knew full well that jaw-dropping grandeur was expected by the upmarket clientele.

At the end of the corridor stood a thick glass door, a potted bonsai standing proud on either side. It was the only one with plants.

Making a beeline for it, Ghita barged in, the receptionist sprinting after her.

Driss Senbel was seated near the window at a teak desk, the wall facing it obscured by diplomas and photographs of the lawyer in the company of the great and the good.

'Forgive me for not making an appointment,' said Ghita, 'I didn't have your number.'

The lawyer looked up from a legal contract. He seemed alarmed at first, but then smiled tautly, waving the receptionist away.

'My dear Ghita, you are a daughter to me, and do not need an appointment. The door is always open to you.'

Ghita sat, or rather she perched, on the edge of a grey leather chair. Coaxing herself to remain composed, she pressed her palms together.

'I am turning to you for help,' she said, 'as my father's close friend.'

Senbel didn't reply at first. He looked at Ghita, his manner taciturn and cold.

'Your father's plan to root out corruption has backfired dramatically,' he replied. 'We all knew it would, and we warned him — but he didn't listen.'

'He is a patriot,' Ghita said, her voice straining. 'He loves his country and is the only one of you willing to stand up against the evil that's eating it from the inside out.'

The lawyer held out his wrists.

124

'You can take me away if you believe I have done anything wrong,' he said.

'It's not you, but the system… and you're part of it.'

'My dear Ghita, if you chop down the forest, nature begins to fight back. It sends pestilence and plague. This may not be nature, but it's the same thing.' Senbel paused, took a deep breath, and sighed. 'The drugs they found… it wasn't a gram or two of *kif*. It was a massive haul, and of heroin at that.'

Ghita's mouth contorted in a snarl.

'You know as well as I do it was planted there!'

'Of course it was.'

'So what are we going to do about it?'

'*Wait*. We have to wait.'

'Wait for what?'

Driss Senbel groomed a strand of hair over his bald patch.

'Your father's assets have been seized,' he said. 'Everything is frozen. His home, his companies, his private jet… *everything*.'

'So let's get them unfrozen!'

Senbel picked a silver letter-opener from the surface of his desk. It had an ivory handle and a hallmarked blade.

'These people we are dealing with,' he said, 'they are extremely dangerous.'

'What people?'

'The ones your father has so enraged.'

'But who are they?'

'They're gangsters, gangsters with the cloak of respectability.'

'Do they have a leader?'

'All I know are the rumours…'

'And what do the rumours say?'

'That they take their lead from a man known to them as the Falcon.'

'I must meet him. I'll plead with him if I have to.'

'He won't listen. None of them will. And in any case, you'll never find him.'

The lawyer ran the blade across his palm.

'The police, the politicians, businessmen, they all live in terror of him,' he said. 'The Falcon controls the system. He *owns* it… even powerful, wealthy men like your father have no hope against him. *Why?* Because his power is not constructed from anything logical. You see, it's power derived from raw fear.'

There was a knock at the door.

The receptionist entered with a memo for Senbel to sign. Striding indifferently through the room, she glared at Ghita as she approached her employer. A moment or two later, she was gone.

'There's a huge storm approaching,' the lawyer said. 'It's going to be a tempest, a perfect storm. All I can do is to warn you. Leave Casablanca. Leave Morocco. Go very far away.'

'And let my father languish in jail?'

'I suppose so.'

There was rage in Ghita's eyes.

'I'm not frightened of this man, this Falcon,' she said. 'I'm not frightened of anyone.'

Fifty-six

TAKING THE SHOESHINE boy's advice, Mortimer Wu went across to Hotel Marrakech and soon found himself installed in the room opposite Blaine's.

Opening the window, he stared out at the flower stalls on the edge of the market. Then he lay on the bed, closed his eyes, and thought back to Hong Kong once again.

An hour or two passed and Wu didn't move.

By remaining completely still, he found that the anxiety and the fear subsided. But as dusk fell over Casablanca, he pushed back his shoulders and pulled himself off the bed.

He glanced down at the market.

The flower sellers were packing up, draining their buckets into the gutters, bundling up the roses for another day.

There were footsteps out in the corridor.

Wu put his ear to the door. He listened and opened it a crack. A man was fumbling for his key at the room opposite.

'Hello,' he said, in a friendly voice — an American voice.

'Good evening,' Wu replied, opening the door wide.

'You new here?'

'Yeah. Just arrived this afternoon.'

'How are you liking the faded grandeur of Hotel Marrakech?'

Mortimer Wu didn't respond to the question. Instead, he asked:

'Is there any hot water?'

'Hot water? Are you crazy?' said Blaine with a grin. 'You're lucky if you get any water at all — hot or cold.'

TAHIR SHAH

'Can you direct me to the shower?'

'Sure. It's all the way down the hall.'

'Thank you,' Wu replied, before withdrawing into his room.

Shutting the door, he slid the bolt firmly into place.

Left standing there, his own door open, Blaine plodded down the corridor to relieve himself.

On the way back, he wondered whether to reach out, to invite the newcomer for a glass of *café noir* down at Baba Cool.

He was about to knock when he heard a commotion down in the lobby. The front door slammed hard, and was followed by the cacophonous cry of cats.

Leaving his room open, Blaine hurried down.

The ever-present clerk wasn't laid out on the floor in his usual state of delirium. He wasn't there at all. Blaine peered on the floor behind the desk, but there was no sign of the clerk.

The cats seemed uneasy.

A few of them had their ears pricked up, alert, poised low as if ready for flight. One or two had leapt up to higher ground and were perched on a high shelf. They were quite obviously spooked.

Eventually, Blaine went back upstairs and slipped back into his room. He cursed the damp, the cold, and the stench. Then his mind turned to Ghita. Even though the thought of her made his blood churn, he wished she were there.

Pulling on his Humphrey Bogart raincoat, fedora in hand, he went out into the corridor again.

Across from his room, the Chinese backpacker's door was ajar.

Rehearsing a line of invitation in his head, Blaine knocked, pushed the door open and swung his head in.

Mortimer Wu was lying on the bed, face up. There was an odd oily, almost metallic smell, and the curtains were drawn shut. Frowning, Blaine flicked on the light.

He leapt back in terror.

The backpacker's throat had been slashed. His clothing and the moth-eaten blanket were soaked in fresh blood.

Blaine screeched. It was a high-pitched, girly scream, the kind from *Tom and Jerry* cartoons when the woman sees the mouse.

He stood there for what seemed like an eternity, his feet rooted to the bare floorboards, every nerve in his body in shock.

Then he panicked.

Something was telling him to get out, to run.

But do so and he'd be a suspect. 'This isn't America,' he thought. 'Things don't work like that here!'

So, shaking, he ran back to his room, grabbed his satchel and the bin liner.

Sprinting down the stairs, he rushed out through the front door of Hotel Marrakech.

Fifty-seven

PATRICIA ROSS HAD spent the day petitioning Casablanca's governor to release Hicham Omary, but without any luck. Baying for blood, he was in no mood for clemency.

At six p.m., she drove back to the Globalcom headquarters, an attaché case under her arm. She was tired, frustrated, and fearful. It felt as though the walls were closing in, as though the enemies were everywhere. As the CEO's assistant, Ross knew it was only a matter of time before the authorities tried to implicate her as well.

On the ground floor, five uniformed police officers were standing guard in a line. Ross was no expert on Moroccan law enforcement, but they appeared to be better equipped than usual, armed with semi-automatic weapons.

Before she could get to the elevator, a plain-clothes officer stopped her.

'Where are you going?'

'Up to my office.'

'At this late hour?'

Ross rolled her eyes.

'We're in the news business,' she said. 'The news doesn't stop.'

'What's in your case?'

'Papers, documents, that's all.'

The officer waved her through. She took the elevator up to the fifteenth floor, placed the attaché case on her desk, and looked out at the lights of Casablanca below. In any other job she might have quit right then, but Hicham Omary had been a mentor to her, a boss with a vision.

She sat down, put her head in her hands, and tried to think straight.

How could she help him?

Without meaning to, she thought of the first time they'd met. It was in Paris at the Musée Jacquemart-André.

Omary had been alone, taking a quick tour through the picture gallery between meetings nearby. They had both been drawn to the same painting, a self-portrait of Nélie Jacquemart, her long, graceful form in profile.

From the first moment she saw Omary, Patricia Ross had been struck by his gentleness, and by his love of fine things.

They had taken tea in the museum's salon and, the next thing she knew, she was working for him in Casablanca.

A dozen memories flashed through, all of them featuring Omary, in an exhibition of courtesy and good taste. She had never met a man like him, either in intellectual capacity, or in the way he always seemed to be three steps ahead of the game. The news business was suited to him more than anyone alive.

Ross glanced at her reflection in the window. She could feel the establishment closing ranks. It was just a matter of time before they took her in. But she knew how Omary had a sixth sense, a sense of how a situation would be played out, a sense learned on the way up from the streets.

Logging into her laptop, Patricia Ross squinted at her emails and swore out loud. Her account had been hacked. Thousands of filed messages were missing. She was about to slam the laptop shut when a random email caught her eye.

It was from Jacques Mart.

She clicked on the message. It was blank, except for a single character way down the page — a question mark, highlighted as a hyperlink. She clicked it, and a website opened. It was password protected.

Without thinking, Ross typed in the name *Jacquemart*.

The screen went blank. Then, a moment later, it came alive with dozens of dossiers, titled with some of the most important names in the land.

'My God, Hicham, you're amazing!' she exclaimed.

Opening ones of the files at random, she found scans of illegal bank statements, secret video footage, and proof of bribe-taking on a grand scale.

At the bottom of the page was an instruction. It read: MAKE PUBLIC AS SOON AS POSSIBLE.

Fifty-eight

FOR MORE THAN three hours Blaine walked the streets, replaying the sight of Mortimer Wu with his throat slashed.

Time and again, he set off back to Hotel Marrakech, each time stopping just short. On the last abortive return, he saw a cluster of uniformed officers standing outside, and the stoned-out clerk being interrogated on the pavement, a fluffy white cat pulled tight to his chest.

Blaine's gut told him to bide his time, because whoever killed the backpacker might still be there, waiting for him. He thought of going to the American consulate and explaining it all. But again, instinct warned against it. He needed somewhere quiet — somewhere he could lie low and think.

He thought of Ghita and her apartment. It may have been wretched, but at least it was silent — the last place he would be disturbed. As for Ghita, she may have been a pain in the backside, but she spoke fluent English.

Making sure no one was following him, and dressed in the fedora and raincoat, Blaine hurried to the apartment building opposite Baba Cool. He slipped into the entranceway and ran up the stairs, groping his way up the curved wall as he went.

There was no light under Ghita's door, but he knocked anyway.

Silence.

Blaine sucked air through his teeth and squatted down on his case, his forehead streaming with sweat.

'Jesus Christ,' he said aloud. 'What do I do now?'

Fifty-nine

AT GLOBALCOM HEADQUARTERS, Patricia Ross copied the dossiers and sent them to Wikileaks, with an embargo until ten p.m. GMT.

Then she sent them to every newshound she could think of — in Morocco and abroad.

After that, she hurried upstairs to the newsroom and cornered Adam Binbin, the only editor she could completely trust.

'What have you got on the line-up tonight?'

Binbin logged on, skimming the schedule as he stirred his tea.

'A Chinese student's been murdered downtown — it's a suspected robbery gone wrong. Then some political stuff and a whole lot of sport — the opium of the people.'

'I need to ask a favour… a big favour,' said Ross, touching a hand to the back of her head.

Binbin took a sip of the tea, picked another sugar lump from the saucer, and dropped it in.

'I've got a huge story that has to go out… *tonight.*'

'Bigger than a murdered tourist?'

Ross leaned in close.

'This is as big as it gets,' she said.

Sixty

GHITA HAD CRISS-CROSSED Boulevard Mohammed V all evening, checking the cafés and the dingy drinking dens tucked away in the backstreets. She might have been repulsed by the derelict men who patronized them, but her mind wasn't on judgement. Rather, it was on finding someone who could lead her to the Falcon.

Behind the market she came to an especially run-down bar. There was no name outside. And, in place of a door, a curtain hung fashioned from what looked like strands of bath chain. Ghita peered inside, into the cumulonimbus haze of cigarette smoke.

In varying stages of inebriation, half a dozen men were reclining on broken chairs, nursing half-empty bottles of Flag Spéciale. A couple of loose ladies were attempting unsuccessfully to drum up business.

On the floor near the bar, a man was having his shoes cleaned. Ghita recognized the shoeshine box, which had a gold cross on the side. She stormed in and tapped Saed on the neck.

'I need to speak to you,' she said urgently.

He looked at her feet.

'I clean those, OK?' he said.

'I don't want my shoes done.'

'*So?*'

'So, I need some information.'

Choking into her hand, her face screwed up, Ghita took a seat at a booth. Saed sat down opposite.

'I'll get you a drink,' she said. 'You want a Coke?'

The boy made a sign to the barman, and a pair of green bottles were slapped down on the tabletop.

'You're far too young to drink that!' Ghita said reproachfully.

'No, no, no…' Saed replied. Lighting a cigarette, he blew the smoke out to the side.

'What would your mother think?'

'I have no mother.'

'Your father then… what would he say? I bet he'd spank you!'

'I have no father. No one to do spanking,' said Saed, downing the first beer in one. 'So I am free.'

Ghita's disapproval eased. She lowered her head subversively, her thumb feeling the curved lines of her iPhone.

'What do you know about the Falcon?' she asked.

The shoeshine boy froze.

'Nothing,' he said quickly.

'I don't believe you.'

'Keep away from the Falcon,' said Saed, wiping the froth off his lip.

'I can't.'

'Why?'

'Because he's had my father imprisoned for a crime he's incapable of committing. I need to know where he's being held.'

'Then look for the police commissioner. You need him. Not the Falcon.'

Ghita frowned.

'*Do I?*'

'Yes.'

'Why?'

'Because he knows everything.'

Ghita's eyes widened.

'Should I give him *baksheesh?*'

The shoeshine boy waved a hand dismissively through the air.

'No, no, just drinks. That's what he wants.'

'Drinks?'

'Scotch.'

'How do you know that?'

'I know everything… like the commissioner,' the boy said, reaching out for the second beer.

Ghita tapped a manicured fingernail to the table.

'And where does the commissioner drink his Scotch?' she asked.

Saed winked at the ground.

'Down there.'

'Where?'

'In the tunnels.'

'What tunnels?'

'The ones under the city. There is a world down there.'

'Is there?'

Saed nodded.

'You don't know that?'

'Apparently not,' Ghita replied curtly. 'When can I go there, to buy him the Scotch?'

The boy shook his head.

'You cannot go there. Only… you know… *working* women can go there.'

'Then will you go?'

'Too young for Club Souterrain.'

'So what can I do?'

'Find someone else.' Saed took a gulp of Flag and lit a second cigarette off the end of the first. 'The American?' he said.

'That imbecile? Oh, God no!'

'One of your friends?'

Ghita's expression soured.

'I don't have any friends,' she snapped.

All of a sudden, 'Yankee Doodle Dandy' blasted out from the iPhone. It was Mustapha.

'*Chéri*, I came looking for you!' said Ghita.

'I know you did. My father told me.'

'When can I see you, my dearest? Will you come for me?'

There was hesitation on the other end.

'Ghita, I must inform you that... that...'

'What?'

'That our engagement is off.'

Sixty-one

THERE WAS THE patter of feet moving up the darkened staircase. They weren't heavy, gruesome steps, the feet of a murderer or of a policeman, but rather they were nimble ones, making almost no sound at all.

Blaine got up and hid himself in the shadows. He had the advantage, as his eyes had had time to adjust to the lack of light.

Taking the last step, Ghita paused. She was barefoot, heels in her hand.

'Can I talk to you?' said Blaine, stepping from a shadow.

Ghita let out a shriek.

'What are you doing here?'

'Something terrible has happened... at Hotel Marrakech.'

'What?'

Blaine tapped a finger towards the door.

'I don't want to be a burden,' he said, 'but could I come in?'

Without a reply, Ghita twisted the key back and forth in the old lock.

'There's something you should know,' she said. 'A little secret.'

'Huh?'

'Do you promise not to tell?'

Blaine wasn't in the mood for games, but he agreed anyway.

They went into the vestibule and the American slumped down on the blood-speckled mattress. He was exhausted, so much so that he hardly even noticed the filth.

'The secret,' said Ghita. 'It's in here.'

She pointed to the wardrobe. Stepping inside it, Ghita jerked away the hatch at the back.

'Follow me,' she said.

Blaine did so, and found himself in the secret apartment. It was made all the more impressive by the low expectations.

'I don't believe this!' he exclaimed, blinking.

'I made a few adjustments, had the place spruced up.'

Lowering himself onto the couch, Blaine put his head in his hands.

'I'm beginning to wish for a life with fewer surprises,' he said.

'What do you mean?'

'Well, this afternoon I met a Chinese backpacker. He was staying in the hotel, in the room across from mine. I was going to invite him out for a coffee at Baba Cool. So I went to his room. But…'

'But what?'

'But he was dead — throat slashed.'

'*What*?!'

Blaine touched a thumb to his Adam's apple and swallowed hard.

'Just like in the movies.'

'That's terrible. What did the police say?'

'I don't know...'

'Why not?'

'Because I ran away.'

Ghita crossed the sitting room to where the American was seated. She looked at him with disbelief.

'You can't run away. I mean... you mustn't!'

'I didn't know what to do.' Blaine paused, staring into space. 'I feel so alone.'

Ghita held up a finger — a finger ending in a manicured nail.

'I know what to do,' she replied.

'What?'

'You must go straight to the police commissioner and explain it all.'

'But I can't go to the police station. They'll arrest me.'

The fingernail waved left, right, left.

'I didn't say go to the station,' she said. 'This is Morocco. You never go through the front door when you can go in the back.'

Lighting a scented candle, the wick flickering in the draught, Ghita lowered her head meekly.

'I'm alone as well,' she said. 'My father's been arrested, framed for an invented crime. I need to find out where he's being held.'

'What did he do?'

Pacing over to the fridge, Ghita took a bottle of chilled Pouilly-Fumé. She opened it and poured a pair of large glasses.

'Drugs,' she said at length. 'At least that's what they've accused him for. They planted them.'

'*They*?'

'The underworld. The gangsters… the ones who control Casablanca.'

'What are you gonna do?'

Ghita took a gulp of wine.

'Save my father. Then get revenge… I mean, justice.'

'What's your plan?'

Ghita looked sheepish. She topped up Blaine's glass.

'To get to the commissioner.'

'The same guy who you're saying I should go talk to?'

'Yes.'

'Isn't that a coincidence… that he can help us both?'

'Morocco's like that,' she replied. 'Many roads lead to the same place.'

Sixty-two

AT DAWN THE next day, Hicham Omary was fingerprinted. Then, handcuffed and shackled, he was led out from the holding cells to a waiting prison van. It was raining, light drizzle, the sound of a distant ambulance siren breaking the silence.

Thirty armed officers had formed a circle around the van. They braced themselves as Omary shuffled towards them, as though he posed a serious danger to honest society. Struggling to walk in the chains, he was heaved up into the back, his head striking the top of the steel doorframe.

The morning's copy of *Assabah*, the most popular daily, was folded on the bench seat. Omary saw the Arabic headline as he clambered onto the bench. It read:

GLOBALCOM PUBLISHES SECRET DOSSIER!

The doors slammed and the vehicle moved away, rumbling out from an entrance at the rear. Threading its way through the backstreets, it was soon on Route El Jadida, heading south on the open road to Marrakech.

'Where am I being taken?' he asked the police officer opposite.

'To a secure place.'

'I need to contact my daughter.'

The officer chuckled.

'Good luck with that!' he said.

Sixty-three

THE EVENING AT Ghita's secret apartment had been long, and loosened with much Pouilly-Fumé. Blaine found that chilled white wine was the best way of dealing with the fear, the fear of being hunted in a foreign land.

He and Ghita sat on either end of the long, ivory-white couch, inching a little closer as the cool wine warmed them. Blaine suggested fleeing back to New York, but Ghita reminded him of the uncertainty likely to face him at the airport.

'Only the police commissioner can help you,' she urged.

'But what if he arrests me right there and then?'

'In an illegal drinking den?' Ghita wagged a finger left and right. 'He wouldn't dare.'

'Why not?'

'Because here in Morocco there's such a thing as hospitality. If you are hosting someone, you have to protect them. It's a duty, not a choice.'

A second time, Blaine suggested absconding home to New York, and Ghita switched on her charm. She stroked a hand down over his arm, looked him in the eye, and managed to coax a single tear to roll south over her cheek.

'I need you,' she whispered, as a second tear tumbled down in the wake of the first. 'I need you more than I have ever needed anyone in my life.'

Sixty-four

SEVEN CONCENTRIC WALLS separated the fortress prison from the natural mountain theatre that lay beyond. Topped with concertina razor wire and with watchtowers at every corner, the camp was regarded as the most secure in the kingdom.

Its forty cells were located far underground and were arranged in such a way that the prisoners had almost no contact with anyone at all. The solitary confinement was so absolute that most of the convicts went insane long before they roasted from the summer heat or froze from the winter chill.

Cell No. 3 was no larger than any other. It was eight feet by eight feet, floored in reinforced concrete, with an iron door leading out onto a slim corridor. The only source of light was a lamp recessed high on the wall, turned on and off depending on the whims of the duty guard. Most of the time it was left off, forcing Hicham Omary to endure the darkness.

Once each day a guard would arrive, open the inspection hatch, and push through a plate of second-rate food. Twice a week he would take out the slop, and shine a light into the inmate's eyes — gauging whether lunacy had set in.

A man of steely resolution, Omary had learned when in life to act, and when to bide one's time. He knew the moment of redemption would come, and that day-to-day survival was the challenge of the moment.

When the food came, he forced himself to choke it all down, even maggots. They were protein and protein provided strength — the currency of survival.

And through the frozen winter mornings, the owner of Globalcom did push-ups on his knuckles to keep warm. From time to time he worried that Ghita may have been taken into custody as well. But, as he reasoned it, anyone foolish enough to mess with his daughter would get what they deserved.

Much of the time, Omary paced up and down, revisiting his life from the very start, as though it were a matinée show.

He thought back to the tenement block downtown where his mother had brought him up alone. And he thought of all the playground fights and the split lips, the early hardship that had made him the man he was. Without the beatings and the bruises back then, he would have been as soft as mush, like everyone else.

'I am Hicham Omary,' he said getting down onto his knuckles for the third time in a day, 'the same Hicham Omary who rose from nothing — the Hicham Omary who can endure anything!'

Sixty-five

THE NEXT MORNING, Blaine woke up on the couch with a dry mouth and a throbbing head. He thought of Wu, the sight of his slashed neck and of all that fresh blood.

Then he remembered the postcard.

Riffling through his pockets, he found it, squinted at the writing and the scrawled map. The thought of holding an object that had belonged to Bogart would, in more normal circumstances, have filled him with wonder.

But the murder at Hotel Marrakech had left him unable to appreciate normality.

He sat on the couch, his bare feet pressed onto the antique Turkish kilim, and he took a deep breath.

Just then, Ghita came through from the bedroom, her hair damp from the shower. She smiled, said something kindly, but Blaine didn't hear. He was staring into space.

'Can I make you some coffee?' she said, repeating herself.

'Huh? What? Oh, yeah, thanks.'

'How do you take it?'

Blaine turned, but his eyes didn't change focus.

'I have to get home to America,' he said all of a sudden. 'I'm not safe here. I don't know what I was thinking. Casablanca, *the* Casablanca, isn't *my* Casablanca. It's not the movie. It's nothing like it — there's no Humphrey Bogart, Ingrid Bergman, or Paul Henreid. There's no Vichy Regime or refugee crisis, no German soldiers, or spies, or Rick's Café.'

Ghita passed Blaine his coffee.

'But there's danger,' she said.

'That's the understatement of the decade.'

'I'm just thinking of protecting you,' said Ghita. 'In Morocco, protection comes from people with power, and that's why we need to find the police commissioner.'

The American hunched forward gloomily.

'I know you're in a tight spot, with your father,' he said, 'but I could be implicated for murder. This is a foreign country, and I'm out of my depth.' He paused, lifted his face, his eyes swollen with fatigue and fear. 'Hell, haven't you seen *Midnight Express*?' he asked.

'Go take a hot shower,' Ghita replied, 'and you'll feel a lot better.'

Blaine sighed.

'OK.'

Fifteen minutes later he was scrubbed clean, with a lavender-coloured bath towel wrapped around his waist. He padded through into the sitting room and hunted through his bin liner for the cleanest dirty shirt, smelling them one by one.

All of a sudden he stopped, put the plastic sack down and picked up his satchel, as if in urgent need to check something.

'Oh my God!' he yelled, his hands tearing fast through odds and ends. 'It was in here last night, I *know* it was!'

'What was?'

'My passport! Jesus! I don't believe it!'

Standing over in the kitchen area, Ghita slipped a coffee capsule into the Nespresso machine and pressed the button.

'I'm sure it's there,' she said over the whirring sound.

'No, no, it's not!'

'Did you leave it at Hotel Marrakech?'

'No, I brought it with me. I know I did! It was right here, in this little pouch.'

'You must have dropped it on the way over. We could retrace your steps.'

Blaine screwed up his face.

'Do you really think anyone would leave an American passport where it was if they found it on the street? Anyway, I trudged around for hours before coming here. All I can do is to go to the consulate and plead for my life.'

Ghita hurried over.

'I warn you against going to the authorities — *any* authorities,' she said. 'The police commissioner is the only one who can help you.'

'And he's *not* the authorities?'

Ghita stuck out a hand and nudged it side to side.

'There's authorities and there's authorities,' she said hesitantly. 'And he's the right kind of authorities. He can help you.'

'You mean, he can help *us*?'

Sixty-six

ON THE STRIKE of noon, twenty police vans rolled up fast to the main entrance of the Globalcom HQ. A stream of officers poured out and took up positions all around the building. More still marched inside and set about shutting Globalcom down.

Patricia Ross had known it was only a matter of time before the governor and his cronies would attack. She had loaded the secret dossiers onto numerous websites, hosted all around the world. They were timed to reveal another document every five minutes, playing out the scandal a little at a time.

Omary would be proud of her, she thought. After all, it had been he who had taught her to allow a news story to develop — the snowball effect.

By thirty-five minutes past the hour, Ross and her colleagues were down on the forecourt. Their hands tied with nylon straps, they awaited processing at the police headquarters on Boulevard Zerktouni.

Behind them, a mass of computer hard drives, plastic files,

and assorted paperwork was shuffled out of the building towards a fleet of waiting vans.

In other jurisdictions the emphasis might have been on sifting through the mountain of data. But, in Casablanca, sifting data was the lowest priority.

The files and the hard drives were instead headed straight to the incinerator.

Sixty-seven

BLAINE DARED NOT leave the apartment until the late afternoon.

At eleven, Ghita had slipped out on an errand, leaving him to brood there alone. When she was gone, he sat on the couch, consumed with worry and fear.

For hours he sat there, rigid like a statue.

He thought about his life in New York, about Laurie, and about Drain-O-Sure, one of a hundred dead-end sales jobs that had sucked him in and spat him out.

Then his thoughts turned to Bogart.

A man with his own demons, he'd been a role model to a generation, a pillar of strength and an idol — the kind of man who guffawed in the face of adversity.

'Damn it!' said Blaine angrily. 'What would Bogie think of me, cowering here like this? I can't hide in here forever. If I'm going to survive the real Casablanca, I'm gonna have to learn to fight back!'

Pulling on his macintosh and fedora, Blaine took a good, hard look at the postcard. Despite the almost illegible script, the directions were just about clear enough.

They led to a bar opposite the Cinema Lynx in nearby Mers Sultan.

Within the hour, Blaine found himself outside Bar Atomic, a haunt of impecunious drinkers dating back to the thirties, when anything with the word 'atomic' in the title was regarded as cutting edge and cool.

The doors were open, the panelled saloon pleasing in its size and shape, with a bar on one side running the length of the room. The walls were hung with old studio prints of Hollywood greats — Gary Cooper and Greta Garbo, Katharine Hepburn, James Cagney and, of course, Humphrey Bogart in trademark *Casablanca* attire.

Behind the bar there were a pair of antique wooden refrigerators, the wall above them peppered with enamelled advertisements — among them Cinzano, Campari, and Ricard.

And between the bar and the back wall lay a hotchpotch of battered tables and chairs, a handful of regulars sitting in silence with their beers and cigarettes.

Blaine took a seat in the corner and soaked up the atmosphere.

A moment or two passed, and then the crusty old barman crept over, doling out green bottles of Flag and ashtrays as he came. He handed Blaine a bottle, wiping the rim of a glass clean on his sleeve.

Every now and then a salesman coursed in as if swept through on the tide.

The first one sold peanuts from a shallow wicker tray. The second offered bras in assorted sizes and colours. And the third was touting all manner of goods — from can openers to bottle cleaners, to oversized dusters fashioned in the shape of the Eiffel Tower.

When the last of the salesmen had washed away, Blaine took out the postcard and, hesitant as to quite where to start, held it up between thumb and forefinger.

'A friend gave me this,' he explained to the barman. 'And it led me here.'

The barman combed a hand back over his hairless head. He frowned, his brow furrowing like a fallow field. Without a word, he returned to the bar, picked out a clutch of fresh bottles from the fridge and dished them out, whether anyone had asked for refills or not.

Nearing the American, he seemed to stoop.

'Come with me, Monsieur,' he whispered.

Blaine stood up and followed the barman through saloon-style swing doors into the toilet. Even by Casablanca's atrocious standards, it was a deplorable place. An advanced case of rising damp had taken hold on every surface. The single squat lavatory was cracked down the middle, as though an enormous weight had been dropped onto it at some time in the past.

The barman pressed a hand to his chin.

'We have waited,' he said.

'Waited for what?'

'For this moment, for this day.'

'I'm not exactly sure what this is all about,' Blaine replied.

The barman pointed to the postcard, to Humphrey Bogart's script.

'It's about that.'

'I know, but what exactly about it?'

His old hands trembling, the barman unclipped an enamelled advertisement for Schweppes Tonic that was hanging above the urinal. Then he picked out a cardboard envelope from the niche behind.

It was mottled with damp and dirt.

'Here it is.'

'What is it?'

The barman seemed confused.

'It's what you came for,' he said.

Sixty-eight

THE SLIM, WIRY body of Mortimer Wu had been taken away by the police. His possessions and the blood-soaked bedclothes were removed too, confiscated as evidence.

After that, the clerk was arrested as a suspect, although he was later released. The only other guest at the hotel was a Slovak in search of a Sufi brotherhood. He had planned to hitchhike eastwards to Figuig to join a fraternity there, but found himself locked up in an interrogation cell instead.

The clerk had thought it strange that the American might have disappeared at the time of Wu's death, especially when he noticed that he had left his precious poster behind.

But Blaine Williams had been friendly to the cats. And, as a cat-lover himself, the clerk thought it unlikely that he could have committed such an act of brutality.

Late in the afternoon, he poured an extra-large bowl of cream and laid it on the floor in the usual spot. Still spooked, most of the cats refused to come down from their perches.

At five minutes to five, a stout man with a Marrakchi accent, a dark complexion, and heavily scarred cheeks, forced the hotel's front door open. His voice was coarse, his eyes intensely cold. Even before he had uttered a word, the clerk had guessed who he was.

'The body?' the man asked, severely.

'Taken, by the police, along with his luggage.'

'He had something that belonged to us, something valuable.'

The clerk dared not ask what it was.

'You can go up and check the room,' he said.

The Marrakchi went up. He didn't need to be told in which room to look, as though he had experience in tracking down the scent of death.

The clerk could make out the sound of floorboards being prised up and the rickety furniture being torn apart.

When he came back down, the Marrakchi looked at the guest register.

'Where is this one, this American?'

'Which?'

'This one... Monsieur Blaine... Blaine Williams?'

'He left.'

'When?'

'Just before…'

'*When*?'

'Just before Mr. Wu did,' the clerk said.

Sixty-nine

BLAINE COVERED THE half-mile from Mers Sultan at a slow pace.

His mind was on the hardback envelope tucked away in his breast pocket, as much as it was on the mental freeze-frame of Mortimer Wu lying there, all lifeless and drenched in blood.

He planned to head back to Ghita's apartment and to open the envelope there, but the closer he got to the building, the more he wondered about her.

All of a sudden, Blaine thought of his grandfather.

He was sitting on his porch slurping iced tea through his gleaming white dentures.

'Don't trust her!' the old man barked. 'That girl's nothing but trouble!'

So Blaine crossed the street and threaded his way through Derb Omar. The textile merchants were closing up for the night, packing away the great bolts of cloth, donkey carts hauling off the mountains of discarded packaging. He passed the Rialto, and Le Petit Poucet, and was about to drop in on Monsieur Raffi when he heard footsteps behind him.

They were coming fast, in a sprint.

Blaine turned sharply.

A plump, dark man in a thick winter coat was running straight towards him, his right hand outstretched, the fingers clutching the hilt of a knife.

Without thinking, Blaine ran — like he had never run before.

Up Mohammed V, and then doubling back fast in the adjacent street.

The figure followed, and was closing in.

Blaine made a left turn back onto the main drag, then darted down the dimly lit Passage Gallinari, a stone's throw from the Marché Central.

He charged down to the end, to where the hookers gathered when it rained. The footsteps had paused at the passage entrance, as though unsure which way to go.

Suddenly Blaine felt a hand grab the collar of his coat. It yanked him back hard towards a doorway, catching him off balance.

He fell, panting, cursing, hands protecting his head.

'Stay down there!' said a voice. 'I think you've escaped him.'

Blaine looked up. He got to his feet.

'Saed?' he stuttered, still panting from the run. 'What are you doing here?'

'Saving you. That's what I am doing,' he said.

Seventy

Up on the fourth floor, Blaine took the shoeshine boy through the wardrobe into Ghita's secret world. He might not have trusted her, but options were limited. And she had trusted him with a key.

Once inside, he went straight over to the counter, poured himself a Grey Goose, and slugged it back in one.

'Why does she hide...?' asked Saed, dazed by the luxury.

'It's something about proving herself to her father.' Blaine paused, poured another vodka. 'If you ask me, she's a complete nutcase.'

He sat on the couch, fingertips pressed together at his chin.

'I don't understand what's happening,' he said. 'Who was that guy — a mugger?'

Saed helped himself to a neat Grey Goose, then another.

'An assassin. But not one from Casa,' he said casually.

Blaine looked up.

'You think he killed the backpacker?'

'Yes.'

'And what does he want?'

'I do not know. But he thinks you have it.'

'Have what?'

'The thing he wants.'

The shoeshine boy's ever-ready smile melted away.

'I need to ask something from you... a favour,' he said.

Blaine felt a tinge of apprehension in the pit of his stomach, as though a demand for funds was about to be forthcoming.

'A favour?' he repeated in a slow, dry voice.

'This looks like a safe place — a secret safe place,' Saed said.

'Yeah…'

'Could you keep something for me, for a few days?'

The American breathed a sigh of relief.

'Sure… although I'm a guest of Ghita's sofa — an invited guest.'

Saed pulled up his T-shirt and unzipped a money belt. Inside it were a collection of random credit cards, foreign currency bills, and an envelope with what looked like Chinese handwriting on the front.

'Will you keep this envelope for me?' he asked. 'The police stop me very often…'

'You don't have to explain.'

Blaine took the envelope and slipped it into his satchel.

The sight of it reminded him of the treasure trail that had ended at Bar Atomic. He went over to his coat, pulled out the dirt-speckled envelope and opened it.

There was another postcard inside.

It bore the black-and-white image of a sleek, open-topped limousine. Rising up behind it was the Shell Petroleum headquarters at the top of the old Avenue de France.

As with the first postcard, the reverse side was blank. And as before, Blaine peeled back the photograph, revealing Bogie's spidery hand.

'I want to find this building,' said Blaine, having glanced at the text. Saed waved a hand towards the window.

'It's just down there, two blocks away.'

At that moment, the door opened and Ghita slipped through the cupboard into the apartment. She was surprised to see the shoeshine boy, who was lying outstretched on the couch.

'He's my saviour,' said Blaine quickly. 'Saved me from an assassin.'

'It sounds as though you've had a colourful afternoon,' she said, walking over to the kitchen and putting down her purse. She took in the half-empty bottle of Grey Goose, raised an eyebrow and looked at her wristwatch.

'While you've been drowning your sorrows,' she said, 'I have been getting information. I've discovered where the commissioner drinks, and the exact location of Club Souterrain.'

Saed waved a hand towards the window a second time.

'It is under the Marché Central,' he said. 'But the entrance is at the Hotel Touring.'

'That sounds complicated,' Ghita said.

'It is more complicated,' said Saed. 'You see, there's a pass code. It changes every night.'

'I thought you were too young to go inside.'

'Yes, I am.'

Blaine sipped his vodka pensively.

'How would you get the code?' he asked.

'I can get it for you,' said the boy in an easy voice. 'I know the person to ask.'

'And will the commissioner be there?'
Saed tapped his watch.
'Of course he will,' he said.

Seventy-one

AT A QUARTER to twelve Blaine crept from the apartment building, past the Marché Central, to the Hotel Touring. His wallet was weighed down with Ghita's spending money, his hair gelled back, and his slim frame squeezed into a borrowed tuxedo, sourced at short notice by Saed.

A throwback to the glory days, Hotel Touring was a favourite with working women who appreciated its hourly rate, and with backpackers who were willing to endure the lice in the name of economy.

Saed was waiting inside the door. He led Blaine down a twisted iron staircase into the maze of subterranean tunnels that criss-cross old Casablanca.

'You got the code?' Blaine asked.

'Yes. It's CIGOGNE. The French word for "stork".'

'When I'm inside, what do I do?'

'Order a bottle of Scotch. Something expensive. Don't ask how much it is. It's better to seem like you can afford it, whatever it costs. Ask for a table near the bar. Tip the doorman as you go in, and the manager who takes you to your table. And when you get in there, ask him to introduce you to the commissioner.'

'Why shall I say I want to meet him?'

Saed stepped around a pair of dead rats.

'Say you want to check the price of Alphabonds,' he said.

'*Alphabonds?*'

'Government bonds. The money of the underworld. Untraceable and as good as cash.'

'What happens if the police commissioner doesn't turn up?'

The shoeshine boy pushed open a reinforced door at the bottom of the staircase. He seemed anxious.

'He'll come,' he said. 'He always comes.'

They walked down a slender tunnel, the walls lined in rusted iron sheets. It was illuminated by bare, low-watt bulbs, and stank of industrial pesticide.

'I can't believe there's anything down here at all,' said Blaine.

Saed stuck out his hand.

'This is as far as I can go,' he said.

'You're leaving me *here?*'

'Keep going down there and turn right at the end.'

'And what then?'

'Then you will be at the door.'

Blaine peered down the corridor. He half wondered whether it was a trap.

'It doesn't look safe,' he said.

Saed didn't reply. He had gone.

'Bastard!' spat Blaine.

He took a deep breath, wiped a hand hard over his face, and quickened his step towards the secret door of Club Souterrain.

A moment before he reached the end of the tunnel, he heard footsteps and conversation. It sounded like a pair of men approaching — deep voices and city shoes.

Panicking, Blaine ducked into a side tunnel and hid in the shadows. Slowing his breathing, he caught a single snapshot of the men as they passed. One was tall, the other short, both well dressed in suits and ties.

When they were gone, Blaine jumped out and hurried the last few yards to where he expected the club's entrance to be.

But there wasn't a door, just a dead end.

That's impossible, he thought. They couldn't have vanished like that.

He searched the iron-panelled walls for a hidden doorway, but there wasn't one. Blaine was about to turn back, when he noticed a faint ribbon of light at the edge of one of the panels.

At first he assumed it to be a reflection. But, looking more carefully, he saw that the light was coming from behind. He put his ear to the iron and listened hard. There was a trace of sound, little more than an indistinct whisper of vibration.

He looked for a handle or a catch, but he couldn't find one. So he knocked gently... once, then again.

A moment passed, and the panel opened inwards very slowly.

Blaine stepped into a small, square chamber.

Lit more brightly than the corridor, it smelled of perfume and cigarette smoke. Each of the walls was covered in a full-length mirror, a perpetual reflection.

A hatch in one of the mirrors opened at eye level, and a doorman's face hung in the shadow behind.

'*Oui, Monsieur?*' he said in a sour tone.

'The club,' Blaine said, faltering. 'Souterrain.'

'*Oui?*'

'Um, er… *CIGOGNE.*'

The word was followed by a *click*, the sound of a lock snapping back, and well-oiled hinges pressing against themselves.

The mirrored door opened. Blaine stepped forward into a small vestibule.

It was dark, hot, and ended in a curtain of crushed black satin. But it was the noise that was most surprising — the wild, rollicking noise.

A doorman held a hand in invitation towards the curtain.

'*Bienvenue, Monsieur*,' he said.

Blaine pushed the black satin to the side and found himself in a realm worthy of his own far-fetched fantasy.

A cavernous salon spread out before him, packed with immaculate waiters and guests. Filled with conversation, with laughter, and with a haze of cigarette smoke, it was lit by a dozen crystal chandeliers.

At one end, the gaming tables were in full swing — roulette, baccarat, poker, and blackjack. At the other, a group of attendants in white jackets were preparing drinks, a blur of cocktail flasks shaking Martinis at the bar.

In the middle of it all, the outsized hands of a female pianist were gently caressing the keys of a vintage grand. An Argentine from the good side of Buenos Aires, she was big-boned and overly hirsute, and she swaggered boisterously as she played.

Impeccable in a white tuxedo jacket and tie, a manager appeared as if by magic.

'*Bonsoir, Monsieur.*'

'Good evening. I would like a table. A table for two.'

'At once, Monsieur. Please come with me.'

Blaine followed the white tuxedo as it weaved between the clusters of lounge chairs, upholstered in pink velvet with gold piping down the sides.

Crossing the room, he thought of Bogart sitting languidly at the bar, head in hands, cigarette screwed into the corner of his mouth. He felt as though he had actually travelled back in time. And, rather than fearing the situation, he was calmed by it.

The manager motioned to a cluster of chairs set around a low table a few yards from the bar. Blaine dug in his pocket and pulled out a large bill, folded small in anticipation of the moment. It disappeared into the manager's pocket so fast that the American was left wondering whether he had given it at all.

'I'd like a bottle of Scotch,' he said. 'A single malt.'

'Certainly, Monsieur. I can offer you a bottle of Glenlivet, twenty-five years old, with a hint of oak.'

'That will do fine.' Blaine paused, then beckoned the manager a little closer. 'I am hoping to invite the police commissioner to join me for a drink.'

'Of course, Monsieur. I shall extend the invitation at once.'

The pianist blew a kiss to a haggard man at the bar and began to play 'Blue Moon'.

A waiter glided up, a silver salver borne high on an upturned palm. He put the whisky, the ice, and soda siphon on the table, and waited for instructions.

'No ice, and a splash of soda, please.'

Blaine took the glass, held it to the light. Touching it to his lips, he tasted the oak.

A woman approached. She was dressed in a long flowing gown, Chinese silk ruched at the sides, with precariously high stilettos.

'Would you like a little company, Monsieur?' she said.

'Er, not right now, I'm expecting a friend.'

As if on cue, the manager returned.

Beside him was a uniformed officer — six foot two, broad at the shoulders, with a walrus moustache and the kind of face that prompted small children to scream.

'I should like to present the commissioner of police.'

In one motion, Blaine introduced himself, invited the officer to sit, and slipped the manager another neatly folded bill.

'Could I offer you a whisky?' he asked, pouring a triple.

The officer took the glass, clinked it to Blaine's, and downed half the liquid. He licked his lips.

'It's good,' he said with a grin. 'Very good.'

Blaine refilled his glass, dispensing with small talk and replacing it with drink.

Within five minutes, half the bottle was gone and the commissioner seemed drowsy.

Blaine seized the moment.

'I'm new in Casablanca,' he said awkwardly. 'And I'm interested in getting my hands on some Alphabonds.'

The officer sipped his drink thoughtfully.

'How many do you want?'

'It depends on the price.' He drew breath. 'How much *is* the going price?'

'A thousand dirhams each, more or less. But I am surprised that they would interest a man like you.'

Blaine cocked his head expectantly.

'Why?'

'Because you are an American, are you not?'

'How did you guess?'

The commissioner lit a cigar, inspected the end, and thought for a moment.

'Because whether he be in Casablanca, Paris, or Timbuktu,' he said without looking up, 'an American sticks out. He doesn't blend in. Why not? Because he can't.'

Blaine may have debated the point, but he knew there was truth in it. The officer was right — while Americans liked to think they are experts in social camouflage, the only place they are capable of blending in is at home.

A few minutes of silence slipped by.

The commissioner sucked on his cigar, and the hookers paraded, one by one, their gowns brushing the gold piping of the chairs. The pianist began playing an old Edith Piaf number, her large, brusque hands vigorous on the keys.

When the number was halfway through, Blaine touched a hand to his jaw.

'I heard that an Asian tourist was killed at the Hotel Marrakech,' he said absently.

'He's lying in the morgue now,' the officer replied with equal disinterest. 'Throat cut clean in two.'

'I wonder who did it.'

'A gangster, a lowlife,' said the commissioner. 'We caught him. He confessed after a thorough interrogation.'

'Oh,' said Blaine timidly, 'that is good news, isn't it? What's your plan for him?'

The commissioner nodded, sucked long and hard, exhaled, then sipped his Scotch.

'When he's been tried and found guilty, he will be taken to the most secure prison in the kingdom,' he said.

'*Will he?*' Blaine asked with interest. 'And where exactly would that be?'

'In the mountains. The prison there is reserved for the worst offenders.'

'Like that Globalcom boss... what was his name? Let me think.'

'Omary,' the commissioner said in a flash. 'Yes, he's been taken there, too. A lot he has to answer for. He will never get out alive.'

'Out of interest,' said Blaine indifferently, 'where exactly in the mountains is the prison located?'

The commissioner drew a breath to speak a name. The word moved up through his vocal cords and onto his tongue. But, just before it emerged into the world, an immensely large man sidled up and kissed the commissioner on the cheeks.

The two men hugged, then embraced again.

'This is my old friend Dr. Weisemann from Hamburg,' said the officer with considerable delight. 'He has a business making ball-bearings for motor cars.'

Blaine extended his hand, waved to the waiter for another glass and another bottle of single malt. As he did so, Dr.

Weisemann's ample backside made landfall on the pink velvet.

The conversation turned to secret Swiss cabarets, and then to German prostitutes. Blaine glanced at his watch. He tried time and again to steer it back to the subject of remote mountain jails, but without any success. After all, Teutonic whoring was so much more appealing to his audience than the ins and outs of the Moroccan penal system.

At two-fifteen, the commissioner stood up, thanked his American host courteously for the drinks, hugged the German, then staggered away towards the door.

A protracted silence followed, after which Dr. Weisemann fluttered a set of distended fingers at the girls clustered near the bar.

'Which one are you going to take?' he asked.

'Oh, er… I'm really not interested in them,' said Blaine.

'How can that be?' Weisemann's eyes widened. 'Is it not ladies you admire?'

'No… I mean, yes, I do like ladies, just not right now, just not tonight.'

Seventy-two

GHITA WAS STILL awake when Blaine arrived back at her secret apartment. She was sitting on the sofa in a bathrobe, her hair pinned up on the crown of her head.

'Please don't judge how I look,' was the first thing she said.

'I'm not judging you,' Blaine replied tenderly.

'Did you get the information... did you find out where they're holding my father?'

'In the mountains. They're keeping him in the mountains.'

'Which mountains? The Atlas or the Rif?'

Blaine pulled his bow tie loose.

'He didn't say. I'm so sorry.'

Ghita began to weep. She covered her eyes with her hand.

'I don't know what to do,' she sobbed.

There was a knock at the door.

'Are you expecting someone?' Blaine asked.

'No... no one except for you knows I am here. No one except for...'

'Saed.'

Ghita unlocked the door and the shoeshine boy stepped in as if he owned the place.

'How was Club Souterrain?'

'Well, the good news is that they've caught a guy who admitted to killing the backpacker.'

'And the *bad* news?'

'That I couldn't find out where Ghita's father is being held — just that it's in the mountains.'

'Which mountains?'

Blaine shrugged.

'Dunno.'

Ghita started sobbing again.

'I have an idea,' said Saed. 'An idea that may work.'

'What is it?'

'I'll ask my girlfriend.'

'You've got a girlfriend?' Ghita and Blaine exclaimed both at once.

'Yes, of course I do. She's older than me, and she works for the commissioner at the main police station.'

'Why didn't you tell us this before? It could have saved a lot of time,' Ghita said witheringly.

'Not to mention a lot of drinking,' murmured Blaine.

Saed filled himself a tumbler of neat Grey Goose and took a long, satisfying gulp.

'You are very lucky,' he said.

'How's that?'

'Because she owes me a big favour — a favour I have been waiting to use for a very long time.'

Seventy-three

FOR THREE DAYS and nights it rained.

It wasn't mild European splish-splash rain, but a full African downpour. The city was flooded right away, the old French drains clogged with decades' worth of dirt and grime. A number of *bidonvilles*, shantytowns, were washed clean away, leaving the impoverished residents homeless and bereft.

Up the hill in Anfa, Casablanca's *nouveau riche* were moaning about what they imagined to be the terrible inconvenience of it all. They sat indoors, cancelling their golf games and flicking through imported magazines.

Down near the port, one of the last remaining Indian traders was bailing the rainwater from his shop. His family had come to Casablanca back in '28, lured by the promises of the French, and by the prospect of a land untouched by low-cost Indian wares. His name was Ankush Singh and, while he himself had never visited the land of his ancestors, he knew it through the stories his grandfather used to tell.

As he chucked out another bucket of dingy grey water, he spotted a pair of sensible, well-made shoes standing at the kerb. They led to slender ankles, and up to fine legs, a pretty dress and, eventually, to a lovely face.

Putting down the bucket, Ankush Singh looked at the girl.

Unable to remember the last time beauty of any kind had visited his premises, he wanted to savour the moment.

'Someone told me that you are a pawn dealer,' she said.

'Yes, I am, but business is a little slow at the moment,' the shopkeeper replied. 'The rain's driven my customers away and there's some flooding down there in the back.'

'Could I come in for a moment?'

'Of course you may.'

Ghita stepped inside, drying her feet on the mat.

'I am rather embarrassed to be here like this,' she said.

Ankush Singh patted his hands on his shirt.

'And why is that?'

'Because I am from a family of means,' she replied. 'My father has run into some trouble and our assets have been seized. I have begged my friends for a loan, but they have all forsaken me in my moment of need.'

'I don't loan money,' Ankush Singh explained. 'But I can give you money in return for an object of value.'

Ghita pulled a tissue from the sleeve of her dress and pinched it to her nose.

'I've sold most of my clothes — practically gave them away. The rest are at our family home and the police have sealed it shut.' She fumbled with the clasp of her necklace — a gold locket, encrusted with diamonds and sapphires. 'This is all I have left,' she said.

Ankush Singh inspected the jewellery with a loupe.

'It's excellent work,' he said. 'Looks stolen to me.'

Ghita stamped her foot.

'How dare you! I am no thief!'

The shopkeeper leant over the counter. He took Ghita's hand in his and turned it over.

'Your palm is as soft as silk,' he said gently. 'You have never done a day's work in your life, have you?'

Ghita blushed.

'I don't need to work,' she said defensively.

The shopkeeper stepped away from the counter and motioned to a chair.

'Please do sit down. May I offer you some tea?'

Before Ghita could refuse, the shopkeeper had lit a burner and was brewing the pot.

'I don't know why, but you look familiar,' he said, looking at her side on. 'Have you come in here before?'

'No, no, never.'

'Are you sure?'

Ghita blushed again.

'I am certain,' she said icily.

'Then maybe your brother or sister.'

'I am an only child.'

The shopkeeper spooned some loose tea into the pot, dropped in a sprig of mint, and a chunk of sugar the size of his fist. He stirred and, as he stirred, he frowned.

'Who is your father?' he asked.

'His name is Hicham Omary. He owns the telecommunications company Globalcom.'

'I knew someone of that name when I was a child,' said Ankush Singh. 'He had a deep scar on his cheek from wrestling with me out there in the dirt.'

Ghita looked up.

'My father has a scar on his cheek,' she said.

'Is it curved at the end?'

'Yes... yes, it is.'

Ankush Singh poured the tea into a pair of small Chinese-made glasses.

'He was always lecturing us about his Berber heritage. He was *so* proud of it. In every game we played, and every fight we fought, he was a Berber warrior protecting his homeland.'

'That's my father,' said Ghita with half a smile.

The shopkeeper reached out and touched her hand.

'I will help you in any way I can,' he said.

Ghita handed him the locket.

'Then would you lend me a little money in return for this?'

Ankush Singh dug a hand down into his underwear and took out a cloth bag filled with banknotes. He passed it to her with his right hand. And, with his left, he returned her the necklace.

'To help the daughter of an old friend is an honour,' he said.

Seventy-four

DURING A BREAK between downpours, Blaine walked along Boulevard Mohammed V in the direction of the Casa Voyageurs railway station.

The main thoroughfare of French-built Casablanca, the street was once the preserve of the most fashionable shops, cafés, and restaurants. For a company to have a headquarters there was a statement of influence and power.

But, despite the new tramway and a coat of fresh whitewash, most of the buildings were in a wretched state, symbols of the despised days of the French Protectorate.

Put up back in '34, the Shell Building stood in pride of place at a little crossroads, once named after General Patton. Like everything else with a French title, it was subsequently renamed. In the postcard there had been a prim new streetlight there, the kerb around it striped in black and white.

Weaving between the parked cars and the mounds of soaking garbage, Blaine made his way to the exact spot where the open-topped limousine had stood in the photograph. A Rolls-Royce Silver Ghost, its liveried driver was holding a door open for a lady in a wide-brimmed sun hat.

Unsure of quite what to do, Blaine went inside.

The building was empty and gutted of its original contents and fixtures. A guardian emerged from the shadows. He had been feeding milky bread to a nest of puppies.

'*C'est fermé*,' he said. 'This building closed.'

The American held up a hand.

'I was hoping something might have been left for me.'

The guardian winced.

'*Quand?* When?'

'About seventy years ago.'

Blaine realized how foolish the sentence sounded before he had even spoken it. He passed the guardian the postcard. Holding it into the light, he moved it close to his eyes. And, after a long wait, he seemed to smile to himself.

'This picture... very old,' he said. 'Cars different now.' He motioned to the passing traffic. 'Small, ugly.' He drew a breath. 'This one... beautiful!'

'I am hoping that an envelope or something might have been left for me,' said Blaine.

'Your name?'

'Oh, it wouldn't be in my name. If anything, it would be in the name of Mr. Bogart.' He took a step back. 'Monsieur BEAU-GART,' he said, enunciating. 'He was an American gentleman.'

'Your father?'

'No, not exactly.'

'Oh.'

The guardian appeared a little displeased.

'Well, yes, kinda,' Blaine corrected. 'My father.'

A big toothless smile welled up on the guardian's face.

'Father, good,' he said.

'Well, do you know if anything was left for him — for my father, Mr. Bogart?'

The guardian shook his head and went back to the pups.

'*Non, Monsieur,*' he said as he went. '*Il n'y a rien ici pour votre père.*'

At Café Berry, across from the Shell Building, Blaine sucked down a black coffee and waved a hand through the suffocating smoke.

The waiter hadn't asked whether he wanted it in a glass or a cup, but had served it in a glass — a sign that he was looking more like a local. After all, most Moroccan men take their coffee in a glass, especially those who while away their lives in run-down art deco cafés.

For fifteen minutes Blaine stared at the postcard without looking up once. He studied every detail, every speck. And he read and reread Bogie's spidery scrawl.

When he finally did look up, he noticed an elderly lady. She was watching him. The only woman in the entire café, her large, meaty frame was stuffed into a flowery dress. Her hands were muscular and seemed somehow familiar. But Blaine was bad with faces and even worse with names.

He glanced down at the postcard, and then up again.

The woman was still looking at him. She grinned anxiously, stubbed out a cigarette and moved over towards him, parting the empty tables with her legs.

'How are you?' she said in a rather hoarse voice.

'Fine thank you, and you?'

'Oh, you know… I'm surviving.'

There was an uneasy pause. Blaine took a sip of coffee and swallowed.

'Do I know you?' he asked.

'Last night… I was playing.'

'*Playing*?'

'The piano.'

The American caught a flash of Club Souterrain and an aftertaste of single malt.

'Of course. The pianist.'

The woman fluttered her strong, masculine fingers.

'Yes, the pianist,' she said.

'Please join me,' Blaine replied.

The pianist introduced herself as Rosario. Then she wasted no time in revealing her background. She had come from Buenos Aires decades before, but had put down roots in Casablanca — roots that had taken hold.

'What brought you here?' asked Blaine with genuine interest.

Rosario looked sheepish.

'A surgeon's knife,' she said.

'A…?'

'A knife.'

The pianist touched a thumb to her pearl earring.

'Gender reassignment,' she said.

'Oh,' Blaine replied, wondering whether to deliver it as a question or an exclamation.

Rosario ordered a coffee. It came in a glass as well.

'Back in the seventies,' she said, lighting a cigarette, 'Casa had the only reliable clinic in the world offering The Operation.'

'Which operation?'

'You know…'

'Do I?'

Rosario jabbed a thumb between the American's legs and made a scissoring motion.

'Excuse me?'

'I know, I know,' Rosario continued, 'even then it was a little shocking, and a little sordid.'

Blaine didn't want to appear impolite, but he couldn't think of anything to say.

'That sounds painful,' he mumbled after a long pause.

The Argentine pianist stubbed out her cigarette and tapped a fresh one from a soft pack. She lit it with a match.

'It was agony,' she said.

'Was it legal?'

She giggled frivolously.

'Of course not,' she responded mischievously. 'But this is Casablanca, a city with far less on the surface than there is underground.'

'And why did you stay here, and not go back to Argentina?'

'I fell in love,' the pianist said. 'Hopelessly and stupidly in love. When I woke up to realize he was a rotten egg, it was far too late. You know how it is. Life traps you.'

'Oh, believe me, I know all about getting trapped,' said Blaine.

'Well, I am guessing you have not come to Casablanca for gender reassignment,' the pianist replied.

Blaine might have smiled, but he did not.

'I have come in search of Bogart,' he said.

'As in Humphrey?'

'Yes.'

'A little before my time.'

Blaine pulled out the postcard.

'I'm living in the past,' he said. 'Following clues. This one led me to the Shell Building across the street.'

'I hear it's going to be turned into a boutique hotel,' said Rosario. 'But if you believe that, you'll believe anything.' She held the writing to the light and squinted. 'My eyes are showing their age,' she said. 'But it looks like it says "Les Cafés du Brésil", that's a little shop on the corner of the Central Market. It's been there for ever.'

Blaine's eyes lit up. He shook Rosario's hand, pressed a couple of coins to the tabletop, and stood up.

'I'll see you around,' he said, as if distracted.

'At the club?'

'Maybe.'

The Argentine pianist pointed to a building adjacent to the café.

'That's where I live,' she said. 'The fifth floor. I'm always ready for a little conversation, or to take a stroll down memory lane.'

Seventy-five

A PAIR OF hobnail boots clattered down the slim corridor before coming to an abrupt halt outside Cell No. 3.

The guard pulled the inspection hatch back with his claw-like fingernails, blinding the prisoner with a stream of low-watt light. He stood there for some time. Omary could hear him breathing, as though he were making up his mind what to say.

'You were on the television,' the guard growled in a slow, cold voice. 'Seems like you are very rich.'

'I am a prisoner,' said Omary. 'And that's all I am.'

The guard flicked a switch to the right of the door, bathing the cell in blinding light.

'You could buy yourself a little luxury,' he said. 'Better food, a blanket, even a chair.'

Squatting at the back of his cell, Omary crept forwards on hands and knees, until his mouth was an inch from the door.

He could smell the guard.

'Bribe my way into a world of luxury?' he said incredulously. 'How dare you?! I'd rather rot to death in here than demean myself by paying you off.'

The inspection hatch slammed shut and the light vanished.

Then the thud of the boots came again, more deafening this time. It was followed by a gushing sound in the distance.

More boots, steel keys rattling, blinding light, and a bucket of ice-cold water was flung into the cell.

Seventy-six

THE SALES ASSISTANT at Les Cafés du Brésil had slipped a hardbacked envelope across the counter, identical to the one hidden in Bar Atomic's toilet. It smelt of roasted coffee, having lain undisturbed for decades in a drawer at the back of the shop. The clerk showed no surprise that it was being collected at long last.

A little later, when Blaine opened it up at Baba Cool, he found a third postcard, bearing the image of a snake charmer standing in front of an ancient minaret. As before, he separated the card from the photograph and found a line and a half of Bogart's almost impenetrable scrawl.

Directions, which began at a place called 'Koutoubia'.

As he sat there pondering the clues and what they might lead to, Ghita arrived.

'I thought I'd find you here,' she said.

Blaine showed off the postcard and explained where he had found it.

'I don't understand how clues could have been left unnoticed for so long,' he said.

Ghita ordered a *nous nous*.

'We're not a young country,' she replied, 'not like your America. Here in Morocco something has to be over a thousand years in age to be considered properly old.'

'But Casablanca's far newer than that.'

'I know,' Ghita replied. 'And that's why it's an embarrassment to most Moroccans, and the reason why they're happy to rip down the buildings without a second thought.'

'But they're jewels… art deco jewels.'

'They may be to you. But to the locals they're ugly, like a monstrous eyesore from the sixties… An eyesore created by colonial oppressors.'

Blaine put the card away and, as he did so, his eyes lit up.

'Did you know that Casablanca was once the gender reassignment centre of the universe?' he said with a smile.

'Gender…?'

'*Reassignment.*'

'I don't understand,' Ghita said.

'Sex change… it's where all the early sex changes were done. I met a guy — I mean a woman — called Rosario, who had her privates chopped off here forty years ago.'

'That's disgusting.'

'No, it's not.'

'Then what is it?'

Blaine thought hard.

'It's a last resort,' he said.

There was a thunderous roar of applause from the back of Baba Cool, and all the tired old men hiding from their wives cheered. Some waved their fists in the air; others slapped their friends on the back.

'What's going on?'

The waiter, who was distributing fresh ashtrays, cocked his head back towards the oversized screen.

'One-Zero to Morocco.'

'Who are they playing?'

Disbelieving that anyone could be unaware of the match, the waiter replied:

'Algeria, Monsieur. Our most bitter rival.'

Five minutes later, Morocco's old adversary equalized and, a moment after that, Saed hurried in, a cardboard box in his hands. He was hawking baseball caps with the Moroccan flag glued unevenly to the front.

'I've sold fifty this afternoon,' he said. 'I got them from a Chinese store in Derb Omar.' He put down the box. 'I'm the champion of champions.'

'Because you're good at selling hats?' said Ghita.

'No, not that. Because I've found out where they're holding your father.'

Ghita froze, her eyes filling instantly with tears.

'*Where…* where is he?'

'In a prison high in the mountains.'

'We knew that already.'

Saed took out a scrap of newspaper. There was something scribbled on the back.

'You read it,' he said, passing it to Ghita.

'Why don't you?'

'I don't read much. Been too busy selling hats to learn.'

'It's the name of the jail — beyond the Gorge of Ziz.'

'Where's that?'

'A long way.'

Blaine held up his hands.

'Wait a minute,' he said. 'What's your plan… to turn up and ask sweetly for them to hand your father over?'

'I'll plead with the guards,' said Ghita. 'I'll beg them.'

'And you really think that'll work?'

Saed put a second scrap of paper on the table. It was larger than the first, and looked as though it had been torn from a child's exercise book.

'I think this will help,' he said.

Ghita looked at the thick, unruly Arabic script.

'It says: *Abdelkarim Hamoudi the goldsmith will repay the favour owed by his grandfather. The password is the name of the Prophet's steed.*'

'The Night Journey,' said Saed. 'The Prophet ascended to Heaven on a horse with wings…'

'It was called Buraq,' Ghita said.

Another chorus of cheering erupted at the back.

'What is the favour the goldsmith is willing to repay?' Ghita asked.

'Am I missing something here?' asked Blaine. '*Who* is the goldsmith?'

Saed seemed unusually serious for a moment.

'When my father died, he left me nothing,' he said. 'Nothing, that is, except for three favours that were owed to him. The first was a favour owed from a fisherman down in Agadir. The second was one owed by a doctor in Oujda. And the third, it was owed by a man up in Tangier.'

'But surely you can't call in a favour if the person it's owed to has died,' Blaine said.

'Of course you can,' Ghita replied. 'Or at least you can here in Morocco. This is a medieval country, you see — a place where the repayment of a favour is an almost sacred duty.'

'A duty of blood,' Saed added. 'The man in Tangier knows that. I found out that the cousin of his wife is related to a man who works as a guard at the prison. If I demand the favour to be repaid, he will help. He has no choice.'

'Even if it's breaking the law?' asked Blaine.

'Of course. You see, repaying a favour... having the burden removed from a family's shoulders, is a great blessing.'

Saed reached over and touched Ghita's sleeve with his hand.

'I want to help you,' he said.

'But why?'

The boy grinned mischievously.

'Because when you have saved your father, perhaps you will remember me.'

Ghita leaned forward and pressed her lips to the shoeshine boy's cheek.

'You may be filthy and rough on the outside, but you have a heart of gold,' she said.

The American rolled his eyes.

'How are you gonna get to the mountains?'

'You would have to drive,' said Saed.

'But you don't have a car.'

'I think I know where to get one,' Ghita said.

Seventy-seven

THE NEXT DAY, Blaine was near the old Shell headquarters when he thought of the Argentine pianist. Crossing the street, he went up to her apartment building and took the wooden elevator up to the fifth floor.

At the sound of the buzzer, a small dog began barking inside, as though it had been patrolling. It was followed by a gruff woman's voice telling it to hush, then the clattering of fake pearls.

The door swung back.

Rosario stood in the frame, clutching a nervy chihuahua to her breast.

'I was passing and thought I might drop by,' said Blaine.

'What a nice surprise, please come inside.'

She led the way into a small, cluttered apartment — a sanctuary dedicated to the wonders and mysteries of the female form.

The walls were covered mostly in nudes — some photographs, others hand-drawn. The sitting room was strewn with sculptures in bronze and glass. Some were studies of female genitalia, others a little more abstract.

There were potted plants galore, and books, pamphlets, and yet more books, and dozens of cushions, some embroidered with sequins.

On the back wall, mounted in a sumptuous golden baroque frame, was an oil painting of a nude woman. Life-sized and leering, her arms were outstretched as though she were reaching out to embrace the world.

The pianist tossed the chihuahua onto the couch.

'It's Coccinelle,' she said theatrically. 'The first celebrity to undergo Dr. Burou's blade.'

'She's beautiful,' Blaine said.

'Ah, she was a dream, a sensation, a real star.' Rosario pressed a hand to her hair. 'She was so brave… such a pioneer.'

Blaine sat down on a chaise longue. The dog climbed onto his lap and licked his face.

'Stop that Popsi! Stop that at once! Oh, I am sorry,' Rosario exclaimed, 'but he craves the attention of men.'

She went off into the kitchen, returning with a pot of tea and a bottle of cheap cognac. Pouring an equal amount of each into two mugs, she sat primly on a low chair and rearranged her skirt in the name of modesty.

'Casa's very damp at this time of year,' she said in a loud voice. 'It gets into your bones.' She sipped her cognac tea. 'Are you going to be in town long?'

'I'm not quite sure,' Blaine said. 'I'm here on a kind of mid-life crisis.'

'You don't look old enough for a mid-life crisis,' said Rosario with a smile.

'I guess it's come early.'

'Oh.'

'Anyway, I don't really know what's gonna happen,' said Blaine. He sipped his alcoholic tea thoughtfully. 'By the way, you were right,' he said, pulling out the postcard.

'Right about what?'

'About Les Cafés du Brésil.'

The Argentine pianist added a little more cognac to their mugs and glanced at the photograph.

'Marrakech?' she asked.

'I guess so.'

'A pleasure dome of wonder and delight!' Rosario sang. She gazed up at the sumptuous form of Coccinelle, let out a sigh, and sipped her tea. After a full minute of silence, she said: 'Talking of Marrakech, a little bird told me that you were at the Hotel Marrakech the other day when the student was…'

'*Murdered.*'

'Yes. Murdered.'

'That's right, I was.'

The pianist frowned.

'I heard it was very horrid,' she said.

'And I heard that the police had arrested a gangster and got a confession out of him.'

Rosario leaned forward and crossed her ankles.

'Did the student give you anything?' she asked insouciantly.

'No. We only spoke for a moment. The next thing I knew he was lying there with his throat slashed. It was unbelievable, like right out of Hollywood.'

'How terrible.'

'I don't understand how the murderer could have passed me, or got out without me spotting him.' Blaine took in the flowery print on Rosario's dress as his mind replayed the events.

He felt as though he could trust her.

'Do you know why a gangster would have wanted him dead?' he asked.

'Well, my little bird said it was because he had something to deliver. He was a mule — a mule carrying something that didn't belong to him.'

'What?'

'A passport.'

'Is that really worth a life?'

'It seems as though this one was. You see, so my bird tells me, it's a very special passport.'

'How special?'

'A red laissez-passer issued by the UN. And what was so special about it was that it was signed and countersigned, but blank — just waiting for a name and a photograph.'

'*So?*'

'So it could guarantee almost anyone free passage anywhere on earth.'

'It all sounds so familiar,' said Blaine wryly.

The pianist poured a little more tea into his mug, followed by another dribble of cognac.

'Are you quite sure you don't have it?' she asked.

Seventy-eight

WITH THE SUN dazzling in the bright blue sky, Ghita directed the driver of a petit taxi towards the old French residential quarter of l'Oasis. Blaine sat beside her on the back seat, wishing he had been firmer and gone straight to the American consulate to report the loss of his passport.

'I told you six times,' Ghita said in a matter-of-fact tone, 'I don't know anything about cars. They all look the same to me. So I appreciate your advice.'

The taxi stop-started its way in heavy traffic past the hulk-like French Cathedral of Sacré Cœur. An art deco gem to some, and a colonial monstrosity to others, it had been deconsecrated decades ago, and turned into a centre for the arts.

'Hey, wait a minute!' Blaine shouted. 'There's the American consulate! I'm getting out here!' He signalled for the driver to pull over, but Ghita spat something fast in Arabic and the driver locked the doors and jerked the pedal to the floor.

'What are you doing? I need to go there! Let me out!'

'There'll be plenty of time later.'

'It's Friday afternoon. If I don't get in there now, I'll have to wait till Monday.'

Ghita touched a hand to her eye and coaxed out a small, shiny tear.

'Then couldn't you wait, just until after the weekend?'

'Give me one reason why I should!'

'Well, I know you don't know my family, but I'd be very grateful for your help…'

'In springing your dad from a high-security jail?' Blaine balked. 'Are you absolutely out of your mind?'

'But…'

'No way! There's no way I'm gonna get wrapped up in a plan like that!'

'But I have no one else.'

'Well… take Saed with you.'

Ghita pretended to weep.

'But Saed's too young to drive.'

Blaine turned to face her. She looked away.

'You can't drive?' he asked accusingly.

'*Me… drive?* Why would I ever need to? I have a chauffeur.' She paused, gritted her teeth. 'I *had* a chauffeur.'

'This is ludicrous,' said Blaine.

Ghita motioned to the taxi driver to stop.

'I'm hoping you'll change your mind.'

'Believe me, nothing on earth could get me to.'

'Will you at least wait until you have seen the car?' she asked.

They got out, crossed a wide avenue lined with eucalyptus trees, and made their way to a large brick warehouse.

As soon as he saw them approaching, the guardian ran up, wheezing. He kissed Ghita's hand, shook Blaine's vigorously, and led the way through a side entrance and up an iron staircase.

'This is my father's little collection,' Ghita said.

'*Collection?*'

They stepped onto a platform and the guardian yanked up a lever mounted on the wall. The lights came on.

Arranged in a grid below — six rows of six — was a priceless assortment of classic cars.

There was a 1948 Aston Martin DB1 in racing green, and a pristine D-type Jaguar in steel blue. Beside it was a 1931 Packard with running boards, and behind it, a 1937 Bugatti Atalante.

Although she had little interest in cars, Ghita felt smug.

She pointed a hand to the last row — six scarlet sports cars, all in mint condition.

'I like those ones,' she said. 'I like the way they sparkle.'

Blaine held a hand to his mouth for a long time, and eventually remembered to breathe.

'This is… it's… it's off-the-scale incredible!'

'It's my father's little secret.'

'But how come they haven't been seized along with everything else?'

'Because no one knows about them, except my father, me, and the guardian.'

The American stepped forwards to the edge of the iron viewing platform and squinted hard. He took in the Ferraris and the open-top tourers, the sleek limousines, and the space-age Cadillacs, from the days when Detroit built monsters of steel.

Then, suddenly, he stopped — motionless.

'How could that be?'

'Hmm? What is it?'

With care, Blaine stepped down the narrow staircase onto the warehouse floor. Moving forwards as though in a dream, his feet gliding over the scrubbed grey flagstones, he walked through the lines of cars. They were all shining like new, but none of them caught his attention.

In the middle of the last line, he stopped.

Before him, open-topped, with a tan leather interior and walnut trimmings, was a 1925 Rolls-Royce Silver Ghost. It was finished in bright poppy red.

Blaine took the envelope out from his jacket pocket and removed the black-and-white postcard. He knew instantly it was the same car. All that was missing was the young lady in the wide-brimmed hat.

He showed the card to Ghita, who had followed him down to the Rolls.

'I can't believe it,' he said. 'It's… like…'

Ghita squeezed her hands together.

'Fate,' she replied. 'It's like fate.'

'I just can't believe that your father owns the object that is so much the attention of my thoughts.'

'He loves his cars,' said Ghita frivolously.

'But why does he keep them secret?'

'Because of my mother.'

Ghita opened the front passenger door to the Rolls-Royce. She sat down and beckoned Blaine to climb in. He sat beside her, his hands caressing the walnut wheel, the scent of fine leather conjuring memories.

'Fifteen years ago, my mother was driving home from Marrakech,' Ghita said softly, 'she was in a vintage Mercedes. She loved it, and drove very fast, twisting and turning

191

through the little towns on the outskirts of Casablanca. As she neared Settat, a dog ran out into the road. She swerved… hit a wall. And she was killed outright.'

'I am sorry,' Blaine said.

'My father always blamed himself. It didn't make sense because it was my mother's driving, not the car, that was to blame. But he was broken. After that, he put all his energy into his company — Globalcom.'

Ghita sniffed again, more theatrically than before. 'He's all I have left,' she said. 'I *must* help him — whatever the danger.'

Leaning forward, Blaine touched her arm. He wanted to say something to make her happy, to reassure her.

'We will go to find him,' he said.

'*We?*'

Blaine smiled gently.

'I promise to help you,' he said.

Seventy-nine

Monsieur Raffi was standing outside his shop, a fresh newspaper held between open hands. He was reading the obituary of an old friend, the dean of the university, a man distantly related to his long-departed wife. Tutting to himself, he folded the paper and set about opening up the shop.

Once the wooden shutters were up, and the multitude of door locks opened, Raffi flicked on the lights and breathed a sigh of relief. He had not slept well the night before, woken by a nightmare that the shop had been ransacked, the precious collection hauled away by thieves.

Slipping into his red satin chair, he closed his eyes for a quick catnap before the morning rush — a rush that never quite came.

He dreamed of the good old days when the boulevard was spotless, the flagstones clean and unbroken, the air tinged with a blissful yellow light.

And he dreamed of an elegant French woman, immaculate in white, with a wide-brimmed sun hat throwing a shadow over the right side of her face.

She was strolling along easily, oblivious to the gauntlet of lecherous shopkeepers, an apparition of beauty, a memory that had endured in Raffi's head for sixty years. Sighing in his sleep, he breathed in deep to catch the perfume trail left behind the vision.

The door to the shop was suddenly thrust open.

A slim figure wearing a rough woollen jelaba was standing in its frame. Raffi woke at the sound. He began to sit up, but the man's right hand shoved him back down.

'Where is he?' the intruder demanded.

'Where? What?' Who?' Raffi strained to make sense.

'The American. The one who came in here. Where is he?'

'Which American?'

'The young man. He was in here last week.'

Monsieur Raffi struggled to stand, but was struck in the face.

'Tell me what you know, or I'll bathe your shop in blood!'

'But I don't know anything about him. Except… except that he likes Humphrey Bogart. That's all.'

The intruder punched him again, far more forcefully than before. The elderly shopkeeper was knocked out, his jaw fractured by the blow. Then, in a whirlwind of revenge and rage, the intruder swept through the shop, smashing everything he touched.

Outside on the boulevard, the new tram rattled by and pedestrians criss-crossed from sunshine into shade and back into sunshine again.

The door to the antique shop was left ajar, but no one thought to close it, or to check in on its owner, a shopkeeper regarded as half as old as time.

Eighty

THE OPEN-TOPPED ROLLS-ROYCE glided out from the garage at l'Oasis and moved slowly down the wide, tree-lined avenues of the French quarter.

Blaine caressed the wheel in his hands and, beside him, Ghita tied her hair down with a silk scarf.

'What a dream to drive,' he said. 'It's as if it can read my thoughts.'

'Maybe it can,' Ghita replied. 'A little well-bred English magic.'

They rolled on, the suspension accommodating the potholes, until they reached the edge of Maârif. Ghita pointed to the angular Villa Zevaco, now a café, in which Edith Piaf supposedly once lived.

'I'll get some sandwiches for the journey south,' she said.

Inside, opposite a long chilled counter laden with gateaux, was a small salon, its tall windows giving onto a garden.

Ghita strolled through to the sandwich counter, bought a baguette filled with Camembert and another of *truite fumée*. As she walked back in the direction of the car, she spotted Aicha sitting at a table with her ex-fiancé.

She felt sick in her stomach, the bitter taste of bile on her tongue. But rather than shirk away, or pretend she hadn't seen them, Ghita strode up, treading her heels down hard.

'Hello,' she said, unable to think of anything else.

The pair looked up from their conversation. They froze. Aicha's face contorted into a scowl.

'Keep away from me!' she snarled. 'I told you: in my eyes you are dead!'

'Ghita, please leave us,' Mustapha said in a low voice. 'We are all suffering because of your father's stupidity.'

'You think you know what suffering is?' Ghita riposted, the veins on her throat engorging with blood. 'My father is languishing in a mountain prison... *Why*? Because he had the guts to stand up to a system rotten to the core — a system that you all defend! I may have lost you as friends in my moment of need, but I am a thousand times stronger for it!'

Turning on her heel, Ghita walked out to the Rolls-Royce.

Unable to resist the sense of curiosity, Aicha and Mustapha watched as she tossed the sandwiches in the back and got into the passenger seat.

And, making certain her former friends got an unobstructed view, she leaned forwards and kissed the American on the mouth.

'What was that for?' asked Blaine.

'For revenge,' Ghita replied.

'I don't understand you.'

'How could you? You're an American.'

Blaine looked into Ghita's eyes.

As attracted as he was to her, he was maddened by almost everything she said or did.

'I need you to understand something,' he said, easing the car into first. 'You need me a great deal more than I need you right now.' Ghita stretched out her left hand and laid it on his right as it cupped the gear stick.

'I won't forget it,' she replied.

Eighty-one

BEFORE HITTING THE open road, Blaine zigzagged his way through the ferocious Casablanca traffic to Ghita's apartment.

He parked the Silver Ghost on the corner and took a table outside Baba Cool. There was just enough time for a quick *café noir* while Ghita threw a few essentials into the

Louis Vuitton portmanteau. She may have been separated from her fortune, but the way she acted no one would have known it.

The sun was filtered through palm fronds, the air scented with *shisha* water pipes. Even before Blaine could order, the waiter slid a couple of ashtrays and a glass of the house special: coffee as thick as crude oil.

'It's an old one,' said a wizened figure suddenly beside him. 'I remember when all the cars were like that.'

Blaine raised his coffee and drank to the old days, and he found himself thinking of Monsieur Raffi, a champion of all things past. Once Ghita had appeared, he drove the short distance to the antique shop and parked outside.

'This will just take a minute,' he said. 'There's someone here who would appreciate the sight of this car very much.'

Blaine jumped out and ran round to the front door. To his surprise, the antique shop was shuttered up.

As he stood there, the butcher next door stepped out into the light, a bloodied meat cleaver in his hand.

'He's closed up... gone away.'

Blaine held out his hands.

'Why?'

'He was attacked... beaten up. His shop was vandalized.'

'Who by?'

'I don't know. But it's not safe... not like it used to be.'

'I can't believe it. Poor Monsieur Raffi.'

The butcher wagged the cleaver towards the car.

'There are thieves everywhere,' he said. 'Watch out!'

Eighty-two

An HOUR LATER, Blaine was stop-starting through gridlocked traffic in search of the highway to Marrakech. The lack of road signs and straightforward traffic sense were getting to him. He had tried to buy a map of Casablanca, but had been forced to settle for one of the entire country.

'I'm no good at this, I'm afraid,' said Ghita defensively.

'How does anyone ever find their way around?'

'Well, they either know the way, or I suppose they take the bus.'

'Do *you* take the bus?'

Ghita's eyes widened at the thought.

'*Quelle horreur*, no!' she replied quickly. 'I sit in the back with an iPhone and magazines.'

Tired of inching forwards at a snail's pace, Blaine motioned towards a slender side street veering off to the right.

'What do you think's down there?'

'I have no idea.'

'Shall I brave it?'

'Yes, yes,' Ghita said enthusiastically. 'I think it looks familiar. Take it…'

Blaine turned the wheel sharply and the Rolls-Royce Silver Ghost banked silently. The street telescoped very quickly from slender to narrow, and from narrow into a piste. With insufficient width to turn around, Blaine had no choice but to continue, the Rolls's suspension doing well over the ruts and bumps.

'Oh my God!' Ghita exclaimed.

'What? What is it?'

'I remember why I know this road.'

'Why?'

'Because it leads to a *bidonville*. We took some designer outfits there once. They were from the previous season, entirely out of style.'

'What's a *bidonville*?'

Before Ghita could reply, the open-topped car descended down a steep incline into a bustling shantytown. An army of children were sword-fighting with sticks in the dust, their mothers crouching in front of shacks, scrubbing at great tubs of laundry. There were goats and chickens, cows and dogs, all of them ambling about in a stew of life.

The poppy-red convertible crawled forwards beneath dozens of low-hanging washing lines, as people swarmed from their shacks and surged around it.

'What do I do?!' asked Blaine frantically.

'Just keep going and stay calm. It's got to lead somewhere.'

'A track like this? It's getting narrower.'

'This is so embarrassing,' said Ghita.

Blaine drove on.

Past the fish seller and his huddle of paw-licking cats. Past a mosque with a low minaret with its enormous loudspeaker bolted on the side. And on past many more shacks built from breezeblocks and crumpled iron sheets.

A little further on, they came to a lane edged in towering eucalyptus trees and a high wall.

'I wonder what's behind that,' said Blaine.

'It's a little palace,' Ghita replied. 'I was received there when we handed out the clothes.'

'A palace *here*…? Seems unlikely. This is the end of the world.'

Ghita pulled the scarf tight to her head and tied it again.

'A British writer lives there,' she said, 'in a fragment of paradise.'

Eventually, after fording an ocean of raw sewage and mud, the Rolls-Royce emerged at a sign pointing the direction of Marrakech.

'Thanks be to God!' exclaimed Ghita.

Blaine gave her a stern look.

'From now on please let *me* navigate,' he said.

'It wasn't that the track was too narrow,' she said, 'but that the car was too wide'.

'I can't believe you're trying to defend yourself!'

Ghita took out her Rouge Allure and applied a thick coat to her lips.

'There's something you have to understand,' she said, after a pause.

'What?'

'That the future is written.'

'Written? What? Where's it written?'

'On our foreheads.'

'Huh?'

'It's written there on the day of our births.'

'That doesn't make sense.'

'Of course it does, and all Muslims know it.'

'Well, if it's written on your forehead, why can't I see it?'

'Because it's invisible, of course.'

Blaine rolled his eyes.

'I don't think I'll ever understand Morocco,' he said.

Eighty-three

WITH CASABLANCA FAR behind, the Silver Ghost purred down the highway towards Marrakech. Ghita was silent for a long time, her mind on her father.

'This is all my fault,' she said grimly.

'What is?'

'That my father has been arrested and thrown in jail.'

'It sounds to me as though he had it coming to him,' Blaine replied. 'After all, he was pitting himself against a crooked system.'

'Not that. I don't mean that.'

'Then?'

'A few days ago, when he threw me out to live in poverty, I was absolutely livid — more furious at him than I have ever been. And so I went to Sidi Abdur Rahman.'

'*Sidi...*?'

'Sidi Abdur Rahman. It's on the edge of Casablanca... a shrine where witches live. They'll tell your fortune, sort out your problems.' Ghita paused and looked out at the horizon. 'Or they'll get you revenge,' she said.

'Is that what you asked for?'

'Yes. I sacrificed a chicken in the name of vengeance.'

Blaine grinned and, after a few minutes of silence, he asked:

'Do you really think that you're responsible?'

'Yes, I do.'

'Well, can I tell you something?'

'What?'

'You strike me as a pretty mixed-up girl, but that's the stupidest thing I've heard in a long, long time.'

'And what about you?!' Ghita barked. 'You're so messed up that you came to Casablanca in the hope of finding a dead American actor. Is that "normal" behaviour? It sounds to me as though *I* am the sane one!'

They sat in silence for a long time, the tyres grating over the ruts of rubber between the concrete slabs.

At Settat, Blaine stopped the car at a truckers' roadside café.

The walls were covered in blackened grease, the floor scattered with chicken bones and grime. A handful of truck drivers were hunched in the shadows, sucking on the ends of bones or drawing steadily on their cigarettes. There was an ambience of doom and gloom, as though everyone inside had hit rock bottom.

'I'm not eating here,' said Ghita abruptly. 'I'd rather not eat at all.'

'Where's your sense of adventure?'

'It's far away from here.'

Blaine pulled out a chair.

'C'mon, sit down.'

With great reluctance, Ghita took off her scarf and laid it on the chair. She sat or, rather, she perched on the edge.

Two mutton tagines were slipped onto the table by a waiter with one eye. He grunted something indistinct and blurred away into the shadows. Ghita broke a small crust of bread, touched it into the sauce, and pretended to nibble at it.

'I'm full,' she said.

'I don't believe you. I can feel you're starving.'

'Really, I'm not.'

'I don't know how you survive in your own country,' said the American.

'I survive very well because I'm not a trucker, and so I rarely have cause to patronize establishments like this!'

'What's wrong with it?'

Ghita sat up and dropped the bread.

'I've just thought of something,' she said.

'What?'

'When I was a child, my parents had a Berber maid. She was called Habiba, and was like one of the family, living with us from before I was born until I was ten. Then, one day, she said that she was to be wed in an arranged marriage — and so she had to leave us. We were heartbroken, but my father gave his blessing and let her go. He used to say that she was the most trusted person he knew.'

'So what became of her?'

'She moved to a little village outside Marrakech and she had children of her own. I visited her two or three times as a child. Each time we would have to leave, I would cling to her. I couldn't bear being parted from her.'

'Is she still there?'

'I think so,' Ghita said. 'And I don't know why, but something inside is telling me to find her now.'

Blaine unfurled his map and traced a finger down through the desert.

'We're here,' he said, 'and Marrakech is here.'

Ghita leaned forward.

'And this is Habiba's village, just beside the river.'

'It's on the way.'

'And the prison... it's way up here in the mountains, south of Marrakech. It's going to be freezing up there.'

'Maybe I shouldn't have chosen a convertible.'

Ghita pressed a hand to the back of her neck.

'What's a little discomfort,' she asked, 'in the name of style?'

Eighty-four

TEN MILES SOUTH of Settat, a police officer stepped into the road and flagged down the Silver Ghost. He was wearing reflective Ray-Ban aviators and a pistol on his hip.

'I haven't done anything wrong,' said Blaine as he slowed the car, 'I was below the limit.'

'Drive a nice car and believe me, it happens all the time,' Ghita said. 'Pull over and I'll speak to him.'

The officer saluted, and then asked for the car's documents.

'What are you stopping us for?' Blaine asked in English.

'*Un infraction.*'

'Infraction? What does that mean?'

'That you were going too fast,' said Ghita.

'But I wasn't.'

'*Quatre cents dirhams*,' said the officer, as he began to write a ticket.

'Don't worry,' Ghita whispered. 'It's a little game. Just give him this,' she said, passing him a folded-up bill. 'Slip it down his sleeve.'

'What?'

'His sleeve, it has to go down his sleeve.'

'Why?'

'Because then he can't ever say he actually took a bribe.'

The policeman handed back the car's *carte grise* and, as he did so, Blaine stuffed the fifty-dirham note deftly into his sleeve. He expected an outcry, or to be arrested for attempting to bribe an officer of the law. But, as though he had pressed the right button on a giant automaton, the patrolman stepped back, saluted, and waved them on.

'That worked like magic,' Blaine said as he accelerated.

'Of course it did. A little bribery keeps the system working smoothly,' Ghita told him. 'It's a good thing. Without it, how would the poor police survive?'

'By spending their salary perhaps?'

'Oh no... no, no, no,' Ghita replied. 'They get a pittance. It's not nearly enough to live on. The bribes just top up their wages. And the officers out on the highway share what they make with the others at the police station.'

'So everyone gets a cut?'

Ghita nodded.

'I can't think of a fairer system,' she said.

They drove on in silence for a good many miles, the nut-brown farmland giving way to the baked red clay of the desert escarpment. The road snaked down towards the plateau below. As it did so, the landscape gradually opened out, revealing the Berber heartland of Morocco.

It was vast and flat, like the bottom of the ocean, interlaced with boulders and scrub. There were shepherds tending raggle-taggle flocks and withered old men clinging to donkeys. Walking alongside, their wives were laden with buckets and great bundles of sticks.

'I had no idea Morocco was this beautiful,' said Blaine all of a sudden. 'To tell you the truth, I hadn't ever thought about it. Because all I ever thought about was Casablanca.'

'Casablanca's not Morocco,' Ghita replied.

'So what is it?'

'It's a tiny little splinter of a huge continent — of Africa.'

'It's so vast,' the American said. 'This landscape rolls on forever. I can see till the end of the world.'

'You've got to remember something,' Ghita said, 'and when you return to New York, you must tell people about it.'

'What's that?'

'That Morocco is not just another Arab country. It's a crossroads — between Africa and Europe, and between Arabia and what lies west, beyond the Atlantic. But...' Ghita said, her voice touched with an undertone of pride, 'beyond all else, it's Berber.'

'What's Berber?' Blaine asked, glancing over at her.

'The original people of this kingdom were the Berbers. They come from different tribes with different customs and dialects, but they are Berber first and Moroccan second.'

'Are you one… a Berber?'

Ghita adjusted her scarf.

'Yes, of course I am,' she said. 'From a well-known family.'

'Well known for what?'

'For their bravery and their sense of honour and…'

Ghita was about to say something else when another police officer jumped out from nowhere and flagged them down.

'I can't believe this!' snapped Blaine.

'Don't worry, I have another fifty-dirham note,' Ghita said, folding it up small.

A minute later, the bribe had been delivered and they were on their way again, the Silver Ghost gathering speed as it cut across the red desert.

By the time they reached the turn-off for Habiba's village, they had been stopped half a dozen times and had paid something each time.

The road divided and subdivided, and was soon a patchwork of repairs, ruts, and deep potholes. Blaine navigated between them as best he could.

'Take a left here,' Ghita cried out.

'But it's a dirt track. It can't lead anywhere.'

'Trust me. I know it's up there.'

The Rolls-Royce advanced down a narrow track, lined on either side with cacti and thorny scrub. After a mile of little fields, they reached a farmstead.

A pair of gruff old dogs lurched out from the long afternoon shadows and made for the tyres. Then a multitude of children surged out from ramshackle homes, whooping and jumping at the sight of a car.

'Keep going up here,' Ghita said, 'then turn left at the end.'

'When was the last time you came here?'

'About ten years ago. But it hasn't changed at all. All these people are Berbers — the best people on earth.'

'You're just saying that because you're one of them,' Blaine grinned.

Ghita returned the smile.

'What nonsense!' she said.

Blaine steered the Rolls up a steep incline and through a tremendous herd of sheep.

'Now where?' he shouted, amid the bleating and the dust.

'Up there, towards the brow of the hill.' Ghita pointed to a tumbledown adobe home in the distance. 'That's it.'

Long before the car reached the end of the track, a woman had emerged from the house. Her face was weather-worn, with a square jaw, a faded pink scarf tied down tight over her hair. She was crying, her hands flustering to wipe away the tears. Running to the car, she began kissing Ghita even before the door was open.

When Ghita got out, the two women hugged, kissing each other on the cheeks, cooing greetings and hugging all the more. The American was introduced. He shook hands, smiled broadly, and was swept inside.

The farmhouse comprised three cramped rooms: a small bedroom, an even smaller kitchen, and a living room in which guests were received.

Before he could say a word, Blaine was ushered to a long banquette and encouraged to sit. Refusing to be seated, Ghita followed Habiba into the kitchen. They spoke excitedly in the high-pitched lilt used to pass on gossip and urgent news. From time to time there was a loud exclamation.

After a considerable time, the two women came out from the kitchen. Ghita took a place opposite Blaine on a second banquette, while Habiba sat at the edge on a wicker stool and began the laborious business of preparing mint tea.

The tea was poured in silence, passed out, sipped, and thanks were given to God.

'Isn't she surprised to see you?' asked Blaine softly.

'No, no, not at all. She said that she was expecting me, that she had seen me coming in a dream.'

'Where's her husband?'

'He died a year ago.'

'I'm sorry.'

'Don't be. She's thrilled — she despised him. I half imagine that she poisoned him.'

'And where are her kids?'

'Her son's gone to Meknès to work in the brick kilns, and her daughter has recently married a doctor near Marrakech.' Ghita paused. She sipped her tea, and then she said: 'Habiba insists that we stay the night with her. Not to do so would be very rude.'

As soon as a second round of tea had been poured, Habiba led Ghita into the kitchen again, for more gossip. Anxious to stretch his legs, Blaine went outside and walked behind the house.

The sun was slipping below the ochre-red horizon.

As he stood there, awed by the natural beauty, he imagined his grandfather standing beside him. He could smell the old man's aftershave, Old Spice, and feel the warmth of his skin.

'What am I doing here, Grandpa?' he said. 'It's ridiculous.'

His grandfather touched him on the arm.

'You're following your heart,' he answered, 'and a man who follows his heart can never go wrong.'

The sun vanished and, gradually, the pink glow dissipated, shadows melting into dark. Blaine listened to the chorus of dogs in the distance, and to the bats darting through the evening air.

When it was pitch black, he went back inside and found the little house illuminated by candles. Ghita and Habiba were still chatting, hardly drawing breath as they rooted through the past.

At length, an olive tagine was brought out from the kitchen. Bubbling and squeaking with heat, it was set down, and spoons were passed out. Only when the guests had feasted sufficiently did the host taste the dish.

After the meal, a long silence prevailed, and then Habiba ambled into the kitchen to prepare more tea.

As soon as she was gone, Ghita got up and sat down beside Blaine.

'She's told me something.'

'What?'

'You remember I said that my father regarded her as our most trusted friend?'

'Yes.'

'Well, three years ago he was frightened that someone — I don't know who — would try to bring his empire to its knees. So he came here without telling anyone, and brought a box with him. He asked Habiba to look after it, and to give it to me were I ever to come.'

'What's in it?'

'I don't know. Nor does she — she's never opened it.'

'Where is it?'

Ghita motioned to the dirt floor.

'She buried it under there.'

BEFORE DAWN HABIBA was up, drawing water from the well. Then, at first light, she took a tray of bread a mile and a half across the fields to the communal oven, and brought it back once it was baked.

The two women had slept the night in the bedroom, while Blaine stretched out on the banquette. He woke to the scent of fresh-baked bread, eggs, and an endless supply of sweet mint tea.

Through half-open eyes, he scanned the room, wondering where to find the bathroom. He hadn't relieved himself since the truck stop.

'There's a squat toilet in the little lean-to at the back of the house,' said Ghita, reading his mind.

The American raised an eyebrow, surprised that she had adapted so readily to the reduction in luxury.

'This is what we call the *bled*, the countryside,' she said. 'It's sacred to all Moroccans, whether they're from here or from the city. Its simplicity reminds us that we are all equal.'

After breakfast, Habiba fetched a shovel from the barn and set about digging up the sitting-room floor. She refused to allow Blaine to help her, insisting that it was her duty, a solemn duty she had undertaken to Mr. Omary.

It took half an hour to excavate the wooden box.

The sides were stained red from the dirt, and the top was battered where the shovel had struck it hard. Reaching down, Habiba removed it, praised God, and passed it to Ghita.

'Open it up!' said Blaine enthusiastically.

Ghita paused to mumble a prayer, and then prised off the lid.

Inside were three thick bundles of hundred-dollar bills, each one the size of a brick. Beneath them was a letter and locket.

Ghita ripped the envelope open and scanned its text.

'My darling daughter,' she read, 'as I have always told you, Habiba is one of our family, and the bond we share with her is more highly valued to us than with anyone else we know. I am writing this letter at a time of grave danger. I can feel that forces here in Casablanca are conspiring against me. I don't know who they are, or what their motive is, but I fear them. For this reason, I have entrusted this box to Habiba. I am certain that at a time of catastrophe you will seek her out. Inside, you will find enough funds to see yourself through turbulent times, and the locket your mother wore every day of her life.'

As she reached the end of the letter, Ghita's eyes welled with tears.

'Baba, wait for me,' she said, 'I am coming!'

Eighty-five

ONCE AGAIN, STANDARD-ISSUE boots marching over flagstones woke Hicham Omary from his sleep. Kept in perpetual darkness, he had no idea whether it was day or night.

For a full week he had not left the cell. In that time, he had revisited a thousand memories and pondered all kinds of philosophical questions, the kind for which there's never quite time in the haste of normal life.

He found that by breaking the years down into an intricate flowchart of events, he could keep himself amused for hours at a stretch. The exercise drove out boredom — the curse of solitary confinement.

The boots moved in a rhythm, steel tips striking down hard on the stone. The sound grew louder as it approached Cell No. 3. Then silence. A set of keys clattered in a primitive music of their own. Omary listened, waiting for the inspection hatch to open, and for the blinding shaft of low-watt light.

But this time, another key was selected.

It sounded quite different as it slipped into the lock. It was larger and was serrated on both sides. Hicham Omary hadn't been in the prison system long, but long enough to learn the ritual of keys.

For it was they alone that could deliver freedom.

The cell's tempered-steel door was pulled open fast. Jerking both hands over his eyes, Omary blocked the light, as his lungs expanded with what smelled like fresh mountain air.

The guard ordered the prisoner to stand.

Omary did so, adrenalin coursing through his bloodstream as he struggled to make sense of what was going on. A grating sound followed — metal rasping on metal. His hands were cuffed behind his back, then attached by chains to the fetters around his ankles.

After that came the blindfold.

Not a puny, half-hearted blindfold from a children's birthday party, but a military-issue one of triple-thick hessian with four straps.

Disorientated, the fetters cutting into his ankles and the handcuffs into his wrists, Omary was led inch by inch down the corridor.

At the end, he was turned around six times to the right, and six to the left. Swaggering like a drunkard after a night on the town, he was taken calmly into the interrogation cell and forced down onto a stool.

There was warmth, glorious warmth from the interrogation lamps — lamps he could only feel but not see.

Omary listened.

He made out the call of the muezzin far away, although uncertain which prayer it could be calling. And, much closer, he heard the sound of a lighter clicking, being tossed onto a desk, and the stink of a cheap cigarette.

The interrogator drew a chestful of smoke into his lungs, exhaled, and signalled to the guard to lock the door. He had worked in the prison service for thirty years and prided himself on being able to get the results desired by the authorities in Rabat.

Resting the cigarette on the edge of the desk — a desk speckled with little burns from a hundred other nights — he leafed through the dossier.

'It says that you have a liking for heroin,' the interrogator said in a chill, well-practised voice.

'Does it?'

'Yes, it does. And it says that you have made a fortune in working for the criminal underworld.'

Omary flexed his back to relieve the pressure on his wrists.

'Are you expecting me to confess to invented charges?'

'No. But I am expecting you to answer my questions.'

The interrogator stood up.

He walked around the table and untied the blindfold. Omary's eyes were flooded with a tidal wave of high-watt light. Eager to avoid it, he glanced sideways and found himself focusing on the walls.

They were festooned with all kinds of equipment.

There were wooden batons and straps, a harness for suspending a prisoner upside-down, electric cables and tourniquets, syringes and a box of broken glass, a variety of blades and pliers. In an arrangement high on the back wall were a selection of what looked like meat hooks. And, on another hook, an apron was hung. It had been drenched in blood — some of it old, some of it new.

Unlike the movies, where interrogation rooms are usually pristine, the one in which Hicham Omary found himself was filthy from use. Like the apron, the tools and equipment were spattered in dirt and dried blood.

His focus jolting from one detail to the next, Omary's gaze ended at a drain just near the door. It was clogged with what looked like a lump of human skin and matted hair.

Eighty-six

By TEN A.M. the Silver Ghost was back on the highway, and by noon it was swerving its way through the rip-roaring traffic of Marrakech.

All around, there were mopeds veering to and fro, like a game of 3D *Space Invaders*. There were donkey carts, too, and throngs of bicycles, and water sellers ringing their great brass bells, and beggars weaving through the traffic in their wheelchairs.

'Which way?' asked Blaine at a crossroads.

'That way, straight — towards the great minaret of Koutoubia.'

'That's Koutoubia? *Fantastic*! That's where I've gotta pick up the trail for the next postcard.'

Ghita was about to rein the American in, but she cautioned herself. As he had reminded her — she needed him more than he needed her.

'We'll go there first,' she said, 'to get your postcard, and then we'll go and find the goldsmith.'

Blaine eased the car to a halt.

'Just park up there on the pavement,' Ghita said.

'But I'll get towed.'

'This is Marrakech, not Miami,' she replied. 'The police can be reminded that they are on our side.'

'So I've noticed,' said Blaine.

Mounting the kerb, he steered the Silver Ghost up to within a few feet of the mosque wall.

'Koutoubia means "Booksellers",' said Ghita, 'because there used to be bookstalls here.'

'When was that?'

'About a thousand years ago.'

Blaine wasn't listening. His mind was on the postcard. He pulled it out and did his best to decipher the text on the back.

'It says to ask at the "Old Lady".' He turned around and peered up at the great square minaret. 'This must be the Old Lady,' he said, 'but who to ask?'

Ghita frowned. She took the card from Blaine.

'This was clearly written by a man in love,' she replied. 'I can always tell.'

'Tell what?'

'When a man is in love.'

'*Huh?*'

'You men are so poor at concealing your feelings.'

'So, who was Bogart in love with?'

'With the Old Lady, of course.'

Blaine nodded towards the mosque.

'*That* Old Lady?'

'Would a drunk American actor really have been in love with a mosque?' said Ghita.

'I guess not. So, where's the Old Lady we need?'

'*La Grande Dame*, the Mamounia, of course.'

Eighty-seven

A MASTER IN the art of anticipation, the interrogator could predict exactly the pain threshold of anyone trussed up in the seat before him.

His wife had spent decades begging him to stop, to find a less severe career. But as he told her time and again, there was nothing quite so satisfying as extracting information from the lips of the unwilling.

Omary circumnavigated the questions and tried to gauge where they were leading, if anywhere at all. He was asked about his father and his grandfather, about his income and his schooling, and about the scar on his right cheek.

The examination lasted an hour or more, but was nothing more than a warm-up for things to come. Lighting another cigarette, the interrogator blew out — the grey smoke billowing like a storm cloud into the light.

'Now, Mr. Omary,' he said, his tone deepening, 'you are to tell me about the heroin. Where did it come from?'

His muscles fatigued with lactic acid, Hicham Omary struggled to keep his cool. He was damned if a two-bit torturer was going to ruffle him.

'I'm a businessman, not a drug dealer,' he replied.

'I am looking for correct answers,' the interrogator said. 'And if I don't get them, I shall use the equipment.' He waved a hand towards the apparatus hanging on the walls. 'I have a special treatment for everyone they send to me,' he said.

'Do you expect me to make something up, something to incriminate myself?'

'I expect you to speak the truth.'

'Then listen to me. I don't know anything about the drugs I'm supposed to have bought or sold. And you know it as well as I. You can see it in my eyes. But if you'd like to continue this little charade, we can. You can pull out my teeth with those pliers. Or you can electrocute me with those wires, or cut me into little pieces with the knives. But my response is not going to change.'

'My superiors in Rabat are waiting for your confession, and I have vowed to get it for them. But I think a few more days in the hole will soften you. You will return there now and be put on half rations, and a nice cold bath twice a day.'

The interrogator called out to the guard and, a moment later, Omary was hobbling forwards down the corridor. The blindfold had been left off, allowing him to look into the other cells as he went.

Unlike his own cubicle, the others had bars rather than a full steel door. The walls of the first were painted in black and white spirals, a ploy to drive a sane inmate mad. The next was spattered with a profusion of dark dried blood, from a suicide.

In the first cell, the prisoner was huddled up on the concrete floor. In the second, a convict was standing with his head in his hands. And the man in the third cell was tethered by a metre-long chain to the wall.

Staggering forwards, Omary caught eye contact with him for a fleeting moment. The man's eyes hung in an empty face, swollen with illness, with fear, with nights of treatment in the torture cell.

Until that moment, Hicham Omary managed to remain composed. But the sight of real terror, of a life hanging by a thread, was too much to bear.

As soon as he had been kicked back into his cell, the shackles removed, and the door slammed shut, he broke down and wept like he had never wept before.

Eighty-eight

THE ROLLS-ROYCE SILVER Ghost ran along the ancient crenellated ramparts of the Marrakech medina. Coral pink and crumbling, the city walls were straight out of *The Arabian Nights*. Their entire surface was peppered with little square holes, used from time to time for scaffolding — and always by swallows for their nests.

Turning left through an arched gateway, Blaine took a sharp right into the forecourt of La Mamounia.

Ghita may have spent her life being chauffeured about, but the precise location of '*La Grande Dame*' was one she could describe with her eyes closed.

'My father always says this is where his heart lies,' she said quietly, as the zigzag shadows of palm fronds tumbled over the car.

Cloaked head to toe in white robes, a pair of towering guards swept forwards, opened the doors, and bestowed greetings.

Climbing the mosaic steps, the guests were showered in pink rose petals. And, once they were inside, a retinue of bearers offered moist towels, mint tea, and fresh desert dates.

'I guess it helps if you turn up in a Rolls-Royce,' said Blaine in a whisper.

No sooner had the words left his mouth than a suave man in a hand-tailored suit hurried up. His hair was smoothed back, grey like a turtle dove, his complexion lightly tanned. The personification of sophistication, he was like a Hollywood leading man playing a hotel manager.

Without wasting a moment, he embraced Ghita.

'What a wonderful surprise, *ma chérie!*' he declared. 'How are you, my dearest, dearest Ghita?' His expression faltering, he breathed in sharply. 'But how awful what we have heard about Monsieur Omary. My prayers and those of the entire staff go out to him.'

Ghita gave thanks, and then presented Blaine.

The general manager shook the American's hand firmly, the signet ring on his little finger catching the light.

'Will you be requiring your usual suite, Mademoiselle?'

'That would be wonderful, thank you, Laurent,' Ghita said, 'and a single room as well for my friend.' She paused, glanced up at the crystal chandelier as it caught the afternoon light. 'We are here on something of a treasure hunt. I believe that a former guest may have left an envelope for us.'

'Would it be in your name, Mademoiselle?'

Blaine held up a hand.

'No, not exactly. It would have been left in the name of a Mr. Bogart... a Humphrey Bogart.'

The general manager beckoned the duty manager from the shadows and whispered something into his right ear.

'We will look into the matter,' he said, in a reassuring voice. 'Now I must insist that you are my guests for lunch. I know that your father has a fondness for Don Alfonso's cuisine.'

He led the way through the main body of the hotel, recently refurbished by Jacques Garcia, the celebrated French *décoriste*. There was a solemnity about the place, a sense of power. The ambience had been achieved through dim lighting, miles and miles of silk, and meticulous understatement.

At lunch, the menus were brought forward by a *maître d'hotel*, but were waved away by Don Alfonso, who was horrified by the thought of Ghita Omary being offered anything available to any ordinary guest. Exclaiming his joy, he hurried into the kitchen to prepare a special meal, one that might satisfy the discerning taste of Mr. Omary himself.

Against the gentle sound of birdsong on the terrace, Blaine asked about Bogart.

'Hollywood has had a long love affair with La Mamounia,' the general manager replied, twisting his rings as he spoke. 'Hitchcock filmed scenes in *The Man Who Knew Too Much* here. And we have hosted almost every star you can think of, from Charlie Chaplin to Humphrey Bogart.'

As if waiting for his cue, the duty manager stepped forward, bowed, and offered a silver salver to Blaine.

'This was found in the archive, Monsieur.'

Squared on the salver's burnished surface lay an antique envelope in ivory white. The words 'To Be Collected' were written in large black script over the front, and were complemented by Bogart's signature.

'That's it!' said Blaine quickly. 'Thank you!'

Sliding the blade of a butter knife along the top edge, he removed a fourth postcard.

It showed a fine villa set amid ample gardens.

As before, he began to peel away the back. But unlike the previous postcards, this one didn't appear to have a secret message, just Bogart's signature and a number — 07698.

'Would you mind?' said the manager, motioning for the card.

Blaine handed it to him.

'Villa Mirador,' he said.

'Where is it?'

'In Anfa, Casablanca's *quartier majestique*. It was there that the Allied Summit was held early in 1943. When it ended, Churchill brought Roosevelt down here to stay at *La Grande Dame*, and to paint the snows of the Atlas, as viewed from the balcony of his suite.'

'Villa Mirador,' said Ghita absently. 'I've been to receptions there. It's the residence of the American consul, even now. Quite a house — one soaked in history.'

The general manager propped up the postcard on the silver pepper mill.

'What are your plans, Mademoiselle?' he asked.

'We're going to the mountains to…' She fell short of finishing the sentence and touched a finger to her cheek. 'To see an old friend,' she said.

Eighty-nine

STANDING AT THE heart of Marrakech, itself the beating heart of the desert, lay the great square of Jma el Fna.

Its name, meaning 'the Place of Execution', hinted at a macabre sliver of history. Nudged up at the side of the medina, the square was peopled by tourists and by storytellers, by healers and by acrobats — the one corner in the kingdom owned by everyone whose feet passed through it.

Ghita led the way between the knots of entertainers drawing crowds in the late afternoon. She didn't like the square, thought it stank, and regarded it as a place where thieves and conmen vied for business beneath the African winter sun.

She pointed to a medicine man decked out in pale blue Tuareg robes, a trace of gold embroidery running the line of his collar. Laid out on a carpet before him was an array of home-made potions and tonics, and all manner of curious ingredients.

There were dried chameleons and ostrich eggs, lumps of charred black bark, red beetles, sulphur, mercury, and an assortment of mauve-coloured stones.

'Look at him,' Ghita grunted. 'He's more likely to kill you than cure you.'

'And that said by the woman who went to a witch in the name of revenge.'

'That was different. It was magic, *real* magic, the kind that works.'

As Blaine looked at the Tuareg's ingredients, he got the feeling that someone was watching him.

He turned around quickly.

'What is it?'

'I don't know. I just feel kinda uncomfortable.'

'It's the thieves, they're everywhere,' Ghita said.

They made their way through hordes of people, past the food stalls that were being set up for the night, and into the gaping jaws of the medina.

From the first step inside its labyrinth, Blaine sensed a thousand layers of life, laid down through centuries.

Wherever he looked there were objects on sale — giant brass trays and ewers on ornate stands, rough woollen carpets from the Middle Atlas, boxes of fossils and little phials of perfume, saffron and antimony, plastic buckets, tortoises, and jars of mixed spice.

There were water sellers too, in flame-red shirts, and old men on crutches begging for alms, children selling chewing gum a stick at a time, fortune-tellers and donkey carts.

'This is incredible,' Blaine called out. 'It's just like *Casablanca!*'

Ghita rolled her eyes.

'But this is no movie set,' she said.

They stopped for a glass of tea at a café so small that there was only space for them. As they sipped the straw-coloured liquid, the owner's little son played for them on his flute.

'In the US, we'd call this VIP treatment,' Blaine said.

Ghita wasn't listening. Her mind was on rooting out the go-between.

'We have to find the house of the goldsmith,' she said.

'You've got the address, right?'

'Yes, but this is Marrakech and things aren't that simple. It's a matter of bouncing through the maze until you get lucky.'

All of a sudden, Blaine reached out and touched Ghita's arm.

'Call me crazy, but I'm getting that feeling again.'

'That you're being watched?'

'Yeah. It's so strange. I can feel someone watching us.'

Leaving the café for another couple to enjoy, they strolled on through the labyrinth. Dodging oncoming obstacles and droves of bewildered tourists, they made slow progress.

From time to time Ghita would show the paper Saed had given her to a shopkeeper, and would be waved on a little further into the mayhem.

At a hammam to the right of the main thoroughfare, she was directed down a smaller street, then another.

'This is more like it,' said Blaine. 'It's as if all the people have been vapourized.'

Just as Ghita was about to reply, a figure stepped from the shadows of an arched doorway. In his hand was a knife, poised at waist-height.

As he moved into the light, Blaine caught sight of his face. Poised on a neckless head, it was emaciated and dark, his cheeks hollow, his front teeth missing.

'Give me the papers!' the man demanded in English.

'What papers? You've got the wrong people!' Blaine replied.

'We're tourists!' Ghita cried.

'No, you have come from Casablanca. I know who you are!'

'Oh my God,' said Blaine, his stomach knotting.

'Give me the papers!' the man ordered again.

He stepped forward and, as he did so, a donkey cart rattled past from the right. It was laden with firewood destined for the hammam.

Without thinking, Blaine seized a plank and struck the man with all his strength just below the shoulder.

Then, grabbing Ghita's hand, he pulled her in the direction from which they had come.

They ran through the medina's twisting streets.

Past carpenters' workshops and tailors, and communal bakeries, down streets where boys were playing marbles in the dust, up slopes, and along the slenderest of passages.

'They'll find us,' said Ghita, as they ran.

'So what do we do? Go to the police?'

'*Hah!*'

'Then?'

'We need to blend in with everyone else,' Ghita said quickly, as she ducked into a clothes shop. Five minutes later, she and Blaine emerged wearing jelabas, the hooded robes favoured by all Moroccans.

They slipped into a quiet alleyway to talk things over.

'I don't understand why they want me,' said Blaine. 'The Chinese guy didn't give me anything.'

'Are you sure he didn't slip something into your bag?'

'I'm positive.' Weaving his fingers together, the American cracked his knuckles. 'The only person who gave me anything was Saed.'

'*What*?'

'A little packet. More of an envelope, really. He asked me to keep it for a few days.'

'Where is it?'

'At the Mamounia.'

'Even though he's helping us, I never trusted that kid!' Ghita said angrily. 'Those boys are all the same.'

'I'd defend him,' Blaine replied. 'But I'm the one who's had my passport stolen.'

Ghita leaned forward and touched his hand.

'I have a tiny confession to make.'

'What are you talking about?'

'Your passport…'

'*Huh*?'

'Your passport… it was I who took it.'

Ferreting a hand down into her underwear, she produced it.

The American's face flushed with rage.

'How dare you?!'

'I'm sorry. I'm so incredibly sorry. It's just that I needed you. I needed your help.'

Fuming, Blaine turned his back.

'I'm going to Casablanca tonight,' he said. 'Gonna take the late train.'

Ghita took half a step towards him. She was very close.

'I feel so alone,' she said. 'As though the world is lined up against me.'

'Yeah, well, if you steal people's passports you don't deserve much better.'

Resting an arm on his shoulder, she coaxed him around.

'Please forgive me,' she said. 'I don't deserve it, but I am begging you, from the bottom of my heart.'

Blaine gritted his teeth. He tried to think of something hurtful to say, but nothing came. So instead, he took a step backwards, towards the wall.

'I find myself liking you less and less,' he told her, 'which is quite impressive because I never liked you much at all.'

Ghita smiled, her smile erupting into a fit of laughter.

'You're so silly,' she said.

AN HOUR LATER, after clinging to the shadows, Blaine and Ghita were directed to a narrow doorway, a stone's throw from Dar el Glaoui, one of the city's great ancestral palaces.

On the ground floor, a pair of young boys were learning their prayers. Their sister was doing her homework, huddled over a textbook, a blunt pencil in her hand.

Ghita asked where they might find the goldsmith.

The girl seemed uneasy at seeing strangers. Closing the book, she slipped into a back room and spoke quietly to someone behind a curtain.

A man appeared.

He had a sympathetic face with a long brow, his grey-blue eyes hidden behind wire-rimmed frames. He must have been seventy but could have passed for someone much younger, the only tell-tale sign of age being a patch of grey hair at the side of his head.

'*As salam wa alaikum*,' he said as soon as he saw them. 'Peace be upon you.'

'And peace upon you,' Ghita replied. 'We have come to meet El Hajj Abdelkarim Hamoudi, the goldsmith, sent here by a mutual friend.'

'I am Abdelkarim,' he said, holding still as though waiting for the name of the mutual contact.

Ghita took a step towards him. She wanted to whisper and needed to be close.

'I greet you in the name of Buraq,' she said. 'In the name of the Prophet's steed.'

The goldsmith didn't move. His expression was taut and unflinching, as though a pause button had been pressed.

It was a full minute before he moved.

Then, very slowly, he looked down at the floorboards, touched a hand to his mouth.

'Come with me,' he said.

Ninety

'DO YOU UNDERSTAND the gravity of that word to me?' the goldsmith said when he had prepared tea upstairs.

'Yes, I do,' Ghita replied. 'And, believe me, I would not utter it in anything more than the grimmest of circumstances.'

Abdelkarim Hamoudi removed his glasses and cleaned them on his cuff. Then he furled the stems around his ears, blinked once or twice.

'Please tell me the nature of your situation,' he asked.

Ghita leaned forward, her face catching the light.

'I am here on a matter of life and death,' she said. 'It concerns my father.'

'And who exactly *is* your father?'

'His name is Hicham Omary and he…'

'He was on the television,' the goldsmith broke in.

'Yes, that's right. He was accused of a crime he certainly did not commit. I promise it with all my heart.'

The goldsmith poured a little more tea, inspecting its colour as he did so. He praised God, as if drawing strength from above.

'And tell me what you need from me.'

'As an only child it is my grave duty to come to my father's aid. It is a matter of family honour, as I am sure you will understand.'

'But what can I do?' the goldsmith asked again.

'I understand that your relative works in the prison where my father is being held,' Ghita said.

The old man frowned. He sighed, took off his glasses and wiped a hand over his eyes.

'By speaking the name of the Prophet's steed you have activated an ancient duty, a duty that has rested on the shoulders of my entire family for generations. It is my duty, *our* duty to help you,' he said.

'Thank you,' Ghita whispered sombrely.

'You must understand something though,' he said. 'If I help, it is not out of fraternity, but out of ancestral duty.'

'Thank you…' said Ghita softly. 'Thank you from the bottom of my heart.'

The goldsmith looked away.

'Return here just after dawn and I will give you your instructions,' he said.

Ninety-one

BACK IN CASABLANCA, Rosario went shopping for fruit and veg at the Marché Central, as she did three mornings each week.

She liked it when the seasons brought new produce, relishing the sense of anticipation and expectation as the fruit improved day after day until it was gone for another year.

Having lived in Casablanca for so long, no one gave her a second glance as she meandered through the market, or through the backstreets near to her home.

It was true that there were rumours about her — that she was a spy, or that she was somehow cursed to live a life in limbo, as neither quite a woman nor quite a man.

In front of the market she crossed the street, the smooth handle of a wicker basket hanging from her arm. She greeted the flower sellers as she entered, and they held up roses as they always did, hoping for an easy sale.

One of them even blew her a kiss.

Turning left, Rosario made her way over to the stalls where the fresh produce was on offer. It was all laid out in a great rolling carpet of wares. She made a beeline for a man who was threading shallots on a string. Slightly built and elderly, he had patchy grey hair and a hint of moustache running the length of his upper lip.

In the middle of his forehead, nudged up against the hairline, was a small, leathery blotch of skin, a *zebiba*. Resembling the side of a prune, it signified piety, a brow pressed down in prayer five times each day.

Spotting the Argentine pianist, he dropped the onions, reached out, and kissed her hand.

'If only my wife would leave the mortal world,' he mumbled, 'I would propose to you without wasting another moment.'

'You are talking nonsense, Yasser, just as you always do.'

'But see how my eyes well with tears for your love.'

'The tears are from the onions and not from passion!' Rosario snapped. 'And you are a scoundrel, and you know it as well as I.'

The onion seller wiped his brow with a thumb.

'I pray as God has instructed,' he said. 'And this is a mark of that.'

The pianist bashed the onion seller with the side of her basket as she passed him.

'We both know very well that you have got that by cheating — by grinding pumice on your face at night.'

'Shhhush!' Yasser hissed. 'The shadows have ears.'

Rosario laughed — a shrill, girlish laugh. She bought a kilo of tangerines from the next stall and wandered out through the market's rear door.

Less than a minute later, she was ambling down a side street on her way to the port. One of the fishermen there had promised her the pick of his catch. Glancing at her watch, she saw she was running late, and fishermen were particular about punctuality.

Quickening her step, she thought back to Dr. Burou and his sweet smile. In a strange way Rosario still felt him close by, even though he was gone — having perished twenty years before in a boating accident on the coast.

All of a sudden, she heard a sound.

The sound of large feet pounding fast over stone.

She spun around, and found a knife pressed to her throat. The blade was short, haphazardly sharpened, held by a slender figure in a voluminous woollen jelaba, the kind worn by shepherds up in the Atlas.

'Where's the American, the one who came to see you?!' he said, his voice hoarse with rage.

'I don't know!' Rosario shrieked. 'Leave me alone!'

'Tell me, or I will sever your windpipe!'

The pianist leaned back. She felt the assailant move back with her, the blade rigid against her throat.

'I'll count to five,' he said. 'Then I'm going to kill you. One… two… three… four…'

Struggling for breath, Rosario managed half a step backwards.

Then she twisted her body to the right, catching her attacker off balance. In the same movement, she jolted the weapon from his fist and into her own hand.

Deftly, and without thinking, she thrust the blade in between his ribs, the sixth and the seventh — coaxing it in as deep as it would go.

In her mind she saw herself as a young, uniformed officer in Buenos Aires, learning unarmed combat from a robust American marine.

Glancing left and right, Rosario wiped the blood off her hand with a square of lace and hurried in the direction of home.

Ninety-two

As NIGHT DESCENDED over Marrakech, the great square of Jma el Fna came alive.

Arranged down one side, the food stalls were doing brisk business, with tourists and locals packed at the trestle tables, clouds of meaty smoke billowing up into the desert sky.

Against a backdrop of drums and iron castanets, they dined on sheep brains and boiled snails, on roasted chunks of fatty mutton, offal, and shellfish.

Looking down at it all from the terrace of a good restaurant, Ghita and Blaine toasted the goldsmith with a bottle of dry local wine.

'Can you hear the music?' Ghita asked.

'How could I *not* hear it?'

'They're Gnaoua. Descendants of slaves brought to Morocco centuries ago down the pilgrimage routes.'

'Their music... it's...'

'*Bewitching*?'

'Yes.'

'It gets into your soul… and drives you mad.'

'I know what you mean,' said Blaine.

Uneasily, Ghita traced the tip of her finger around the top of her glass.

'When I was a child, my parents used to bring me here,' she said. 'My father would say that this square was the navel of the world, that it was somehow connected to our ancestors, and to the beginning of time. I used to beg him to let me lie down on the ground right beside the Gnaoua.'

'Why?'

'Because only then can you soak up the vibrations. To understand their music, you have to feel it in your bones.'

'I can't imagine *you* wanting to lie down out there… to get dirty.'

Ghita smiled.

'One night when I was about twelve my father brought me down here after a dinner at La Mamounia. We watched the dancers and the drummers, and I began to feel dizzy, as though I were about to collapse. I lay down over there at the edge of the square.'

'Were you all right?'

'It's so strange to think of it now. But it was as if something entered me. An invisible force. I went into a trance, my body trembling, my eyes rolled up into my head. My father shook me hard, calling my name over and over, but I couldn't break free. I was completely under their spell.'

Ghita took a sip of wine, her gaze fixed on the square below.

'For three days I was lost,' she said. 'A doctor was rushed down from Paris. He rubbed my body with ointment, injected me with drugs, and even did a scan of my brain. There was no hope. My parents resigned themselves to the fact that their daughter might never recover. But then Habiba suggested that they seek the help of the witches at Sidi Abdur Rahman.'

'Where you had the curse put on your father?'

Ghita bit her lip.

'Yes, that's right,' she said.

'And so what happened?'

'Well, a *sehura*, a witch, was brought to our home. As soon as she saw me, she knew that my soul had been unhinged from my body, and that a jinn had entered me. She said the only treatment was for a very special incense to be burned around me, while incantations were spoken.'

'Did it work?'

'It went on for three days and nights, the witch sucking the jinn out from me a little at a time. Eventually, I was healed, but was so weakened that I had to rest in bed for weeks. Before she left, the *sehura* told my parents that the jinn was so powerful that it was impossible to exorcise it entirely.'

'So there's still some of him inside you?'

Ghita nodded.

'That's right,' she said.

'And you believe in this… in jinn I mean?'

'Yes, of course. All Muslims do, because it's written in the Qur'an. You see, when God created man from clay, he created another life force as well — from smokeless fire. They can change their form as they wish, and they live all around us, invisible most of the time.'

Blaine looked down at a group of Gnaoua as they flounced through the throngs of people, the deafening clatter of their music conjuring a magic of their own.

'There's something unearthly about them,' he said.

'I'm frightened,' Ghita replied.

'Of the jinn?'

'No... well, *yes*... of them too. But I'm frightened about what will happen to my father.' She looked across at Blaine, taking in his damp hair and clean-shaven cheeks. 'The wealthy live very well in Morocco,' she said.

'So I've noticed.'

'It's shameful, I know.'

'Why's it shameful?'

'Because you begin to think it's all quite normal, and that those without the means to buy champagne are somehow beneath you.'

'Maybe all of this has happened for a reason,' Blaine said. 'It's been sent as a reminder — a reminder that you're no better than anyone else.'

'I think you're right,' Ghita replied. 'And I think it's my duty to change, just as it is a duty to save my father.'

On the table between them the candle began flickering in the draught. Blaine cupped a hand around it.

'The greatest thing in life is to get out of your comfort zone,' he said.

'Do you speak from experience?'

'Well look at me... Until a few days ago I was trapped like a rat in a dead-end life back in New York,' he said. 'And when the dead-end life caved in, I took a plunge. I jumped and...'

'*And...?*'

He leant forward.

'And that's how I met you,' he said in a tender voice.

Touched by a tingle of electricity, Ghita returned his smile.

'It's time to go back to the hotel,' she said. 'We have to get up before dawn. The goldsmith will be waiting.'

Ninety-three

STANDING IN HER kitchen, Rosario stripped off her dress and washed her hands first with detergent, and then with diluted bleach.

The water pressure was much better than in the bathroom, and the lighting was brighter there, too.

As she soaped her hands a second time, massaging the liquid between the fingers, she saw the face of her attacker leering at her.

It was everywhere she looked, like a twisted apparition.

Drying her hands, she padded through into the cluttered sitting room and poured herself half a mug of cognac.

Coccinelle watched her from the frame, her expression disapproving.

'I had to do it, my darling,' Rosario explained defensively. 'He was going to kill me!'

She took a gulp of the liqueur, wiped the back of her hand over her mouth, and gulped again. The brandy having warmed her chest, she could breathe more easily.

The killer's face was there again.

Lolling back on the couch, she studied the face — taking in the broken capillaries across the cheeks, and the small, penetrating eyes. The thought that someone was prepared to kill her was distressing but, for Rosario, it wasn't new.

She looked up at Coccinelle and, as she did so, she got a flash of Dr. Burou. He had altered the path of both their lives, turning menfolk into ladies with a knife.

The surgeon disappeared, swapped for a memory of the Cordobazo. It was during the ugly days of the civil unrest that the pianist had been forced to flee her homeland.

But all that was half a lifetime ago.

Rosario had been little more than a boy then. A boy called Héctor. Trained by the government to kill, he had turned his schooling against the men who had taught him the art of instant death.

For six months he targeted government officials, assassinating one after the next, until he was finally captured, tortured, and was himself left for dead.

He had only survived because of a remarkable stroke of luck.

The jailer had been a boyhood friend of his grandfather and managed to smuggle him out on the condition that he leave Argentina and never return.

It had been while chained up in the infamous Caseros Prison that he had made himself a solemn vow. If he were ever to be freed, he would track down the doctor he had heard of in a far-off land, the doctor who offered men rebirth, as the women of their dreams.

Ninety-four

THE MUEZZIN'S CALL rang out over the silent maze of the Marrakech medina, calling the faithful to remember their duty to God. It was still quite dark, the streets damp with a light dew, the doors and shutters of every home locked for the night.

Dressed in their jelabas, the hoods pulled down over their heads, Ghita and Blaine made their way through the twisting lanes until they reached the goldsmith's home.

The door opened as they approached, and he ushered them inside.

'The arrangements have been made,' he said, his voice heavy. 'But in order for the guards to look the other way they will need to be paid something.'

'A bribe?'

The goldsmith nodded.

'How much?'

He calculated.

'Two hundred thousand dirhams.'

'I understand,' said Ghita.

'Good. Now, take this paper and follow the map I have drawn. You must be at the liaison point by the *dhuhr* prayer. If you are late then you will have no hope. And if you are caught, you must not reveal my identity or that of my cousin. Do you swear it?'

'I swear,' said Ghita. 'On my mother's grave.'

The goldsmith pulled the curtain from the window and peered out for a moment.

'Once inside the prison you will only have a few minutes to take your father,' he said. 'As soon as you get outside, you are on your own. You must recognize that the entire system will be searching for him... and for you. They will hunt you both, and will stop at nothing until the prisoner and his accomplices have been caught.'

BEFORE SETTING OUT for the Atlas, Ghita sat on the balcony of her suite, staring out at the snow-capped mountains in the distance. She had broken down in tears half a dozen times during the night, and now began sobbing again. The sense of despondency came from worrying about her father as much as it did from self-pity and guilt.

Blaine knocked at the door.

'All packed and ready,' he said.

Ghita wiped her eyes. She craved a shoulder to cry on but was too proud to break down in front of the American.

'I don't want to be the spectre of doom,' he said, 'but you heard what the goldsmith said. Break a prisoner out of jail and they'll be hunting not only him but you.'

'I know the risks, but I have no choice.'

'D'you have a plan?'

'My father will have one. He always does. But he needs to be free to make it work.'

Blaine touched Ghita on the shoulder. He wanted to hold her but feared that she would lash out.

'Break him out of jail and neither of you will ever be free,' he said. 'You'll be hunted like vermin. Is that what you want?'

'It's a risk — one I have to take,' Ghita said. She closed her eyes, then blinked. 'I have to ask you a small favour.'

'Another one?'

'Will you teach me to drive?'

Ninety-five

THE PRISONER IN the next cell had been beaten to within an inch of his life. His back had been lacerated, and he lay on the concrete floor, groaning.

Hicham Omary called out to him.

'Brother, what's your name?'

After a long silence, there came a frail voice.

'Saad. My name is Saad. And you?'

'I am Hicham.'

'Peace be upon you, brother.'

'What are you in here for?'

'For speaking my mind. And you?'

Hicham Omary clenched a fist and touched the first knuckle to his lips.

'For standing up against a rotten system,' he said.

'They will try to break you.'

'I know.' Omary swallowed hard. 'But it takes a lot more than a dark cell and a beating to break me,' he said.

Ninety-six

ON THE OUTSKIRTS of Marrakech, Blaine steered the Silver Ghost off the main road and eased on the brakes. He got out and walked round to the passenger's side.

'Climb over and adjust the seat,' he said. 'Now, when you're ready, turn on the engine.'

'How do I do that?'

'Press that button.'

Ghita pushed a thumb to the starter and the seven-litre engine fired up.

'Look down at your feet and you'll see three pedals. The one on the far left is the clutch. That's for engaging the gears. Then there's the brake in the middle, and the accelerator on the right.'

'Which one do I press first?'

'It depends what you want to do. We want to move off. So, you push down the clutch, and shift this lever into first, like this. Then, slowly, you release the clutch and press down the accelerator.'

Ghita thrust her right foot down and the car shot off, slamming hard into a sand bank, where it came to an abrupt halt.

'Why's it so complicated?'

'Because it's an old car.'

Ghita burst into tears.

'I'm never going to be able to learn so quickly,' she lamented. 'There's only three hours until I have to be at the rendezvous point. I feel so helpless.'

Blaine got out and walked around the car again.

'I'm not gonna spring your dad,' he said. 'So don't even think of asking me. I will drive you up there though, but…'

'*But?*'

'But if you give me any grief, I'm swinging round and heading for home.'

A few minutes later, the crimson Silver Ghost was heading across the plateau in the direction of the snow-capped Atlas. On either side of the road there were olive groves, the gnarled trees throwing shadows on the dust.

After the frenetic pace of Marrakech, the countryside was soothing to the senses, as though they were travelling back in time.

As they neared the foothills of the Atlas, the groves gave way to rugged little fields planted with maize and wheat. The road forded rivulets and streams as it climbed gently upwards, against a backdrop of adobe villages, each of them sprinkled with laughing children, donkeys, and with mud-brick homes.

By early afternoon they had passed the great waterfall of Ouzoud, reached Azilal, and found themselves on the narrowest of tracks.

'Check the road map with the one the goldsmith sketched,' Blaine called out, as the Rolls-Royce careened through the dust.

'There should be a right turn!' Ghita shouted. 'A few miles from here. Then after the lake it's a zigzag all the way down to the meeting point.'

When the dust subsided, they stopped to buy pomegranates from a farmer. Crouched in the shade of a

245

walnut tree, he took their money, blessed them, and pointed a wiry old arm in the direction of the lake.

As they picked up speed, Ghita broke open one of the fruits and burst into laughter as she did so.

'What's so funny?'

'I was just thinking about you.'

'What about me?'

'That you sold drain-cleaner to old people!'

'What's wrong with that? At least it was a job.'

'Well, you must have been so…'

'*So…?*

'So embarrassed.'

'At what?'

'At having such a lousy career.'

Feeding the steering wheel through his fingers, Blaine felt his back warm with anger.

'I've had to pay my own way since I was seventeen years old,' he said. 'Unlike some people… I put myself through college, worked three jobs and went to night school — all at the same time.'

'And after all that studying, the best job you could get was to sell bleach to geriatrics?'

Blaine steered the Rolls round a steep bend to the left, his expression souring.

Suddenly, he slammed on the brakes, clouds of dust billowing out all around.

'Get out,' he said in a quiet, even voice.

'*What?*'

'You heard me. Get out!'

Incensed, Ghita swung the door open and climbed down in silence onto the dirt. As soon as she was gone, Blaine swung the car around and accelerated fast into the distance.

He had rounded three more bends before he stopped.

Slamming the brakes on again, he smacked his hands together in anger, swore as loudly as he could.

Then he did another U-turn.

Gliding up to where Ghita was still standing all covered in dust, he leaned over and opened the passenger door.

She got in without a sound. And they sat there without speaking, without moving.

After a full minute of silence, they looked at each other, their eyes locked onto the other in frozen hatred.

Then, both at once, they threw themselves at one another in a passionate kiss.

Ninety-seven

THE BOOTS ECHOED down the corridor again.

Omary had become expert at working out which guard they belonged to long before he heard the grunt of their owner's voice. The guards may have all had the same standard-issue uniforms and footwear, but they all walked differently.

The most fearful was six foot three, mid-fifties, without an ounce of fat, and with hands capable of crushing stone into dust. Having nicknamed him 'Bruiser', Omary dreaded him because of the way he dehumanized the prisoners. He treated them worse than animals, and thought nothing of beating them senseless for no reason at all.

Even before the guard had unlocked the gate at the far end of the corridor, Omary knew it was Bruiser. He had slow, heavy footsteps — a self-assuredness garnered from three decades of tyrannical rule. It took Bruiser forty-one strides to get from the gate to Cell No. 3.

Omary counted them as he always did.

Counting was a way of keeping oneself sane.

At thirty-seven paces Bruiser stopped. The keys rattled on their chain and the door to Cell No. 2 was opened. Saad groaned for a moment, and was struck for his sins. Then he was cuffed, blindfolded, and hauled away to the interrogation cell.

Crouching on the concrete floor, Hicham Omary coaxed himself to be calm, to believe in the eventual triumph of justice over evil. The worst thing of all was not raw fear, nor the sense of abandonment, but the uncertainty — not knowing how or when it would end.

Ninety-eight

THE ROAD DESCENDED through a forest of green oaks before climbing steeply. Then, winding to the right, it fell away on the other side, revealing the dazzling waters of the lake.

Cross-checking the goldsmith's directions with the road map, Ghita pointed to the distance.

'There will be a little turning on the left,' she said. 'We go past it, and there should be a road on the right. We take that.'

She looked down at the map again, turning it in her hands. There was the sound of a car honking from behind.

The American glanced in the rear-view mirror.

An immaculate black Range Rover with smoked windows was flashing its lights, honking wildly.

'How the hell does he think he'll pass?!' Blaine roared.

'Pull over and let him.'

'There's no space. Not here. I'll have to get round the bend.'

Suddenly, the Range Rover rammed the Silver Ghost. It slowed and then accelerated, ramming it a second time.

'Jesus Christ!' Blaine screeched, as he recoiled from the force.

'Oh my God!'

'What?!'

'It's the guys from Marrakech!'

Blaine changed down into third.

'We've gotta get out of here!'

The Range Rover gathered speed.

It rammed again, and then a fourth time, its sleek engineering more than a match for a 1925 Silver Ghost.

'What are we going to do?' Ghita shouted.

'Outrunning them's not an option!'

The Range Rover pulled back.

Revving ferociously, its driver manoeuvred the vehicle into the oncoming lane, and slammed into the side of the Rolls.

'He'll push us off!' Ghita screamed.

'That's what he's trying to do!'

Blaine jerked the steering wheel to the left. He changed gears again, down to second, flooring the accelerator.

Feeding the wheel fast through his hands, he managed to cut the Range Rover off.

But as the road evened out, it came again, slamming the Rolls harder than before.

'They're going to kill us!' Ghita cried.

Blaine waited for the next turn.

As he expected, the Range Rover drew up alongside again. Just before it smashed into them, he braked full force.

The Range Rover braked, too.

Accelerating through the gears, Blaine pulled out, ramming his attacker on the rear left side, forcing it over the edge.

It plunged down into the abyss.

The American didn't stop.

'I don't want to see,' he said. 'I don't want to know.'

'That was amazing,' Ghita said, overwhelmed.

'It was kill or be killed. There was no choice.'

Struggling to keep focused, Blaine took the road on the right. He saw himself from above, and heard his grandfather's voice asking what the hell he thought he was doing. Rather than embracing the daydream, he forced it out of his mind.

'Make a left here,' Ghita said.

Quite unfazed by the certain death they had left in their wake, she sensed that her coldness worried Blaine.

'It was what they deserved,' she said pointedly.

'*They*? You think there was more than one?'

'Who knows? Who cares?'

The American glanced over and looked at Ghita, whose face was locked forward on the road. He couldn't believe she was so uncaring. But then it was he who had driven the Range Rover off the road.

'We have to pull up when we see a single eucalyptus tree.'

'Like that one?'

'Yes! Stop here.'

'Now what?'

'We wait.'

'I can't believe there's a prison anywhere out here,' Blaine said, turning the engine off. 'It's the middle of nowhere.'

'That's the reason they chose it. Nowhere to escape to.'

'I guess so, but in the movies it's never like this.'

Ghita pushed her hands back through her hair, combing it with her fingers.

'Your love of the movies,' she said, 'its…'

'*Stupid?*'

She leaned over and kissed him.

'It's the sweetest thing,' she said.

THE WINTER SUNLIGHT playing softly on the landscape, Blaine and Ghita waited at the rendezvous point. They arrived at twelve forty-five. There was half an hour until the *dhuhr* afternoon prayer.

'If my life in New York hadn't fallen apart, I wouldn't be sitting here now in this raincoat,' Blaine said, 'in a Rolls-Royce, with a beautiful woman…'

'…in a rocky field, in the mountains of a distant land?'

'Maybe it *is* like out of a movie,' said Blaine.

251

'As for breaking into a jail?'

'Well, that's pure Hollywood. Worthy of Humphrey Bogart himself.' Blaine swallowed. 'I'm sure he would have approved,' he said.

Ghita looked at her watch.

'The *dhuhr* prayer, it'll come soon. I can feel my heart pumping. I just have to keep my head.' She blew into her hands. 'I want to tell you something,' she said.

'What is it now?'

'This is my problem. It's too much to ask of you — to ask of anyone — to help me more than you have. When the goldsmith's cousin gets here, I'm going with him. I have money now, so my father and I will make our own way back to Casa. In any case, if we're trying to be inconspicuous, a vintage Rolls-Royce is probably a little too much.'

Blaine smiled.

'You're going to have to do a lot better than that,' he said.

'For what?'

'To get me to scoot off without you. I'm dug in deep and am rather looking forward to meeting the guy who filled your head with such nonsense.'

'It's not from him,' Ghita replied. 'He's the most sensible man on earth. And he's ashamed of me... of what I've become.'

'Of what you *became*,' Blaine corrected. 'In the short time I've known you, you've changed. Don't you see it?'

'I've had to think for myself.'

'And what a learning curve it's been.'

Ghita touched a hand to Blaine's forearm.

'Please promise me you'll go when the contact gets here,' she said.

The American sighed. He was about to say something when the sound of an engine broke the silence. Firing up the Rolls, he got ready for a quick getaway.

'Do you see them?'

'No, not yet.'

'They'll come around the next bend.'

Thirty seconds passed. It seemed like an hour. Then a shabby pickup swung round the corner, the vehicle rattling to a halt a few yards away in a cloud of dust. The driver waved a hand out of the window.

Blaine returned the signal.

A man got out. He was wearing an officer's uniform, a cracked leather belt tight around his unwieldy waist. He moved slowly, as if with dread, his dark eyes circled with fear.

Ghita got out and walked over to him.

'Peace be upon you,' he said. 'My name is Murad. I am the cousin of Abdelkarim. We have very little time. Do you have the money for the *baksheesh*?'

Ghita took out two of the bricks of American dollar bills that Habiba had given her.

'This should be more than enough,' she said.

Murad took them, weighed them in his hand.

'OK. Now, lie in the back of the truck, and hide under the blankets.'

Ghita went back to the Rolls-Royce. She kissed Blaine, hugged him hard, and made her way over to the vehicle.

Then, climbing in, she began furling a filthy blanket over herself.

Murad laid half a dozen cartons of beef bones onto his passenger. He got into the driver's seat and revved the tired old engine.

A moment before the pickup pulled off into the dust, Blaine cursed. Leaping from the Rolls-Royce, he sprinted over, and jumped in with Ghita.

'Don't say a word!' he said.

Ninety-nine

THIRTY MINUTES PASSED before the pickup reached the first security gate.

Set in the middle of a smooth rectangular plain, the entrance was overlooked by a pair of symmetrical watchtowers, armed guards manning each of them behind bulletproof glass.

After a considerable pause, the vehicle was waved through and began to run the gauntlet between barricades, each of them electrified and fortified with great spirals of concertina razor wire.

A full twenty minutes was spent crossing the plateau, such was its size. Beneath the blankets, Blaine and Ghita clung together as the vehicle jolted from side to side.

All of a sudden, Murad braked.

He got out of the car and called to the crew manning the second security gate.

'What's going on?' Blaine whispered.

'I think we're entering the prison now.'

A siren sounded up on the watchtower. Then a pair of officers climbed down a rusted iron ladder and made a rudimentary inspection. Murad held up his identity badge and waved a hand at the back. One of the guards peered in, grimaced, and beckoned him back to his seat.

Another set of gates followed, and eventually the outline of the prison materialized against the dim mountain sky.

There were watchtowers galore, security lights, and miles and miles of razor wire in concertina, covering almost every surface.

The pickup rolled dead slow down a ramp, its bald tyres pressing against the diagonal grooves in the concrete. The steel gates clanged open, then closed fast, and a guard's whistle echoed loud and shrill.

Too fearful to sit upright, Ghita and Blaine waited for Murad's signal. The beef bones were heavy against them, but they lay rigid, not daring to move.

In the distance a siren sounded — three short bursts, the noise lost to the outside world. Murad steered his vehicle down through a subterranean corridor. It was walled in sheets of steel plate, with a concrete ceiling and floor.

At the end Murad stopped, checked the coast was clear, and only then made his way hastily to the back of the truck. Lifting away the boxes of bones, he was surprised to see the foreigner there as well.

'I can only take one of you,' he said.

'Me,' Ghita replied.

'Then put these on.'

He threw down prison overalls.

'You wait here,' Ghita whispered to Blaine. 'I'll hurry back with my father.'

Murad looked at his watch.

Squinting for a moment, he said:

'We must wait for the change in shifts. It happens on the hour. Your father is kept in the solitary isolation block. It's got the highest security. I will take you directly there, and you will have three minutes to get into the block and to leave. Do exactly as I say.'

Ghita slipped on the overalls and touched Blaine's hand tenderly. The goldsmith's cousin picked up one of the cartons and motioned for her to follow him.

Down a slope.

Through three doors with push-button locks.

Another slope, this time uphill.

Then a corridor, and an electrified fence.

Once through it, Murad opened a steel armour-plated door using a key that hung from the ring on his belt.

He put the box down.

'Quickly, come with me,' he said.

They hurried along yet another corridor, and then another, and through three more steel gates. Once again, Murad looked at his wristwatch.

'We're two minutes early,' he said.

They waited in a doorway, both of them concentrating on the seconds. Ghita caught a flash of childhood memory — the days when her mother was still alive. She was sitting on the edge of a stream in Switzerland with her parents.

A picnic in the mountains. Warm summer air, butterflies, and strawberry flan.

All of a sudden, a shrill whistle sounded.

It was followed by the metallic crunch of gates slamming shut, and the voice of authority bellowing an order.

'That's it,' Murad said. 'We have to move now!'

He led the way, sprinting down the last corridor, Ghita less than a pace behind. Quickly, he jammed a flat-edged key in the lock of the sheet-steel door, '3' written in chipped white paint at the top.

The cell was suddenly blasted with light.

In the corner, where the wretched walls met the floor, a man was hunched over in terror. His eyes were covered by a trembling hand, his face bruised and unshaven.

Ghita was shaking so much herself she couldn't speak at first. She felt as though she was about to pass out.

'Baba?' she whispered, her voice hoarse with emotion. 'Is that you?'

The figure seemed paralyzed at first. But very slowly, he lolled forwards quizzically.

'Baba, it's me... it's *Ghita*!'

They hugged, so tight that they could never be parted, both of them in a flood of tears.

Murad called from behind.

'Hurry! You must hurry!'

'We have to go, Baba! There's no time.'

'*Go? Where?*'

'To safety. I have arranged it. Don't ask me how.'

A look of total disbelief fell like a death shroud over Omary's face.

He began to choke.

'Darling Baba, I have arranged it all.'

'*But how?*'

'Through taking favours and by paying bribes — it was the only choice to save you.'

Hicham Omary let go of his daughter, his fingers gnarled and stiff.

'*No!*' he spat through gritted teeth. 'I shall not run like a dog and be hunted, if corruption was the key that freed me!'

'But Baba... please!'

Hicham Omary turned his back.

'Leave me!' he growled. 'Leave me now! *Go!*'

Ghita stretched forwards to touch his shoulder.

'Please, Baba, please!'

But Omary turned and pushed his daughter away.

An instant later, the door was slammed shut, and the cell was plunged into darkness once again.

BACK AT THE pickup, Blaine peered out from under the blanket.

'Where is he?'

Sobbing uncontrollably, Ghita climbed into the back. She thrust her arms around Blaine's neck.

'He wouldn't come,' she said, still in shock.

'*What?* Why not?'

'Because he's far too proud to run.'

They hid under the blankets and the car rolled out from the belly of the prison, and ran the gauntlet of security checks once again. Ghita cried all the way, with Blaine unable to calm her.

Once the prison was far behind, they poked their heads out from the blankets.

The sun was lowering, the soft winter light illuminating the crags and the mountain scrub.

'I think we're nearly there,' said Blaine. He pivoted round and scanned the road ahead. 'Wow, d'you see that?'

'What?'

'The smoke up there?'

Ghita sat up.

'I wonder what it is.'

'Looks like one hell of a fire.'

The pickup rounded a corner and moved through the plume of dense, oily smoke, drawing to a halt fifty feet from it.

'Oh my God,' said Blaine.

'It's… it's…'

'The Silver Ghost.'

'What could have happened?'

'Must have been the electrics.'

They got out of the pickup.

As soon as they were on the ground, Murad raced away. He didn't stop to say a word.

In silence, Blaine led the way up to the wreckage. The side had been strafed with high-calibre machine-gun fire.

'That's no electrical fire,' he said.

'What are we going to do?'

'Walk, I guess.'

There was the sound of a vehicle in the distance, navigating the mountain passes.

They both turned at once.

'Let's flag it down,' said Ghita.

'D'you think they'll stop?'

'Hope so.'

The car's engine grew louder, straining as it climbed and took the last bend. Blaine put his hands up and waved. Then Ghita jumped into the road and did the same.

All of a sudden a shot rang out, and another, and a third, fourth and fifth.

Lurching forwards, Blaine shoved Ghita out the way.

They crouched down behind the burning wreckage of the Rolls-Royce. A slate-grey four-by-four changed down gears as it sped into view. The driver hit the brakes hard. As he did so, the passenger aimed his weapon — a 9 mm Glock.

He fired off two rounds in the direction of the Silver Ghost.

Blaine swivelled round, scouring the crags.

'What are you looking for?' Ghita said urgently. 'Can't you see, the shots are coming from over there.'

'There's another weapon somewhere — much heavier calibre — the one that hit the Ghost.' He pointed to a blurred figure on a vantage point above the road. 'Looks like he's reloading.'

'Should we surrender?'

Blaine balked at the question.

'Are you crazy? I've seen enough gangster movies to know they'd cut us to pieces.'

'Then what do we do?'

'Pray.'

'For what?'

'A miracle.'

The machine-gunner raised his weapon and took approximate aim. As he did so, the driver of the four-by-four steered his vehicle to the far side of the Rolls-Royce, screeching to a stop.

'We're going to die,' said Ghita in a cold, plain voice.

Blaine narrowed his eyes.

'D'you hear that?'

'What?'

'Another vehicle.'

With time elasticated around them, the pair focused on their hearing. The sound was loud and deep, almost like a racing car.

'Must be their back-up.'

The man with the Glock got out of the car and walked towards them slowly, the Rolls-Royce in between. Blaine picked up a sharp-edged stone and hurled it towards him.

He missed.

The Glock pistol was aimed. But before it could be fired, the machine gun rang out, spraying the ground behind them.

And then, the miracle arrived.

Swinging fast around the last bend came a blur of scarlet.

A 1966 Ferrari Daytona convertible.

Its engine revving as if about to leave pole position, the horn sounded long and hard.

'Get in!' screamed a voice — a young voice.

Blaine and Ghita looked at each other.

'It's Saed!' Blaine yelled.

Without thinking how or why, they leapt into the Ferrari, as it spun round and disappeared in a blinding screen of dust.

'They're sure to chase us!' Blaine shouted.

'Don't worry,' Saed replied fast. 'I know a shortcut.'

'Back to Casablanca?'

The shoeshine boy jerked his head up and down.

'We'll be there in no time!'

'So where did you get your hands on a Ferrari?' Blaine asked, as the road levelled out.

Saed strained to look meek.

'Well, you know how it is.'

'No, I'm not sure that I do... tell me.'

'More interesting is how you knew we were there, waiting to be cut down,' said Ghita.

'Or how your feet reach the pedals,' said Blaine.

The shoeshine boy smiled — a raw, mischievous smile.

'I tied bricks to my feet!' he said.

One hundred

EIGHT MEN AND three women were seated around the oval table in the Globalcom conference room. At the head, Hicham Omary's chair was conspicuously empty. The firm's board of directors were anxious at having been called to convene without their leader.

Glancing at his wristwatch, Hamza Harass motioned to the security guard to leave.

Overweight, and with a horseshoe of thin grey clinging to the back of his head, Harass was sweating — a signal that he needed something for his heart. Slipping a tiny silver box from his pocket, he gulped down one of the red pills inside and, in his own time, addressed the room:

'Ladies and gentlemen, thank God at last we've been permitted to re-enter our offices,' he began. 'Despite this fact, the authorities have confiscated computers, files and everything else they could haul away with them. I want to thank you for making yourselves available, and to start by saying how saddened we have all been by the sudden fall from grace of our chairman.'

'Who would have thought he would have had such an interest in Class A drugs?' mumbled the man on Harass's right.

'C'mon,' said François Lassalle, the only Frenchman on the board, 'what planet are you from? This is clearly a set-up!'

Patricia Ross held out her hands. She was seated at the side of the conference table, in a special place reserved for her.

'The timing was certainly convenient,' she said quietly. 'Discovered moments after the start of his anti-corruption crusade.'

'Of course he was framed,' affirmed Nadim Lahlou, sitting at the far end of the table. 'We all know Omary's no drug dealer.'

'Is anyone aware of where exactly he's been taken?' asked Driss Senbel.

'To the desert, or the mountains. One of those hellholes they keep ready for terrorists. Does it really matter?' Lahlou replied.

'What matters is what we're going to do to save him,' said Patricia Ross.

The directors allowed their gaze to slip onto the notepads and pencils before them.

None said a word. None, that is, until Hamza Harass stood up.

'Hicham Omary's empire is crumbling,' he said. 'It's lost eighty-five per cent stock value in a week. I'd be surprised if it's still open for business by the weekend. Globalcom's about to be vapourized — wiped off the map.'

'The shareholders are insisting that trading be suspended,' said a slim, bespectacled man on the left of the table.

Harass wiped a hand over his face.

'There may be a solution,' he said. 'A frail lifeline.'

'Coming in what form?' asked Lahlou.

'In the form of a takeover.'

'Are you out of your mind? Sell Globalcom without Omary's blessing? He'd rip out your heart.'

Hamza Harass shrugged.

'From where I'm sitting,' he said, 'it doesn't look as if Mr. Omary has any cards left to play. He's not in the position to agree or disagree to anything at all. By Clause 75 of the firm's company code there is a provision "in extraordinary circumstances that the board of directors are permitted to act in the best interest of the whole".'

'*Meaning?*'

'Meaning that we salvage something from a sinking ship.'

'By allowing her to be chopped up while she's still worth something for scrap?' Lahlou sighed.

Patricia Ross held up a hand.

'Excuse me,' she said, wary of the fact she was not on the board and, as such, hardly worthy of an opinion. 'But as directors of the Omary family firm, ought you not to consider discussing the situation with Mr. Omary's daughter?'

'*Ghita?*' laughed Senbel.

'Yes, Ghita.'

Harass choked.

'As you know, my son was engaged to be married to her. She's a socialite, a socialite with a brain the size of a pea.'

'I've been trying to locate her,' said Ross. 'The Omary mansion has been sealed as you all know. And all her friends appear to have disowned her.'

'Welcome to reality, Miss Omary,' said Lassalle.

Hamza Harass clapped his hands hard.

'Ladies, gentlemen!' he boomed. 'I should like to request that the board reconvene tomorrow at twelve noon to vote on the course of action to take.'

One hundred and one

WHILE HIS PASSENGERS slept, squeezed up together in the front seat, Saed succeeded in outrunning both the gangsters and the police.

The scarlet Ferrari fishtailed through the outskirts of Casablanca, roaring like a monster in a cage. Carving a path through the maze of backstreets, it managed to circumvent the city's evening gridlock entirely.

As he neared the Marché Central, the shoeshine boy did a handbrake turn into a snug parking spot.

Blaine woke up at the scent of burning rubber.

'Wwwwhat's going on?' he spluttered, opening his eyes.

'Casablanca,' Saed announced.

'*Already?*'

'How's that possible?' said Ghita, opening an eye.

Saed slipped the key from the ignition.

'Ferrari,' he said.

One hundred and two

NEXT MORNING, AN army of painters in scruffy overalls were at work on a great hulk of art deco might on Boulevard Mohammed V. They were slopping thin white emulsion hurriedly over its facade. Another team were busy painting the next building, and yet another the one beside that.

Every few yards there stood a worker eagerly sweeping the street, or an electrician struggling to make sense of an outdated junction box.

It was as though a wind of renaissance was blowing in.

Walking down the boulevard, Blaine marvelled at the revival. As he did so, a newspaper seller on the street corner near Marché Central caught his eye. He jabbed a thumb at a passing pickup truck and winked.

The vehicle was pristine and new, its back was filled with bundles of perfectly pressed red flags.

It pulled over.

A squad of men clambered out and got to work hanging the flags.

'His Majesty is coming,' he said with urgency.

'When?'

The news vendor shook his head.

'No one ever knows. That information is a secret.'

'Are we celebrating something?' asked Blaine.

'Yes, of course we are!'

'What?'

'The tramway. It's just been finished. They're testing it now. It'll be like the old days,' said the newspaper seller. 'When Casablanca was famous all over the world.'

His eyes glazed over.

In the short time that Blaine had been away in the mountains, a tram stop had been built opposite the Marché Central. It was complete with electronic ticket machines, turnstiles, and prim steel benches.

As he watched, a tram glided forward without the faintest sound. Unlike before, it was filled to bursting with people, all of them smiling. When it stopped, more squeezed on, but no one got off.

Blaine found himself chatting to an elderly woman with a poodle in her arms. She was French, a *pied noir*, one of the old-timers who hadn't left.

'Look at them,' she said disapprovingly.

'Who?'

'The people.'

'They seem very happy.'

'Of course they are. They're allowed to ride for free.'

'Why's that?'

'Because the tram's not officially open yet. So they ride up and down. It's like a game.'

'Free entertainment,' Blaine said.

'They should be working,' the woman scowled. 'But all they can think of is wasting their time. It's a disgrace.'

The American cocked his head at a giant red flag in the distance, a large green star in the middle.

'The king's coming,' he said.

'I know,' the woman replied, brushing a hand over her dog. 'That's why everyone's working so hurriedly. You see, in Morocco everything's left to the last minute. They have a saying… "Why do today what you could do tomorrow instead?"'

A little further on, Blaine saw a smart gold sign being hoisted into position on the outside of the repainted Shell Building. It read 'Hotel Imperial', and it looked like something out of Miami's South Beach. All that was missing was the lady in the hat and the Rolls-Royce Silver Ghost.

Blaine thought of the burning wreckage, a haze of flames and the stench of smouldering horsehair from the seats.

The guardian was standing outside.

'When does it open?' he asked.

'Next week.'

'That's quick.'

'The owner is in a hurry,' the guardian replied anxiously.

'Because the king is coming?'

He nodded, then looked at the foreigner sideways.

'But how do you know about that?' he said.

One hundred and three

PATRICIA ROSS WAS waiting in the cavernous glass-fronted lobby of Globalcom, the morning light streaming in through a stained-glass frieze. She was dressed in a navy-blue suit, twinset and pearls, her hair tied up on the back of her head.

In the seven years she had worked for Hicham Omary, she had experienced a rollercoaster ride of ups and downs, but never anything as turbulent as this.

At nine forty-five, Ghita came in through the revolving door.

She took a deep breath as she stepped inside, as though the air was somehow thinner. Before she had reached the reception desk, the American personal assistant cut her off.

'Ghita, how are you?' she said, her voice tinged with fear.

'I've been better,' Ghita said, offering her hand.

'Believe me, we all have. These are treacherous times.'

Patricia Ross led the way over to a quiet alcove where they could sit and speak.

'I'd take you up to my office,' she said, 'but it's bugged. The whole place is, except for this one little corner.' She struggled to smile. 'Your father used to tell me that if you want privacy the best spot is the middle of Grand Central Station at rush hour.'

'I saw him,' Ghita said, sitting down, her back to the lobby.

Ross missed a breath.

'Where is he?'

'Incarcerated, up in the mountains.'

'*How* is he?'

269

'Alive. Barely so.' She touched a fingertip to her eye and wiped away a tear. 'We will get our revenge,' she said caustically.

'As I said on the phone, time is against us. We have our backs up against the wall and there's no one we can trust.'

'It's like the assassination of Caesar,' Ghita said.

'All those regarded as loyal betraying the man they once swore to protect.'

'Precisely,' Ghita replied.

'The important thing is for us to stall the board. They're angling to dismember Globalcom, to sell it off a chunk at a time.'

'It's my father's life's work...'

'I know it is, and for that reason you and I have to do everything we can to throw a spanner in the works. I'm ready to do anything — whatever it takes.'

Ghita looked at her father's PA hard, taking in the soft skin around her eyes. Until then she had never quite trusted her.

Patricia Ross held up a document. It was fastened together in a legal binding, with a wax seal and red ribbon on the front.

'The Globalcom company code,' she said. 'Article 72 states that, as the sole issue of Hicham Omary, you have the inalienable right to adjudicate on his behalf.'

Ghita grinned.

'I can't wait to see their faces,' she said.

One hundred and four

ROSARIO PULLED OPEN the door of her apartment and stood in its frame, her face quite rigid and empty of a smile.

'I was passing,' said Blaine, 'thought I'd drop in and see you.'

'Hello… Um, er. Please excuse me, I'm still in my bathrobe. I've not been sleeping well. I blame it on the damp.' The pianist pushed back her thin hair, struggling to seem upbeat. 'Please come inside,' she said, adding, 'I was thinking of you last night.'

The American followed her through to the sitting room, where Coccinelle seemed even more dominant than before.

'I was out of town,' he said. 'Up in the mountains. Just got back yesterday afternoon.'

Rosario motioned to a chair and flopped down in another close by. There was no offer of tea or cognac. The lights were off and the ambience was subdued, cold shadows clinging to the walls like soot.

'I'm a little depressed,' Rosario said, after a tedious pause. 'I suppose I've got the Casablanca blues. They come and go. It's just a question of soldiering on, getting through to the spring.'

'I hear the king's coming,' Blaine said optimistically.

'Is he?'

'Everyone's out there smartening the boulevard up. They're even hanging out the flags.'

The pianist groaned.

'That means the traffic will get worse,' she said.

271

'But the king's coming to launch the tram. It's going to make the gridlock a thing of the past.'

Rosario groaned a second time.

'If you believe that, you'll believe anything,' she said, getting up. Crossing the room, she stood beneath the portrait of Coccinelle, as though following a stage direction. 'I have something I would like to ask you,' she said, 'and am not quite sure how to begin.'

'What is it?'

'Well, you see, although I love Casablanca, there's no way for me to leave.'

'What do you mean?'

'In your country you would say that I have a "history"… reasons, private reasons, why I can't return to Argentina, the land of my birth.'

'Is it because… you know… because of Dr. Burou?'

'No, well, yes… and because of other things,' she said in a voice burdened with memory. 'I left Buenos Aires when I was young, at a time of terrible friction — friction between the state and the people.'

'But that's all changed,' said Blaine.

'It may have, but the files are never closed.'

'I'm not sure that I follow you.'

Rosario went over to the window and, standing on tiptoes, peered out at the street.

'When you came in, was there anyone loitering down there?'

'No, I don't think so. Are you expecting someone?'

'No. I'm not.'

Blaine scratched his head.

'What was it that you wanted to ask?'

'Do you remember the other day we spoke of the murder at the hotel?'

'Yes.'

'And I said that I'd heard the dead man was a mule, carrying a special passport?'

'I remember.'

'Well, I understand that it was entrusted to you, or that you were passed it in some way — perhaps without even knowing.'

'What? That's absurd. We only spoke for a moment about hot water — or, rather, the lack of it.'

The pianist cracked her knuckles.

'If you have the passport, your life is in danger, too,' she said. 'It may sound melodramatic, but it's the truth.'

Blaine had a lump in his throat.

'Is life in Casablanca always this intense?' he asked.

Rosario let out a sigh — a sigh mixed with a laugh.

'*Always*,' she answered. 'Haven't you seen the movie?'

'I watch nothing else.'

'Then you'll know how it is.'

'It's brutal,' said Blaine.

'But at the same time, it makes life anywhere else seem drab.'

'So why do you want to leave?'

Rosario looked up at Coccinelle and shook her head, before peering down at the street again.

'Because I can't,' she said.

One hundred and five

THE MEMBERS OF the board were seated in their usual positions, all except for Hamza Harass. He had helped himself to the chairman's seat — the only one with armrests.

A long Montecristo cigar was clenched between his front teeth, an accessory as much as it was a smoke. In his own time, he clipped one end, lit the other, and exhaled a lungful of dense, grey smoke.

'My dear friends and fellow directors,' he said, 'I now have the papers for you to sign in order for the future to begin. And it's a future which bodes very well for us all.'

He glanced over to Patricia Ross, for her to hand out the documents. Finding her chair empty, he thrust the papers towards the middle of the table.

He was about to congratulate himself when the door to the boardroom swung open wide.

Ghita Omary entered quickly, Patricia Ross behind her.

She strode over to where Harass was reclining, Montecristo in hand, and motioned for him to move.

A moment later, she was seated in her father's chair, hands on the armrests, eyes locked onto the stupefied members of the board.

'Good morning to you all,' she said aggressively. 'First, I would like to thank you all for your support in these trying times, and to Mr. Harass for keeping my father's seat warm for me.' She smiled, allowing the smile to dissolve into a scowl. 'Forgive me, but the situation is so precarious that I shall dispense with pleasantries. As you are fully aware, Globalcom stock is in a tailspin. We have to act fast to steer this ship around.'

'Miss Omary,' said Harass, inspecting the end of his cigar, 'thank you for your interest, but I do believe your presence is not permitted, let alone required.'

Ghita winked at Patricia Ross.

Rooting through her attaché case, the American PA pulled out the legal document.

'Article 72 of the company code clearly states that Miss Omary has the full and inalienable right to lead Globalcom in lieu of her father.'

Harass held up his hands as though he were about to be shot.

'I do believe we are well past the point at which we might be saved by your efforts, Miss Omary,' he said. 'I assume you are not cognizant of the JFT bid?'

'*JFT*?' Ghita repeated in a voice so shaped by anger that it was barely comprehensible.

'A consortium of industrialists,' Harass replied, 'formed for the purpose of acquiring Globalcom.'

François Lasalle held up the document that had just been circulated.

'The firm will be stripped of its remaining assets,' he said, 'and sold off piece by piece to the highest bidder.'

Ghita dug her long fingernails into the leather upholstery.

'And who exactly is the leader of this cowboy outfit?... *J...F...*'

'*T*... JFT,' Hamza Harass broke in. Sucking hard on his cigar, he smiled smugly. 'I am proud to declare that it is I, my dear Miss Omary,' he said.

Her blood boiling, Ghita stood up and thumped the walnut veneer with her petite fist. Considering its size, it made an impressive sound.

'You may think me a worthless excuse of a woman!' she shouted. 'But, in the name of my father, the man who gave you all responsibility and made you all wealthy, I ask that you extend to me seventy-two hours.'

'What are you going to do with it?' asked Driss Senbel arrogantly. 'Go shopping in Paris?'

Some of the other board members broke into a laugh.

'Why not?' Harass said, pushing back his shoulders. 'It will give us time to put together the last details, and to go shopping ourselves. For, as you may be aware, the Omary mansion and its contents are about to be auctioned.'

One hundred and six

LATE THAT AFTERNOON, Blaine and Ghita sat on the cramped terrace of Baba Cool, cigarette smoke billowing out from the interior intermittently. They were holding hands under the table, neither of them entirely focused on the other.

'Somehow I have to pull a rabbit out of a hat,' said Ghita.

'And what hat would that be?'

'The one my father has left me.'

'I don't know that I follow you,' said Blaine.

Ghita's grip tightened.

'My father used to tell me that his success was based on one skill.'

'Which is…?'

'The ability to flip a handicap into an advantage.'

'And how do you do that?'

'He said the key was to fully understand the situation you are in.'

'So what *is* your situation?'

'Well, my father's in jail, and a complete crook called Harass is trying to break up his business empire and sell it off. Our family home is going to go up for auction any minute, to pay for fines supposedly now owing to the state.' Ghita took a sip of her coffee, then pushed the glass away. 'That's my situation,' she said.

'There must be someone who can help. Who's got the power?'

'Well, I haven't,' said Ghita.

'So who does?'

'The Falcon.'

'And what do we know about him?'

'That he controls the system.'

'And?'

'And that he holds all the cards.'

'So we need to get to him…'

'And then pressure him to turn things around.'

'But how do we put pressure on someone that we know nothing about?'

Ghita reached under the table and touched Blaine's hand again.

'By using the influence of someone else.'

'Great… but who?'

Ghita smiled — a vindictive smile.

'I have an idea,' she said.

One hundred and seven

CLINIQUE MOGADOR SMELLED of cut-price disinfectant, the kind bought wholesale down near the port. There was a coldness inside, a sense of detachment, as though no one who worked in its fusty wards was trying very hard at all.

Monsieur Raffi was lying in bed on the fifth floor, his head partly bandaged, his arm in a sling. He shared the room with four other men, each one suffering a considerable wound.

His eyes were closed, but he was not asleep, his mind daydreaming of an afternoon half a lifetime ago — an afternoon spent up in a grotto shielded from the Mediterranean shore.

Through a great deal of hustling, Blaine had tracked the old shopkeeper to the fifth floor of Clinique Mogador.

With no one on duty, he showed himself in, a box of Turkish pralines in his hand.

At first Blaine didn't recognize Raffi with the bandages on. But as he drew closer, he noticed something familiar on the nightstand — the black-and-white studio shot of Humphrey Bogart.

It was resting against a small blue vase in which a dying rose was poised. Blaine stood there, his shadow looming over the bed, half wondering whether to take the last step.

A draught swept through the room and Monsieur Raffi opened his eyes. He saw the American, frowned, then blinked in slow motion.

'My dear friend,' he said very gently, as if too fatigued to speak.

'I brought you some chocolates. I was very sorry to hear...'

'That I had been attacked?'

'Yes.'

'Well, the world isn't as safe as it was. Or that's what they say. I don't believe them of course, because we don't have world wars any longer, just muggings like this.'

'Are you in pain?'

'Find me a man as old as I am who isn't in pain.'

'Do you know who did it?'

'A thug.'

'What was he after?'

The old man let out a cough.

'You... it would seem.'

'*Me?*'

Raffi nodded.

'He smashed up the shop. Maybe it was a sign — a sign to pack it all in.'

Blaine took a seat on a fragile chair positioned at the end of the bed.

'I'm so extremely sorry,' he said. 'But if it makes it any better, they came after me as well.'

Monsieur Raffi sat upright as much as he could manage.

'How terrible!'

Getting to his feet, Blaine walked over to the nightstand and picked up the photograph.

'I found it,' he said.

'Found what?'

'The postcard.'

He took it out of his jacket pocket and held it up, turning it to the light.

'That's Villa Mirador.'

'So I was told.'

'Did you go over there?'

'No, not yet.'

'Then what are you waiting for?'

One hundred and eight

A VOLUPTUOUS WOMAN with ample cleavage was lying in a marble bath, swathed in bubbles. Clusters of scented candles were burning around the edge, throwing shadows over the crimson curtains and the stucco walls.

She was smoking an Egyptian cigarette in a long holder, while a pedigree Chow Chow licked the perspiration from her face.

Suddenly there was the sound of music, Edith Piaf's 'Non, je ne regrette rien'.

The woman, whose name was Samira, but who was known as Mimi by her friends, reached out for her iPhone. Her eyes widened at seeing the name on the display.

'Hello, my darling,' she cooed. 'I want to see you! Can we meet tonight?'

On the other end, a man's voice grunted flattery, then excuses.

Stubbing out her cigarette with one hand, Mimi used the other to toss the iPhone onto a loveseat on the other side of the bathroom.

'Men!' she exclaimed in the direction of the Chow Chow. 'They are the real dogs of this world!'

One hundred and nine

THE RED PETIT taxi rattled up past the lighthouse and took a left and then a right just before the Corniche.

The driver forced his foot down hard so as to climb the palm-lined avenue, which led up to the crest of the Anfa hill. He turned again and steered gently round past a series of villas, each one a little grander than the last.

A few feet short of the most magnificent one of all, he drew the battered vehicle to a halt. A moment later, a pair of security guards wearing dark-blue baseball caps stepped into the road. They were waiting for a name, or an explanation.

'I'm kind of on a mission,' said Blaine.

'A mission?'

'It's gonna sound a little strange. You see it concerns Humphrey Bogart and this postcard.' He paused, stepped up onto the kerb and held up the picture of Villa Mirador. 'Is there someone I could speak to, an official or someone like that?'

One of the guards spat a handful of words into his walkie-talkie. Then he disappeared into the security booth and got on the phone. Fifteen minutes passed and he called out:

'Your identification, Monsieur.'

Blaine slipped his passport through. It was examined, photocopied, examined again, and then returned.

The second guard waved a hand at a solid steel door. It opened electronically.

'You can go in,' he said.

Stepping through an airport-style detector frame, Blaine found himself in a sprawling garden, a lovely bow-fronted villa set back a short distance from the gates. He walked up to the building slowly, his eyes taking in the art deco details, the wrought ironwork and the building's gently curving lines.

It was the house from the postcard.

As he approached the front door, an American man stepped out. He was middle-aged and bespectacled, and had an engaging face, the kind that puts others instantly at ease.

'I am George Sanderson,' he said amiably, 'the American consul here in Casablanca. I understand you showed an old postcard of Villa Mirador to the guard.'

Blaine extended his hand, held eye contact, and strained to appear sane.

'I was thinking this moment through on the cab ride,' he said, 'going over my opening gambit. And heck, to tell you the truth, I couldn't think of anything that would sound plausible. So I'll just run with it.'

The consul touched a fingertip to his chin.

'You'd better come inside,' he said.

They went through into a small room on the left of the main door. The walls were hung with formal black-and-white portraits, a number of them featuring Churchill and Roosevelt. The Stars and Stripes stood on a stand to the right of a desk.

Sanderson took a deep breath.

'Here's your chance,' he said. 'Hit me with what you've got.'

Blaine took out the postcard and held it in his right hand.

'I was drawn to Casablanca by my love for the movie,' he said. 'And through my appreciation of all things Bogart,' he paused, held up the card. 'I have followed a treasure trail of clues the great man laid down, clues in the form of postcards like this.'

The consul took the postcard and examined the reverse.

'Do you know what this number — 07698 — signifies?' he asked.

'No, I don't. Do you?'

A maid shuffled in with mint tea, poured it, and then shuffled out.

Sanderson held the glass of tea and breathed in the steam. Then, slowly, his focus moved towards the window and the gardens beyond.

'When I became consul here,' he said, 'I was given all the usual briefings about the city and about this house. It's quite an extraordinary place. As you may know, the Anfa Summit was held here back in '43. Churchill and Roosevelt ran the Allied war effort from this very room. It's a great chunk of history.'

He stood up and stepped into a shaft of yellow sunlight near the window.

'And the thing is,' he went on, 'with houses like this, there are all sorts of marvels. You may not realize it, but your postcard is one of them.'

'One of what?'

'Of the marvels.'

The maid shuffled in again, this time with a plate of gingerbread. She laid it on the desk without a word, and was gone.

'One of the stranger fragments of information entrusted to me,' Sanderson said, 'concerned Humphrey Bogart. I am sure you know better than I that he was here in North Africa entertaining the troops.'

'That's right. He was with his wife, Mayo. They fought like cat and dog.'

The consul nodded.

'So I understand.'

'What was the fragment of information… the one entrusted to you?'

'That one day, someone might turn up and claim the lost treasure of Humphrey Bogart.'

Blaine broke into a grin.

'What is it, a bottle of Scotch?'

The consul shrugged.

'I don't know. But I have a sense that we are about to find out.'

One hundred and ten

THE BOOTS ECHOED down the stone corridor, waking Hicham Omary from a light sleep. He recognized the feet inside them instantly as those of his nemesis, Bruiser.

Following Ghita's break-in, Omary had fallen into a gloom of terrible despondency. He was losing weight fast, and his bones ached. Were he not so stubborn, he might have regretted ever taking on the system.

Standing in the darkness, he coaxed himself to be strong.

First came the keys rattling on their chain, then the sound of the lock mechanism turning, and hinges creaking open.

And then a tidal wave of blinding light.

'Turn around!' ordered Bruiser, striking Omary's shoulder with his cane. 'Hands behind your back.'

The prisoner crossed his wrists and waited for the nickel-plated handcuffs. But they didn't come. Instead, a pair of rusted old D-lock cuffs were slammed over his wrists and locked twice.

Omary may not have seen them, but he could feel the difference. They were colder, tighter, and somehow far more fearful than simple, self-locking handcuffs.

Then came the fetters and a blindfold made from extra-thick hessian. Like the cuffs, they were different.

By the time he was led out from his cell, it was clear that Omary was not en route to the interrogation cell.

'What's happening?'

'You're being moved,' said Bruiser.

'Where to?'

'Do you want me to ruin the surprise?' he said.

One hundred and eleven

GEORGE SANDERSON DISAPPEARED into the back office and was gone a long time.

When finally he reappeared, he was clutching a tan-coloured dossier. It looked extremely old, the faded binding covered in dust and speckled with damp.

In small, neat script on the front was the number: 07698.

The consul placed the folder on the table, blew away the dust, then opened it slowly.

Inside were a series of letters and photographs, most of them showing Bogart and his wife performing for the troops. The consul shuffled through the papers, his forehead knotted in concentration.

'What is it you're looking for?' asked Blaine.

Sanderson didn't reply, not at first.

Then, after a minute or two, he pulled out an envelope. It was labelled 07698 and was pasted shut, Bogart's signature scrawled over the seal.

'The plot thickens,' he said, as he drew the blade of a letter-opener down the side.

Blaine leaned closer to get a better look.

'Is it a letter?'

The consul removed the single sheet of paper, the crest of the United States embossed on the top. Holding it between his hands, he rotated it clockwise.

'It's a map,' he said.

'To the Scotch?'

As before, Sanderson didn't reply.

Instead, he paced out of the room and gave an inaudible instruction to the maid. A few minutes later, one of the guards from the front gate was standing in the doorway of the room. He was holding a shovel.

'Let's go outside,' said the consul.

'You think it's buried here somewhere?'

'Look at the map. The house is here, and the terrace there. This line is the curve of the garden wall, and that's the tall palm there. It just wasn't quite so tall when this plan was drawn.'

'And that?' asked Blaine, pointing to a circle bisected with a line.

'That's what we're searching for, I guess.'

Counting fifteen paces from the edge of the terrace, and twenty-two from the wall, they found themselves at the sundial.

'It must be under here,' said Blaine.

Using all his strength, the guard pulled away the dial and began to dig.

Ten minutes later, there was a little mound of dark brown soil, and a hole two feet deep beside it.

All of a sudden, the shovel hit something hard.

'It sounds like wood,' said Sanderson.

The guard speeded up, his face streaming with sweat. Carefully, he dug around the sides of what appeared to be a casket.

He lifted it out onto the lawn.

Fastened with a pair of rusted iron padlocks, the wood was overlaid with curious metallic motifs.

The guard brushed off the dirt and, when instructed to do so, knocked off the locks with the shovel.

'Are you ready?' Sanderson asked.

'Couldn't be more so,' replied Blaine.

The curved lid was pulled back, the hinges so rusted that they needed force to part them.

'I don't believe it,' said the consul.

'It looks like another box.'

'It's made of metal.'

'I think it's lead.'

They lifted it out and unfastened its clasp.

Inside it was a third box, also made from lead, but this time reinforced with a thin layer of wood.

Blaine opened it, to find a package the size and weight of a telephone directory.

'The treasure?'

'Not whisky after all.'

Sanderson carried it inside and led the way through to the main reception room.

On one side there was an antique Érard grand. Across from it was a fireplace and a group of formal chairs.

The packet was put on the coffee table and opened up.

It contained something wrapped in a long strand of discoloured muslin.

Blaine unwound it inch by inch.

Inside was a book, handwritten Arabic in the elegant Maghrebi style of centuries ago. It was not bound, but rather enveloped in a sheet of coarse goatskin.

Turning it over in his hands so that the spine was on the right, Blaine pulled the covers apart. His eyes focused on the now familiar script of Humphrey Bogart, a line or two of text inserted on a loose sheet.

'Can you read his writing?'

Blaine held it to the light.

'I was presented this down in the desert by a fellow chess player, who made sure I couldn't read it before he passed it on. I leave African shores shortly and have decided that it belongs here on the Dark Continent, a prize for the man who can make sense of my trail — Humphrey Bogart.'

The consul flicked through the pages. A great many were inscribed with mathematical diagrams and symbols.

'It looks like witchcraft,' he said. Getting to his feet, he tramped through to the kitchen.

A moment later he returned, followed by the maid. He tapped a finger towards Bogart's treasure.

'Zeinab, can you read any of this?'

The maid opened the book at the title page. Her face froze and she began to whimper, a whimper that quickly turned into a high-pitched scream.

'What is it?' asked Blaine urgently. 'What's so frightening?'

'You must bury this book and never think of it again!' Zeinab exclaimed, hyperventilating.

'But why?'

'Because it is a pact with the Devil!' she said.

One hundred and twelve

GHITA TOOK A taxi to CIL, one of the old French quarters patronized by the city's bourgeoisie.

There were no designer clothes shops there or little boutiques selling jewellery or shoes, but there was something far more in demand by the jet-set ladies from Anfa — Chez Louche.

An extrovert of the most sensual nature, coutured from neck to toe in pink satin, Laurent Louche was the most sought-after man in town. His clients booked weeks and, sometimes, months in advance, to be pampered and pored over in his salon. An appointment at Louche was an entrance ticket into the most exclusive of sororities. Merely being seen in the salon was in itself a mark that one had arrived.

Laurent Louche specialized in obscure beauty treatments — the kinds that only ladies with abundant free time and extraordinary wealth could afford. These included caviar facials, and gold-leaf face masks, bull-semen hair treatments and even snake massage.

The more extreme, the higher the price, and the more the clientele demanded them.

Ghita had dressed up in a profusion of couture, pieces that had not found any takers on the streets downtown. Her scarf was by Fendi, and her dress by Chanel, the hat a Fleur de Paris creation, and the belt was Hermès. A gift from Ghita's father, it was far too precious to sell, even by a spiteful daughter.

Unlike the Ghita Omary of old, she now felt self-conscious at being so overdressed. But she knew very well that the only way to be taken seriously at Chez Louche was to be way over the top.

Swaggering towards the entrance, she allowed the pair of towering Nubian guards to pull the doors apart, while the Chinese dwarf attendant scattered rose petals at her feet. More importantly though, she made an effort to appear completely nonchalant and bored by it all, as if she had seen it a thousand times before — which of course she had.

Her foot hadn't taken a single step through into the leopard-skin interior when Laurent Louche himself waddled up and air-kissed Ghita's cheeks.

'My darling!' he swooned. 'Where *have* you been? I have been worried sick about you!'

'Monaco,' Ghita replied conceitedly. 'But it is so tiresome in winter. You know how it is.'

'So drab,' screamed Laurent. He gave a snigger. 'But who has been doing your hair my darling? Not that monkey at the Salon Mustique?'

He snapped his fingers and a gaggle of fledgling attendants slipped out from crevices. Dancing around her with garlands and scattering yet more petals, they directed Ghita to a throne-like seat, and the business of beautifying began.

Laurent himself swanned about, fussing over his clientele; he lavished superlatives, and his own inimitable wisdom.

'You must leave him, but only after taking him for every penny he's got,' he told a pretty Italian woman dressed in pea-green silk. And he said to another: 'What do you think beauty is for, if not as a tool to get what you want from a man?'

One of the reasons that Chez Louche was such a financial success was that its proprietor decided what treatment he would administer to each woman who came through the door. He would not have dreamt of allowing them to decide for themselves.

By rationing the most expensive techniques, he created an insatiable demand. A day didn't go by without a craggy matriarch from the good side of Anfa begging for one of the more extravagant procedures, and being turned away.

A team of fourteen staff laboured at the throne on which Ghita perched, a glass of chilled vintage Krug in her hand.

After forty minutes, Laurent Louche glided up with an antique mirror. It had once been owned by the English mistress of Napoleon III. He held the glass to Ghita's face.

'Mirror, mirror on the wall, who is the fairest of them all?' he giggled.

'You work wonders my darling,' she said.

Louche blushed and fell at her knees, his lips pressed gently to the back of her hand.

Choosing the moment, Ghita looked into Laurent's eyes and blew him a kiss.

'I have a favour to ask you, my dearest,' she said.

'If it's not a big one I shall be cross.'

'I feel awful at asking anything of you at all,' Ghita said, moistening her lips with champagne.

Laurent Louche tapped a fingertip to his ear.

'Whisper in here my darling,' he said, 'and your wish shall be my command.'

One hundred and thirteen

UNCERTAIN QUITE WHAT to do with Bogart's treasure, Blaine took it back to the secret apartment and hid it in his satchel.

The fact that Ghita had solicited services from the witches of Sidi Abdur Rahman suggested she might be unnerved at the thought of having a black-magic manuscript in her home.

The American was about to put the satchel on the shelf in the hallway when something caught his eye.

The bottom edge of the bag had a small tear along it, where the two main seams joined. He didn't remember ever noticing it before. Taking it through to the window, he prised the two seams apart. Strange, he thought, it's out of shape. Without thinking, he delved his fingers into the hole.

A moment later, he was holding a booklet.

Its cover was red, adorned with a globe, a laurel wreath, and the words 'United Nations Laissez-Passer'.

One hundred and fourteen

THE PRISON VAN was constructed from armoured steel, the kind used in bullion trucks. It had a bullet-proof glass windscreen and a sealed compartment for the convict. There was even a spray nozzle mounted on the ceiling, through which nerve gas could be piped in the event of an attempted break-out.

The van made its way through the gauntlet of security checks, but never once were the doors opened, for fear that the prisoner would try to escape.

Hicham Omary spent the entire journey crouched on the floor, his hands still cuffed behind his back. Thankfully, the blindfold had been untied at the last minute before he was loaded in.

For the move, Omary had been dressed in fluorescent orange overalls. In the unlikely event he managed an escape, it would be easier for a sniper to spot him and to bring him down.

But escape was the last thing occupying Omary's thoughts.

Incarceration had taught him to mind-wander. Staring at a fixed point on the floor or the wall, he would begin the spiral down through layers of interwoven memory. The technique tended to take him to the bedrock of his youth, played out in the carefree streets of Casablanca's downtown.

All of a sudden, he was playing marbles in the dust.

There were three of them — Adil, Hassan and Hicham. For an entire summer they spent almost every minute together. How old could they have been?

Omary squinted to see the detail. *Seven? Eight?*

They always went to the same place — a disused cinema across from the old Christian church, not far from the Hyatt. Through that long, scorching summer they had made it their den.

They called it Dar Majnoun, 'House of the Possessed'.

Sometimes they used to rip up the floorboards and set fire to them, or smoke cigarettes cadged from the old winos in the nearby bars, or scrawl their names on the walls with sticks blackened in the fire.

For Omary, the den was part of his own fantasy, of being a Berber warrior, protecting the family's homestead in the centuries before the Arabs came.

One night they all cut their forearms with a penknife and pressed the wounds together, swearing an oath of lifelong fraternity, a friendship bonded by blood.

The van hit a bump and Omary's memory was jolted fast-forward.

He was much older now — twenty-two or -three.

He had a little office in Derb Omar, not much more than a lean-to up on the roof of a disused warehouse. But to him it was the beginning of great things.

He could see himself in there as though it were yesterday.

Piles of papers from deals he had already done. There were boxes of stock — plastic toys from Hong Kong and women's lingerie from southern Spain. And there were half a dozen tea crates packed with vials of cheap perfume.

They were minuscule, holding no more than a few drops of the precious liquid, and so were affordable to the middle class. Omary, who had dreamt up the scent himself, called it l'Eau de Topaz. The fragrance was a massive hit — so much so that the black-market price was ten times what he sold it for.

The van took a sharp turn and the floor rattled hard.

Where were Adil and Hassan right then, he wondered? Where were his blood brothers in his time of need?

Omary frowned, then let out a slow sigh. He knew the answer but had somehow suppressed it, forcing it to the back of his mind.

Hassan had been arrested for stealing a Frenchman's car and gone to jail, so beginning a career of petty crime. Their paths had crossed from time to time in the early years, Hassan begging for cash or imploring him for a job. Each time he turned up he was more derelict, ravaged by the woes of drugs and drink.

And Adil?

He had stowed away on a cargo ship to Copenhagen, and had sent a smudged postcard from Vladivostok a year or two later. He claimed to have found true love with a girl from Ukraine — a girl with emerald-green eyes. Omary had written back to the address at the bottom of the card, but he never heard anything more.

There was a rumble of thunder in the distance.

Then the rain started as a light shower, but quickly turned torrential. The clatter of it on the roof was somehow comforting, as though it was a link with nature, a reminder that there was more to life than incarceration in cell blocks conjured from concrete and steel.

The road descended a steep incline, the tyres whirring as they corkscrewed down through a series of sharp turns.

Concentrating hard, Omary could just about hear the guards up front.

They were discussing a local soccer team, their accents from the villages in the hills outside Marrakech. He struggled for a deep breath and coaxed his head down towards the sheet-steel floor.

The lower down he crouched, the less strained his breathing.

For a long while, the vehicle rumbled down an even stretch of road. It sounded like a highway. But, as far as Omary could tell, they hadn't stopped at a tollbooth.

Suddenly, an alarm sounded in the distance — a high-tech electronic buzz. It was followed by a grating noise, a series of clunks, a thud, and by a whistle sounding off.

The brakes were jolted hard, and the prison van stopped.

Then the ritual of opening the doors and securing the prisoner followed.

It took an age.

Each time it was acted out, Omary laughed to himself. If the recent experience had taught him one thing, it was that prison was nothing like it was in the movies.

In reality, there was none of the James Bond bravado, the death-defying stunts to win freedom, or the sarcastic one-liners spat at the guards.

Real incarceration was an agony of uncertainty and jaw-dropping boredom, tempered with zeal... the zeal to go unnoticed.

Omary was taken straight to a holding cell. It was spacious, very cold, and smelled of sulphur.

On the far wall were arranged half a dozen wooden batons. They were well worn but good quality — imported — with nylon straps to allow them to be swung from the officer's hand.

A guard with a wart-ridden face took the prisoner's fingerprints. After that he made him sign five or six blank sheets of paper. Omary assumed that they were for producing false confessions, if needed at a later date.

An hour later, he was in his new cell.

It was large, fifteen feet square, with a squat toilet in the corner and a broken wooden packing crate — a piece of furniture that could be used as a stool, or almost a bed.

Best of all though, there was a view of the outside world. It wasn't much — not more than three or four inches across. But if he pressed his nostrils up to it, Omary could breathe pure air.

Breaking down in tears, he fell to his knees.

'Thank you, thank you!' he whispered over and over. 'Thank you for this luxury!'

One hundred and fifteen

THE NURSE WAS doing her rounds, passing out little green pills to everyone on the fifth floor of Clinique Mogador.

Propped up with three pillows, the bandage on his head now gone, Monsieur Raffi took his ration and gulped them down. He was about to close his eyes for a snooze when he heard a voice. A voice in English.

'I might have been killed!'

The shopkeeper looked up, rummaged for his spectacles.

'*Ah, bonjour, Monsieur Américain,*' he said.

Blaine's expression was uncharacteristically stern.

'I know it was you who hid it!' he shouted.

'Excuse me?' replied Raffi.

'I could be lying in a morgue right now!'

Monsieur Raffi took off his glasses, wiped them on the sheet, and slipped them on again.

'I do not follow,' he said, blinking.

Blaine moved closer, his shadow inching up over the bed.

'You hid the UN passport in my satchel,' he said indignantly. 'That time I brought it in and put it on your chair.'

The shopkeeper blinked again. He moistened his lips.

'Oh,' he said. 'How ever did you guess?'

'That it was you?'

'Yes.'

'Because of a little receipt that I found in the back.'

'*A receipt?*'

'For a silver cigarette box. It bore your signature.'

299

'Ah,' Raffi said once again. 'I wonder how that got in there.'

He took a sip of water, rinsing it around his mouth.

'I should never have accepted the passport as payment,' he said. 'I knew it would lead to nothing but danger.'

Blaine sat down beside the nightstand.

'If you knew, then why did you give it to me?' he asked gruffly.

'Don't you see?' the old man asked.

'*No*, I don't!'

Monsieur Raffi shifted in the bed.

'Because that passport is of such value to so many people that it raised... how can I say...? It raised the stakes.'

'What stakes?'

Raffi took in Bogart's face on the nightstand, the strand of cigarette smoke curling up from his hand.

'You came to Casablanca in search of adventure,' he said. 'And that document was nothing more than a catalyst, a cast-iron guarantee.'

'That I found instant death?'

'That you found adventure!' Raffi exclaimed. He began to choke, then wiped a hand to his mouth, clearing his throat. 'After all, the worst crime is to live a wasted life — a life of mediocrity, one untouched by uproar.'

'But I could have been killed!' Blaine exclaimed, repeating himself.

'Surely it was a trifling insignificance, for it opened a door to a memorable experience.' Monsieur Raffi coughed and then swallowed. 'As for your reward, it's the passport itself,' he said. 'I'm sure you'll find a use for it — I certainly shan't.'

Blaine frowned.

'But what of the murdered student?' he replied.

The shopkeeper shrugged.

'These things happen.'

'*Murder*?'

Raffi shrugged again.

'Oh yes,' he said with nonchalance, 'it happens all the time.'

'But why did they kill him — if he didn't have the passport?'

'I dare say he had something else.'

'Something worth killing for?'

'Of course.'

His gaze moving fitfully from the bed to the nightstand, Blaine found himself looking hard at his idol, Humphrey Bogart. There was something so confident about him. It was as though every trial and tribulation he had ever endured was marked on his face. Yet despite all the scars of life, he was calm, aloof.

Blaine blew into his hands.

'I'll never understand this city,' he said.

One hundred and sixteen

GHITA MAY NOT have known the Falcon's identity, but she did know the ways of men.

Given an opportunity, the male gender always resorted to the same predictable pattern. They craved stimulants, attention, and adrenalin thrills. And they hankered for the gentle comfort of the female form. But, of course, for a man with power and wealth, one woman is never quite enough.

It was for this reason, Ghita felt sure, that the Falcon would have at least one mistress in tow. As she pondered it, the lover was likely to be a woman with a raw sense of self-preservation, and looks that were on the wane. Such a woman could, she mused, be the key to dismantling the gangster's realm.

And who better to track her down than Casablanca's greatest expert on the fairer sex — Laurent Louche? Having been a regular client since she was a child, Ghita knew that she could rely entirely on both his discretion and consummate skill.

Less than a day after whispering into his ear, she was provided with a name and address.

The details of Mademoiselle Mimi.

Unsure how best to make first contact, Ghita decided to write a letter. Handwritten on heavy-grade writing paper, the script was confident and neat.

Mimi was cooing over her Chow Chow when it arrived, brought by a young private messenger — none other than Saed. She signed for it, took it inside, and held the envelope to the light.

Intrigued, she ripped it open, lit an Egyptian cigarette, lounged back in her chair, and read:

My dear Mimi,

I believe that all women have a duty to one another — a duty to defend ourselves from the venomous and ill-intentioned desires of men. Part of this duty is to look out for each other, and it is in this spirit that I am writing to you now.

I have it on the very best authority that the gentleman with whom you are amorously engaged has taken a new and much younger companion. She intends to usurp your coveted position.

And I understand that the gentleman in question intends to relieve you of your lodgings and the gifts he has showered upon you, and bestow them instead on his new love... Mademoiselle Fifi.

For now, it is imperative that you do nothing, not until I contact you again with instructions.

Yours sincerely,
G. O.

Feeling faint, Mimi allowed the letter to fall to the floor, where it was sniffed eagerly by the Chow Chow, his nose picking up the scent of Chanel No. 5. Then, pressing her small, delicate hands to her face, Mimi wept like she had never wept before.

After that, drying her eyes on a square of printed Thai silk, she began to brood.

Half a dozen times in the next hour she reached for her iPhone and began to make the call. But each time, something cautioned her to stop — the need for the perfect revenge.

One hundred and seventeen

THE NEXT MORNING, Blaine and Ghita were sitting in Baba Cool trying to come up with a plan, when Saed hurried in. Putting down his shoeshine box, he drew up a chair.

'I have got good news,' he said softly. 'News about the Falcon.'

'What is it?' asked Ghita.

'Every month the money is collected... all of it... the money from the Falcon's business. And it is counted. Then they take it away, from Club Souterrain.'

'Is that the good news?' Blaine asked.

Saed signalled to the waiter for a *café noir*.

'No.'

'Then what is it?'

'The handover... it is tonight.'

'What time?'

'Twelve o'clock... midnight.'

'That doesn't give us much time,' Blaine said. 'I don't know what we can do. It's not as if the police are going to be interested in arresting them all.'

Saed added four sugar lumps to his coffee. He took a hesitant sip... and added two more.

'The police are paid to look away,' he said.

'There's only one thing we can do,' broke in Ghita all of a sudden.

'What?'

'Film a full confession.'

'And give it to the police?' Blaine asked.

'No, better than that — we'll put it out on the news.'

'Sounds easy,' Saed grinned sarcastically.

'He's right,' Blaine sighed. 'The odds are stacked wildly against us.'

'So what do we do?' asked Ghita.

Saed drained his coffee and waited for the sugary sludge at the bottom to slide into his mouth.

'The red book...' he said. 'Get the red book.'

'Which red book?'

'The red book with the numbers. It has all the secrets... the Falcon's secrets.'

'What does it look like?' Ghita asked.

'It is just a little red book.'

'And where do we get it?'

'At the handover. It travels with the money.' Saed tapped the table with his thumb. 'Something else,' he said.

'What?'

'From the nightclub you cannot enter the money-counting room.'

'Why not?'

'Too many guards.'

'So then?'

'Must go the long way,' he said.

'Which is?'

The shoeshine boy smiled a Cheshire Cat smile.

Foraging in his underwear, he brought out a crumpled scrap of paper.

'I made a map,' he said.

'A map of…?'

'Of the tunnels.' The shoeshine boy paused, tracing a finger in a roundabout way from one side of the paper to the other. 'To get to the money-counting room you go like this… under the club and along.'

'Where did you get that from?' Ghita asked.

'I cannot tell you,' Saed said. 'Big secret.'

'There's a lower network, under Club Souterrain?' Blaine mumbled.

Saed nodded.

'Casablanca's biggest secret,' he said.

One hundred and eighteen

AT TEN P.M., Rosario left her apartment and made her way through the backstreets to work. Dressed in a flowing blue silk dress and matching heels, she was wearing her best paste earrings, with a full-length woollen coat to keep out the cold.

The pianist wasn't feeling well. She was upset after the brawl down near the port. But, like everyone else at Club Souterrain, she knew it was the one night that she had to turn up. The last Thursday of the month was when the club's owner was there.

The curious thing about the club was the secrecy that surrounded it. The staff were forbidden ever to discuss the day-to-day running practices, the clientele, or what went on behind the steel security doors at the back.

Everyone knew there was an underhand side to the business, but no one had ever told Rosario what was really going on. She knew almost nothing about the Falcon, except that he was a gentleman of means, who preferred to keep to himself.

As the pianist climbed down the staircase from Hotel Touring in her heels, Saed was leading Ghita and Blaine to a manhole cover in the Hyatt's parking lot, a crowbar stuffed down his shirt.

Assuming they were hotel customers, the guard at the gate had greeted them with a smile and got on with his work.

Forcing his full weight down on the crowbar, Blaine managed to dislodge the iron cover. It came away with ease, as though it had recently been removed.

A tubular shaft descended into the earth. It was awash with cockroaches and spiderwebs.

Blaine shone his torch down the hole.

'There are handles,' he said.

'I'm not going in there,' Ghita whimpered. 'Not for anything.'

The American touched a hand to her arm.

'Not even to get your old life back?' he said. 'Not even for your father?'

Saed went first, his small hands swinging from one rung to the next.

Then it was Ghita's turn. She let out a pained squeal as she went.

After her went Blaine. He struggled to pull the manhole cover back into place before lowering himself down the shaft.

The further they went, the more the cockroaches, until there were so many that they all melded into a seamless, seething landscape of them. Taking his lead from Saed, Blaine switched off the lamp and allowed his eyes to adjust to the subdued light.

They descended for five minutes, until they reached the main sewer pipe. There was a residue of pungent sludge at the bottom.

'It's raw sewage,' said Blaine.

Ghita gagged, and moaned a little more, but coaxed herself to be brave.

'I'm pleased I didn't wear my Jimmy Choos,' she said.

One hundred and nineteen

FORTY MEN WERE toiling away in an underground warehouse behind Club Souterrain.

Each of them was dressed in special overalls, without pockets, and were forbidden to wear anything underneath. The leader of the team was a dark, crow-faced man called Larbi. Having worked for the Falcon for almost a decade, he was one of the few men in a position of responsibility.

'Those last bales of banknotes have to be counted again,' he instructed.

'But they've been counted once already,' one of the men replied.

'*Twice*. They must be counted twice. And that's an order.'

Larbi jerked a thumb to the counting machines. The men started feeding the wads of notes through them a second time. There was a sense of anticipation and of fear, as though they were being watched.

And of course, they were.

Mounted on the walls were at least a dozen surveillance cameras. Some of them had wide-angle lenses, while others focused close up on the hands operating the counting machines. The room had been specially designed by a team brought in from Corsica. It could be hermetically sealed and flooded within a matter of minutes, or pumped full of poison gas in the event of a raid.

At half-past ten, Larbi clapped his hands.

'Hurry!' he yelled, breaking over the noise of the counting machines. 'And make sure the bundles are double-tied!'

He noted down the result of the first count in the red ledger. The rows of columns were tight with numbers, dates, and code names.

At that moment, a mousy man in a beige polyester suit and cheap city shoes shuffled into the warehouse through an armoured door. He had a rough, unwashed appearance and was severely stressed.

'He's here,' he said. 'And he wants to know the total.'

Larbi gave a number, rounding it up.

'Is that all?'

'No, we're still waiting for the Marrakech deposit. It should be here any minute.'

'They are cutting it close.' Pulling up his polyester cuff, the mousy man glanced at his watch. 'He's not going to be pleased.'

'How's the club tonight?'

'Busy. There's a cruise ship full of Russians docked at the port.'

Larbi wiped a hand down over his face.

'We'll be ready on time,' he said.

One hundred and twenty

'CAN YOU HEAR that?' said Blaine, as they walked double speed through the tunnel.

'*What?*'

'Listen.'

'It sounds like a vibration... like music,' said Ghita.

'The Argentine pianist,' replied Blaine. 'She must be up there playing in the club.'

'That means we're getting close.'

'We have to climb up to that level. We are far below them,' said Saed.

He took out the map, squinted at the converging zigzags in the torchlight.

'Can you see a ladder?'

'Where?'

'Over there. It should be on the right.'

The American skimmed the beam over the wall, sending the cockroaches into frenzy.

'There!'

'Thank God for that.'

They hurried over.

The torch in his right hand, Blaine climbed as fast as he could. He slammed his fist up on the hatch, once, twice.

'It's no use,' he called down. 'It won't budge!'

Saed looked at the map.

'If we go on, and then double back, it will take far too long,' he said.

Blaine slapped his hands together heatedly.

'If only we had something to work on the rust,' he said. 'It hasn't been opened in years.'

'I could go back and get a knife,' Saed said.

'We don't have time for that, either. Let's try to make use of anything we've got. Empty your pockets.'

The shoeshine boy rooted about and, a moment later, pulled out a golf ball, a rusty nail, three inches of metal twine, and a glass eye.

'All I've got is some money and this,' said Ghita, fishing a small bottle of clear liquid from her purse.

'What is it?'

'Hand sanitizer.'

The American climbed down, took the container, and clambered up again.

With care, he squeezed the gel into the groove. Then, with all his strength, he pounded at the hatch.

It moved a fraction.

Blaine squeezed more gel and thumped again. Suddenly, the hatch popped open.

'*Alhamdulillah!*' Ghita exclaimed.

They climbed up and closed the hatch behind them.

ON THE UPPER level, they found themselves at the spot where several tunnels converged. Saed led the way down the widest one, map in hand. Much drier than the lower level, it hardly stank at all.

After a relatively straight stretch, it curved around sharply to the left, before arcing back to the right.

They took another left, then a right and, gradually, the passageway tapered until it became so narrow that they were forced to advance sideways.

All of a sudden, it ended.

'This is where our luck runs out,' Blaine said.

He shone the light on the walls, examining every inch of the brickwork.

'We'll have to go back,' said Ghita. She turned and, as she did so, Blaine reached out and grabbed her arm.

'What is it?'

'Wait.'

The American put his hand on the facing wall and ran it down the bricks slowly, in concentration. Then taking a step back, he lunged at the wall with his shoulder.

A door swung open.

'Casablanca Magic!' he whispered.

They stepped through, and found themselves in a bright, modern-looking corridor. It was damp-sealed, and illuminated by hundred-watt bulbs. There were voices in the distance, and the churning sound of counting machines.

Allowing his breathing to shallow, Blaine led the way.

Behind him was Ghita. She was so close that he could feel her warmth. Saed was just behind her.

They tiptoed down the corridor and arrived at a steel door. Mounted at its centre was a wheel, the kind used on submarines.

In the distance was the sound of a large vehicle reversing.

Blaine put his ear to the steel. He closed his eyes, counted to three, and rotated the wheel to open the door.

The counting room.

From the limited vantage point, Blaine could make out bales of banknotes, dozens of them, all piled up squarely on one another. His eyes widened as the adrenalin hit again.

'Jesus Christ, d'you see all that?'

'And there's the same amount again over there,' said Ghita.

'Sounds like they're counting the money.'

'Must mean they are getting it ready to move.'

'Follow me,' said Blaine, creeping down an alley between the bales. They towered from floor to ceiling like the walls of a fortress. He motioned to the far end of the warehouse. 'We've got to get over there if we have a chance at getting the red book.'

Just then, a second armoured door swung open without the faintest hint of sound. It led through to the club.

A suited man with thin, grey hair entered the warehouse. He was smoking a cigar, his face taut with anger.

'The transfer vehicles are here!' he hollered. 'Get this paper out of here immediately!'

Larbi looked at the wall clock.

'Yes, sir!'

Crouched down in the passage between the bales, Ghita couldn't believe her ears.

313

'It's *him!*' she whispered. 'I know it's him!'

'*Who?*'

'The Falcon.'

'How do you know?'

'Because I *know* him!'

'Huh?'

Ghita craned her neck around the end of the passage. An oversized counting machine was obstructing much of the view. But she could see the floor. The foreman was wearing a pair of sneakers, and the other man was in handmade shoes — in indigo leather.

'I can't believe it,' said Ghita, almost collapsing. 'Harass is the Falcon... the man who runs Casablanca's underworld?'

Blaine didn't understand.

'Who? What?'

'I'd know those awful shoes anywhere!'

Blaine frowned.

'*Shoes?*'

'He's my father's best friend. He *was* my father's best friend. The man whose son I was about to marry, the guy who now chairs the board of Globalcom!'

All of a sudden, the Vertu phone cradled in the Falcon's fingers buzzed. He looked at the number, cursed loudly, then took the call.

'*Bonsoir chérie*, no, I can't talk now. I'm very busy. Yes, later... maybe later. I'll try to do my best.'

There was a sound from the other side of the steel door.

'I am going through,' he said. 'Make sure all of this is ready to leave in fifteen minutes. Is that understood?'

Larbi looked back at the team running bills through the counting machines.

'Fifteen minutes!' he snapped.

The Falcon stepped through the armoured door, down a short passage, and into Club Souterrain.

It was in full swing.

There must have been three hundred people in there — gamblers, drinkers, carousers of every sort. In the middle of the salon, Rosario was crooning at the piano, a half-empty glass of vodka martini on a coaster beside the music stand. Her hands were playing 'Blue Moon' again, but her mind was far away.

She was thinking about the night she had undergone the knife in Dr. Burou's clinic, about going to sleep a boy and waking up a girl.

The *click click click* of the roulette ball broke through for a moment, and was followed by a wave of cheering and laughter, by expletives, and by the sound of the croupier raking in the chips.

At the bar, a huddle of waitresses were attending to their orders. Their low décolletage might have been scandalous elsewhere in Casablanca, but at Club Souterrain, scandal was unknown. The house had one rule and one rule alone: any behaviour, however depraved — if acted in the name of decadence — stayed within the club.

Gentlemen clients had been known to strip naked and parade about wearing nothing more than a feather boa, or to down an entire bottle of bourbon before spewing their guts out over the red velvet furniture.

And no one ever said a word.

Although, of course, this didn't stop the club from filming the illicit activities through secret cameras. There were sixty of them, positioned so discreetly that none of the staff was even aware of their existence.

Weaving his way through the room, the Falcon greeted the regulars, before checking the running totals in the betting pits. The kind of man who was incapable of trust, he was all the more mistrustful on a night when the funds were moved.

The Falcon perused the figures on the clipboards one by one. He showed no emotion. He never did. As far as he was concerned, emotion and gambling were quite incompatible, two elements to be kept absolutely apart.

He checked his watch.

Three minutes to go.

He signalled to the barman to send a round of free drinks to the Russians.

'Make sure they leave with enough cash that they return tomorrow night,' he told the duty manager in a stony voice. 'And tomorrow, suck them dry.'

He turned and slipped back through the rear entrance.

As he did so, Ghita made her move. She had spotted the red bound register lying on a desk to the right of the telephones. Nimbly, she scurried out, snatched it, and retreated into the passageway, between the two lofty walls of paper money.

'I got it!' she whispered.

Blaine hugged her, and the three of them beat a hasty retreat.

They were about to step through into the tunnel when Ghita tripped. She flew forward, landing on her side, blood streaming from her knee.

Larbi heard the commotion.

In an instant, he had roused the guards.

A moment after that, Ghita, Blaine, and Saed were lined up against the back wall. A guard in black uniform was bearing over them, a semi-automatic rifle in his hands.

'What's going on?' the Falcon shouted as he entered.

'I caught these three in here. They were trying to take the register.'

Hamza Harass strode purposefully through the warehouse.

'My, oh my!' he exclaimed. 'Now this *is* a surprise!' He paused, put a hand to his mouth in thought. 'Or perhaps it isn't a surprise at all. Tell me, my dear, who are your friends?'

Ghita didn't reply. She was too angry to speak.

'Leave her alone!' said Blaine.

The Falcon grinned.

'Oh, that's the last thing I'm going to do,' he said. 'Believe me, I'm not going to leave any of you alone.'

Larbi was given orders.

The intruders were to be taken under armed guard to an anteroom. It had rubberized walls, no windows, and another one of the submarine-style hatches for a door. Half the space was packed with files and junk.

One by one, they were thrust inside.

The Falcon stood at the hatch, staring at Ghita's face. He appeared genuinely pleased.

'Dear Hicham would be proud of you,' he said. 'And I dare say he'll weep a tear once he learns of your death. But that will be some time… for I doubt news reaches the mountains as quickly as it ought.'

He nodded to the guard, stepped back, and the heavy steel hatch was slammed shut. A second later, a pressure valve was closed, locking the door securely from the other side.

Ghita threw her arms around the American's neck.

'I'm so sorry,' she said, 'and you, Saed, will you forgive me?'

'There's enough air in here to survive for a while,' said Blaine.

Just then, there was a piercing sound.

'Oh no!' bellowed Saed.

'Water!'

'They're flooding the chamber!'

Blaine got down on his hands and knees and struggled to cease the flow streaming out from a duct. He was immediately knocked backwards by the force.

'I can't do it,' he yelled. 'Quickly, look through all this stuff and think!'

They rooted through all the junk — old shelving, bicycle frames and canned food, miles of nylon rope, coloured hosepipes, bottles of bleach, pots, pans, and what looked like an extremely old engine block from a Renault truck.

Melodramatically, Ghita collapsed in the water and started to weep.

'I should have guessed it — that Harass was the Falcon!' she howled. 'I always detested him. To think of it — he was almost my father-in-law!'

The water inched up over the engine block. As it did so, Saed coaxed the others to move to higher ground.

'If we climb up, we may live,' he said.

'For how long? Until someone comes and lets us out?' said Ghita.

The shoeshine boy's face dropped.

'I hope so,' he answered.

Blaine, who had been standing in knee-deep water, glanced down at the deluge, then up at the ceiling. Slapping his palms together, he plunged his hands below the waterline.

'What are you doing?' asked Ghita incredulously, the water now up to her waist.

'I have an idea,' he said. 'But we have to work fast.'

Blaine pointed to a cast-iron ring in the middle of the ceiling. It must have been fifteen feet high.

'Saed, can you get up there, and thread this through?'

The shoeshine boy grabbed the end of the nylon rope and scampered up onto the pile of junk. Within a minute, he had threaded it through the ring and lowered the end down.

Quickly, Blaine tied it around the engine block, fastening it in a half hitch. Then, mustering all his strength, he heaved the engine block an inch at a time, up through the water until it was level with the middle of the hatch.

'What are you doing?' Ghita asked.

'Making a battering ram,' Blaine said, straining to keep hold. 'The only question is how much force we can get behind it.'

Tying the cord, he stepped back into the corner, and thrust the engine block at the door. It slammed home with an almighty *crash*!

'Again!' Saed yelled. 'Do it again!'

Blaine did.

And then again, and again.

Each time the engine block slammed against the steel, it stressed the hinges a little more. He continued, again and again, until his hands were bruised, and until the water was up to his chest. Raising the battering ram a little higher to be clear of the waterline, he thrust it with all his strength.

All of a sudden, the hatch bowed outwards and the water began to drop. Ten more thrusts and the hatch was breached.

One at a time, they crept out into the corridor.

Saed tiptoed through to the warehouse.

But he was soon back.

'They have all gone,' he said. 'And they have taken all the money with them.'

'The music's still playing in the club,' said Ghita.

In the warehouse, Blaine double-checked for the red book.

'It's definitely not here,' he sighed.

Then, lifting his gaze from the desk, he scrutinized the walls.

'What are you thinking?' Ghita asked, taking a step closer.

'Listen, you go back to the apartment with Saed,' he said, 'and I'll follow in a bit.'

'I'm staying with you.'

'No, you're not. Not this time.'

'Why not?'

'*Because…*'

'Because it's no place for a woman?'

Ghita glared at the American.

'Because you need to make contact with the news team at Globalcom. Is there anyone left you can trust?'

'Miss Ross,' Ghita said. 'I can trust Patricia Ross.'

One hundred and twenty-one

BLAINE STRODE INTO Club Souterrain battered, bruised, and soaking wet. He was fearful of being discovered there but, as he reasoned it, if the money had gone, then the Falcon and his henchmen had certainly left, too.

The Russians had moved from the card tables to roulette. A pair of them were seated, mountains of coloured chips piled up on the baize.

The croupier spun as he called last bets.

Not far from the blurred wheel, Rosario was playing a Scott Joplin number, her black gown gleaming, a faint trace of perspiration on her brow.

Reeling about near the bar was the police commissioner. He was drinking with a European man. Each of them had a glass of Scotch in their hand.

Following Blaine's instructions, Ghita and Saed had made their way out through Hotel Touring, and were soon on the street. The exit had been immensely more preferable than the route in through the tunnels.

As she scurried towards her secret apartment, Ghita felt a pang of terrible fear. She couldn't bear the thought of anything happening to Blaine.

Now there were two men in her life to worry about.

Inside the club, the barman was preparing a round of caipirinhas, rolling the limes to get them extra juicy. He had been on edge all evening, as he always was on the nights that the Falcon came in. Pouring a triple measure of cachaça into the shaker, he began slicing the fruit.

Blaine sat down at the bar, his back to the room. It wasn't a minute before a girl approached and asked if he wanted some company. He slipped her fifty dirhams.

'Go and tell the pianist to join me for a drink,' he said.

'Who should I say is inviting her?'

Blaine thought for a moment.

'Coccinelle,' he replied.

At that moment, there was a commotion at the roulette wheel. The manager was called to sanction a particularly large payout to a monstrous bearded Muscovite.

Rosario glanced round at the disturbance and found the hooker's lips whispering in her ear. Slowly, she allowed her gaze to move over to the bar.

A minute later, she was seated beside Blaine.

'Good evening, my dear Coccinelle,' she said with a laugh.

The American kissed her on the cheek.

'Good evening.'

'How did you get so filthy, my dear?'

'I came the long way round.'

'Through the medina?'

The American shook his head.

'Through the sewers,' he said.

'I see,' Rosario replied tersely. 'And what brings you down here, into the shadows?'

'A proposition.'

The pianist giggled.

'I'm far too old to be propositioned by such a handsome young man,' she said.

Blaine took out an envelope from the inside pocket of his jacket.

'I'm willing to give you this,' he said.

Rosario swallowed hard.

'The laissez-passer?'

'That's right.'

'What do you want in return?'

'Something I imagine you can get quite easily,' the American said.

One hundred and twenty-two

MIMI LAY ON her bed, brooding on how best to get revenge.

She kept thinking back to the way she had been wooed, and to the endless stream of gifts. There had been diamonds the size of walnuts, bottles of rare perfume, buckets of caviar, meals at expensive restaurants, and even a pedigree dog.

She looked down at the Chow Chow, who was licking his lips.

'I should send you back to that beast!' she screamed.

There was a knock at the door.

The dog scampered over and began to bark, and Mimi slipped on a silk robe. She had almost forgotten that Ghita had called and invited herself over.

Pacing through the sitting room, she opened the door.

A large box of Belgian chocolates in her hand, Ghita introduced herself.

'For you,' she said.

Mimi invited her in and opened a bottle of Veuve Clicquot rosé.

'I only drink champagne when I am sad,' she said, downing a glass of it in one gulp. 'It helps to dry the eyes from the inside out.'

After a second glass, she opened the chocolates and gulped down a handful as though they were peanuts.

'I hate him,' she said in a cold, fractious voice.

'You're not the only one.'

'But how did you come across this information?'

Ghita picked out a morsel of fudge and tossed it to the dog.

'I have a friend with a salon,' she replied. 'There's nothing he doesn't know… nothing he can't find out.'

'It's not Laurent Louche is it?' whispered Mimi, her eyes glittering at the thought.

'Well, yes, actually, it *is* him.'

'Oh, my dear!' Mimi poured more champagne and held up her glass. 'Once I've got revenge you must promise to introduce me.'

'I promise.'

'Thank you! Now, my dear, please tell me your plan.'

One hundred and twenty-three

THAT AFTERNOON, THE directors of Globalcom met once again in closed session.

As before, Harass was seated at the head of the table. He was still smarting at having heard that Ghita and her companions had escaped. The guards responsible had each lost the top joint of their little finger, Larbi as well. The punishment had been meted out by the Falcon himself with the cleaver he kept in his desk.

Leaning back in the chairman's seat, he surmised that Omary's daughter was a spent force. The important thing now was to take a cleaver to the Globalcom brand — to chop it up, and to sell it off bit by bit.

'Ladies and gentlemen,' he said, leaning back in his chair, 'I have the honour of informing you that JFT's acquisition of Globalcom is now ready to go through. The papers are drawn up and await your signatures. Once this formality has been attended to, we can put the past behind us, and strive towards the future.'

'But what about Mr. Omary?' asked François Lasalle, smoothing a hand down over his hair.

'Omary?!' Harass let out a childish cry. 'He's gone! Finished! Kaput!'

Hamza Harass took a gold Mont Blanc from his inside jacket pocket and swivelled to where Patricia Ross was seated.

'So... where are the documents for us to sign?'

'In Mr. Omary's office.'

'You mean, in *my* office?' he smiled, gave a wink, and stood up. 'I'll go and get them myself,' he said, leaving the room.

Ross reached for the phone, speed-dialling a number.

'He's coming there now,' she said.

One hundred and twenty-four

THE PACKING CRATE may have been damaged beyond repair, but it was a source of enormous joy.

Through his incarceration, Omary had endured loneliness, violence, cold, and appalling food, but it was the lack of anywhere to sit that was the worst punishment of all. We take chairs for granted, perching on them, or reclining back at whim. Yet most of us have never had to consider a life without sitting down.

The increased space was pleasing, too.

There was so much of it that Omary found himself suffering from almost a phobic reaction. He couldn't understand why he had been moved to the new installation, or given what he regarded as luxuries.

He sat on the crate, filled with new vigour.

At two in the afternoon, the guard tramped fast down the corridor outside the cell. The familiar sound of keys jangling was followed by old, rusted hinges opening.

'Get against the wall!' the officer ordered. 'And splay your legs!'

He placed something on the packing crate and was gone. Cautiously, Omary turned around.

Confused, he looked at the object as though it were from another century, another world. Bending down slowly, he picked it up, turning it in his hand.

It was a miniature battery-operated television.

He flicked it on, and the screen came alive to a news station — Globalcom News 24.

Omary gasped. Then he laughed, his eyes welling with tears.

Someone out there wanted him to watch the news. At first, he thought it must have been sent by Ghita, smuggled in with yet another bribe. His eyes narrowed and he felt his back warm with disapproval. But then, as he thought about it, he realized that he had missed something — something important.

On the packing crate there was a note card. He picked it up, held it into the light.

My dear Hicham,
I wanted you to see for yourself the grand plan we have for your beloved firm.

Hamza H.

One hundred and twenty-five

THE GIANT WALL of television screens in Omary's office were trailing the main news story of the hour — that Globalcom was about to be dismembered, its assets acquired by JFT Holdings.

Ghita was sitting on the edge of the desk when the Falcon entered.

Attired in a pinstripe business suit, charcoal grey, her hair was pulled back tight in a bun, her feet strapped into sensible shoes. She had prepared for the moment, coaxing herself to stay composed.

'Good afternoon, Mr. Falcon,' she said in an even voice.

'Ghita! How the hell did you get in here?!'

Harass exhaled angrily.

Glancing fast around the room, he said:

'I'll have security sling you out in a moment. Now, where are the documents I had left here?'

'Is this what you are looking for?' asked Ghita quizzically, holding up the red ledger.

Harass did a double take.

'How did you get that?!' he roared.

'From a friend.'

'Who?'

'Let's just say that she wears a size sixteen.'

'Give it to me!'

'I will. But first I want to know one thing… How did you run the underworld for so long without anyone suspecting?'

Hamza Harass stepped towards the desk. His bitter expression fortified with arrogance, he snatched the ledger from Ghita's hand.

'Because I own the system,' he said. 'I have everyone you could imagine on my payroll — the police, ministers, judges, even prison guards. They all quake in fear at the thought of me — at the thought of the Falcon.'

'And the money you had piled up in your warehouse last night — what's it all from?'

'What do you mean?' Harass glowered. 'It's from my operations, of course.'

'And which operations would those be?'

The Falcon took half a step forward. His face was inches from Ghita's own.

'I have a number of businesses,' he said, with a forced smile.

'Would they by chance include gun-running, drug dealing and protection rackets?'

'What if they do?'

'Please answer my question.'

Harass let out a laugh.

'How else do you expect anyone to amass proper wealth in a country such as this?' he bellowed.

Striding back across the room, he reached for the metal handle. As he did so, Ghita called out:

'One last thing, Mr. Harass! There's someone who would like to speak to you.'

'I don't have time for conversations. The Board are waiting in the other room.'

'Oh, but I do think you have time for *this* conversation.'

Right on cue, the door to the adjoining room opened, and Mimi stepped in. Like Ghita, she was dressed in a formal business suit, her face quite devoid of emotion.

'Hello, Hamza,' she said.

'Er... Um... Hello, Mimi. What are *you* doing here?'

'She wants to know why you have taken another lover,' Ghita said.

Harass cracked his knuckles.

'I don't have time for this!' he yelled.

'You don't have time for Mimi, you mean?' Ghita said. 'And what will you do with Fifi when you are sick of her — throw her out into the gutter as well?'

Mimi stepped forward.

She might have shouted something, or wept, but she was too irate. So she just stood there in silence.

Harass looked at his watch, then at his mistress.

'You're nauseating,' he said. 'Everything about you fills me with disgust!'

Ghita jerked a finger at the wall of TV screens.

As if by magic, the Falcon's explanation from moments before was being replayed. It was followed by footage of him in the warehouse, surrounded by all the bales of money. A voice-over explained how Harass had arranged for the heroin to be stashed at Omary's home — and that it had come from his own narcotics trafficking business.

'You did all the work for us,' Ghita said, motioning to a pile of black boxes. 'I've never seen so many CCTV hard drives in my life.'

The Falcon's brow beaded with sweat.

'I'll have them all erased,' he said. 'The films will never see the light of day!'

Ghita looked down at the floor modestly, then up into the eyes of the man who was so nearly her father-in-law.

'I suppose you could do that,' she replied. 'Except that it just went out live on Globalcom's news.'

One hundred and twenty-six

THE NEXT MORNING, a red petit taxi pulled up at the gates of the Omary mansion. It was a bright day, the light tinged with spring. Ghita got down, followed by Blaine. As they walked over the damp lawn, their hands touched.

A guard was standing to the left of the gate.

Rather than turn Ghita away as before, he signalled to a second guard in the security booth. The gates opened electronically.

'Welcome home, Miss Omary,' he said.

They walked up the drive and over to the porch.

'This is where you live?' said Blaine, visibly shocked.

Ghita blushed.

'If you'd like me to give it up, I will,' she said.

'No... no...' Blaine stuttered. 'I think I could become accustomed to a lifestyle like this.'

They kissed and, as they did so, the front door opened inwards.

'Welcome home, Mademoiselle,' the butler proclaimed. 'I trust you are well.'

'I don't think I have ever been this well,' she replied, 'and how are you?'

The servant appeared baffled. The Ghita Omary of old would never have enquired after anyone except herself.

'I am very well indeed, Mademoiselle. Thank you for asking,' he replied.

Ghita led the way through to the grand salon, pausing to greet the maids and other staff as they approached. She was trembling.

'I feel so humble,' she said, 'so utterly unworthy of all this.'

Blaine kissed her on the cheek.

'Believe me, you are worthy of it all,' he said.

Ghita looked at her watch. Gone was the diamond-pavé Chopard, replaced by a Swatch.

'The court's acquittal went through last night,' she said. 'All our assets have been returned. But, best of all...' she was cut off by the sound of the doorbell. 'Best of all is this!' she exclaimed.

Rushing back through the salon, she pulled the door open and found herself in her father's arms.

Neither would let go.

After the longest hug, Ghita remembered something important. She let go, kissing her father's cheek as they parted.

'This is Blaine, Baba, the most wonderful man in the world.' She stopped, looked at the floor bashfully. 'The *second* most wonderful man in the world.'

'I believe it is you I have to thank,' Omary said, extending his hand. 'For saving me from… from limbo.'

'He's an angel,' Ghita swooned. 'A wonderful, silly, funny American angel!'

One hundred and twenty-seven

THE THUD THUD *thud* of hobnail boots was loud and heavy on the flagstones of the isolation block. It grew louder still, before falling silent outside Cell No. 3.

The inspection hatch opened.

'There's a package for you,' said the guard in a raspy, uncaring voice. 'Can't imagine why they let it through!'

The prisoner took the package.

'Would you turn on the light, so that I could open it?' he asked.

The guard grunted, the one known to Omary as Bruiser.

'Five minutes,' he said, 'then you'll be back in darkness!'

Hamza Harass ripped the wrapping away, and found himself holding an ancient manuscript, furled in goatskin. Thanking God for sending him something to read, he opened the handwritten book eagerly at the first page.

Then he froze.

His expression went from one of fear to one of true terror, and from that to extraordinary distress.

He collapsed, the book in his hands.

'That's your five minutes!' roared the guard, switching off the light.

One hundred and twenty-eight

THAT EVENING, AS they finished dinner, Ghita excused herself, leaving Blaine to explain to her father what happened to the priceless Silver Ghost.

'I will be back in a little while,' she said as she left.

Having heard the story of the attempted break-out, Omary took a sip of Saint-Émilion, savouring it as it went down.

'The most magical thing in the world,' he said, 'is to have children and to watch them as they change.' He paused, holding his glass up in the air. 'I should like to toast you.'

'Even though I'm partly responsible for ruining such a fine old car?' said Blaine.

Hicham Omary waved the thought of it away with his hand.

'That's nothing,' he said. 'Just an object.' Raising his glass a little higher, he said: 'I toast you for the woman you have made out of Ghita — something I was unable ever to do.'

'The credit for Ghita's transformation goes to her, and to her alone.'

'You are so very right,' Omary replied.

One hundred and twenty-nine

FIFTEEN MINUTES AFTER leaving the mansion, the Maybach purred to a halt outside Singh's Pawn Shop down near the port.

Thanking the chauffeur for opening the door, Ghita stepped out onto the kerb.

The shop was closed up for the night, but the lights were on in the room above. Ghita pressed the bell, her heart beating fast.

A face peered down from the window — the face of Ankush Singh.

'Mademoiselle Omary!' he called out. 'I am coming.'

Downstairs, the shopkeeper pulled the shutter open and turned on the lights.

'I heard that your father was freed,' he said enthusiastically.

Ghita nodded. Then she took a little cloth bag from her coat pocket and handed it to the pawnbroker.

'You proved your friendship in a moment of terrible need,' she said. 'And no amount of thanks shall ever be worthy of your kindness.'

One hundred and thirty

THE PRISONER IN Cell No. 3 was found dead the next morning.

The death was put down to a massive heart attack. He was buried in a cheap pine casket along with the manuscript he had been found clutching at the time of his death.

The only family member present at his funeral was his son, Mustapha. Standing there in silence as the coffin was lowered into the ground, he was unable to shed a tear.

One hundred and thirty-one

THREE WEEKS AND one day later, there was the sound of music at the Omary mansion. Unlike the evening of the previous party, no caterer had been hired, nor were there tiaras, diamonds, or swish limousines. The only people invited were real friends — a handful of old ones, and a few new ones as well.

Rosario was the first to arrive.

She was resplendent in a low-cut gown that she had bought in the flea market of Tangier some years before.

'I'm leaving tomorrow,' she whispered to Blaine. 'Wish me luck.'

He gave her a hug and asked if she would play something at the Steinway concert grand.

'What would you like?' she asked.

'Surprise me.'

A moment later, the house was resounding to the lilt of 'As Time Goes By'. As the fingers of the Argentine pianist caressed the ivories, the door opened again and Ankush Singh stepped inside.

Running up, Ghita led him to her father.

The two men hugged and laughed, and hugged again.

'I thought you wouldn't remember me,' said the shopkeeper anxiously.

'How could I forget?' Omary replied. 'After all, I see you every day in the mirror,' he said, touching a fingertip to the scar.

Ghita looked at the clock above the mantelpiece and frowned. She seemed concerned.

'What's wrong?' Blaine asked.

'I'll be back in a moment.'

Walking out into the front garden, Ghita made her way across the immaculate lawn to the great arabesque gates.

Standing on the other side of them was Saed.

He was dressed in a prim dark suit that was far too big, with a ready-made bow tie, and his hair wetted down.

'What are you waiting for?' Ghita asked.

The shoeshine boy's eyes lit up.

'For you to be my date,' he said.

Taking Ghita's arm in his, the two walked back over the lawn and into the house.

Introduced to Omary, Saed was praised for his getaway driving, and was thanked for all he had done. Then he slunk into the kitchen and helped himself to a bottle of cooking sherry.

That was where Blaine found him.

'I believe I still have something of yours,' he said.

Saed struggled to hide what was left of the sherry behind his back.

Taking the envelope from his jacket pocket, Blaine passed it over.

'There was a time in all this that I half wondered what was inside it,' he said.

'You never looked?'

'No.'

'Why not?'

'Because I trusted you.'

The shoeshine boy seemed grateful, almost moved.

'Thank you,' he mumbled under his breath.

They were about to rejoin the party when Saed reached out and touched Blaine on the arm.

'Wait. I want to show you,' he said.

Tearing the edge of the envelope, he removed a dog-eared photo of two smiling people. It was a group shot of a mother, a father, and their baby son.

'My parents,' he said.

Blaine held the picture into the light.

'Where are they now?'

Saed's gaze lost focus on the kitchen's grey tiled floor.

'In Paradise,' he whispered.

The American put an arm around the boy's shoulder and gave him a hug.

'I'm going to make sure that you're never on your own again,' he said.

One hundred and thirty-two

BACK IN THE party, Ghita beckoned for Blaine to follow her. Leading the way through into the library, she closed the door firmly and kissed him.

'Now that you have saved your damsel in distress,' she said seductively, 'what are your plans?'

The American bit his lower lip.

'Well, I guess I could go back to New York and sell drain cleaner for the rest of my life,' he said with a smile. 'Or...'

'Or?'

'Or, I could do this...'

He got down on one knee.

'Miss Omary, will you spend the rest of your life with a wonderful, silly, funny American angel?'

Ghita screamed, then hugged Blaine so hard that his ribs cracked.

'Yes, yes, yes!'

The party rolled on and news of the engagement seeped out. It was toasted with Dom Pérignon.

Then the engaged couple danced to Rosario's music and laughed like they had never laughed before.

At a quarter to one, the butler whispered in Ghita's ear.

She seemed unhappy and even vexed. And, slipping out to the front of the house, she found a man standing there.

His shoulders were slouched forward. Some distance behind, on the other side of the street, another man was standing.

'*Mustapha?*' said Ghita. 'What… what are you doing here?'

'I'm so sorry. I can't express it,' he murmured. 'I had to come to beg your forgiveness.'

Ghita dug her heels into the gravel.

'You want to be forgiven for the fact your father almost killed me… that he so nearly did away with us all?'

'I know it's too much to ask. But I wanted to tell you something.'

'To tell me what?'

'That he ruled over me as a tyrant. Yes, I was spoilt rotten, but I was merely following his orders.'

'And what orders were those?'

'To get to know you… to marry you.'

'But why?'

'So that he could take over Globalcom,' Mustapha said. 'After your father's sudden and mysterious death.'

Ghita cursed loudly and breathed out hard.

'Well, I heard that it was *he* who has left us,' she said, without any emotion.

Mustapha touched a hand to his mouth.

'Believe me, he will *not* be missed.'

Ghita fell silent. She peered into the darkness across the street.

'Who's that — that guy standing back there?'

Mustapha cleared his throat.

'It's Karim.'

'*Karim?*'

'He's… he's…' Mustapha faltered. 'He's my boyfriend,' he said.

One hundred and thirty-three

LATER THAT NIGHT, Hicham Omary poured another round of champagne.

'We have already drunk to my darling daughter,' he said, 'and to this mysterious American who has charmed us all. But now I have a toast that's far more solemn.' He raised his glass, the crystal reflecting the candlelight. 'Let us drink to the city whose blood runs in all our veins — *to Casablanca!*'

There was a resounding cheer, followed by the *ching-ching* of Waterford crystal flutes chiming together. And when the toast was done, Rosario took to the piano once again.

While she played, Omary glanced at the American as though remembering something.

'It seems as though we share a passion,' he said, his voice rising over the music.

'Ghita?' replied Blaine with a smile.

'*Another* passion.'

The American shrugged, then frowned.

'What?'

'Come with me,' Omary said, motioning for Blaine to bring his glass.

They left the others in the salon and went through into an anteroom beside the library. It was entirely empty, except for a wardrobe that covered the back wall, rising floor to ceiling.

Opening the double doors, Hicham Omary disappeared inside.

'Follow me,' he called out as he went.

Blaine had a sense of déjà vu.

341

Climbing into the cupboard, he stepped through into another room.

The lights came on automatically in what seemed to be some kind of museum.

The walls were covered in posters of Bogart and Bergman, and there were all manner of objects on display in a series of large glass cases.

On one side of the room were a roulette wheel and a pair of silver cocktail shakers, a dossier of papers marked 'Top Secret', and an antique movie camera. Opposite them stood half a dozen mannequins, each of them dressed in long, silky gowns. There was a French police officer's uniform, too, with its kepi, and a fez hat, and fake Luger pistol in a glass box.

And, in the middle of it all, as if in pride of place, was another mannequin dressed in an old raincoat and fedora.

Omary waved an arm over the collection.

'I've been an avid collector for as long as I can remember,' he said.

'I never would have guessed it...'

'What?'

'That a Moroccan like you would have cared about *Casablanca*,' said Blaine.

'I'm a Berber,' Omary corrected with a smile.

'So I've heard. Well, a Berber like you then...'

'How could I resist it?' Ghita's father looked at the American hard. 'This room, all of this, it's my secret homage to Casablanca — the city and the film, the fact and the fantasy.'

'It's the past,' said Blaine.

'And it's the future.'

'The greatest story ever told.'

'A Moroccan story,' Omary laughed, 'and a Berber one, too.'

Blaine held his champagne flute up in a toast.

'I think this is the beginning of a beautiful friendship,' he said.

Finis

A REQUEST

If you enjoyed this book, please review it on your favourite online retailer or review website.

Reviews are an author's best friend.

To stay in touch with Tahir Shah, and to hear about his upcoming releases before anyone else, please sign up for his mailing list:

 http://tahirshah.com/newsletter

And to follow him on social media, please go to any of the following links:

 http://www.twitter.com/humanstew

 @tahirshah999

 http://www.facebook.com/TahirShahAuthor

 http://www.youtube.com/user/tahirshah999

 http://www.pinterest.com/tahirshah

 https://www.goodreads.com/tahirshahauthor

http://www.tahirshah.com

Printed in Great Britain
by Amazon

16489166R00203